NOBODY'S CHILD

VICTORIA JENKINS

Bookouture

Published by Bookouture in 2018

An imprint of StoryFire Ltd.

Carmelite House
50 Victoria Embankment
London EC4Y 0DZ

www.bookouture.com

ISBN: 978-1-78681-489-0
eBook ISBN: 978-1-78681-488-3

NOBODY'S
CHILD

ALSO BY VICTORIA JENKINS

The Girls in the Water
The First One to Die

PROLOGUE

'Let's play a game.'

The voice sounded muffled, as though she was hearing it under water. The girl's ears were still ringing from the blow to the head she had suffered earlier and she felt sick with the pain that coursed through her. She had returned to consciousness to find herself bound to a chair, her arms and legs tied tightly. If her eyes hadn't been covered and her vision cast into darkness, she would have recognised too that her short-lived state of unconsciousness had also rendered her sense of sight temporarily impaired. She realised she had never felt scared before, not properly; not like this.

Why were they doing this to her?

'I'll count to three, and after three, one of us is going to touch you. All you have to do is guess which one of us it was. Easy.'

The girl felt tears escape from under the fabric pulled across her eyes. She didn't like this game. She wanted to go home. She tried to cry out, but whatever was stuffed into her mouth made the sound escape as little more than a muted sob.

'Come on,' a second voice said. 'Do it. Touch her.'

Knowing she couldn't free herself, the girl's body tensed, every limb shuddering with fear. This couldn't be happening to her. She had heard about things like this – had seen the stories on TV, things she hadn't wanted to see – but they didn't happen around here. They didn't happen to her.

The sound of a slap, sudden and sharp, cut through the horrible silence that had fallen over the room. The girl felt nothing, but heard a small whimpering sound somewhere else in the room, the sound of a caged animal, trapped and tortured, before a scuffling crossed the floor, the noise falling towards her.

She felt a hand on her arm, shaking, and then a quiet voice that whispered in her ear. 'I'm sorry.'

CHAPTER ONE

'It's looking lovely in here.'

Alex sat on the sofa in Chloe's living room drinking a cup of tea. The last time she had been over to the house had been about six weeks earlier, when Chloe had still been in the process of moving in. Chloe hadn't had many material possessions, so moving from Alex's house into her own rented home had been fairly straightforward and hassle-free. The emotional impact of moving was something both women knew might prove a little trickier to manage. Chloe hadn't lived alone since the attack earlier that year and she was still having nightmares from her ordeal, but she had known she couldn't rely on Alex forever.

'Thanks. I was quite lucky, really – the place didn't need much doing.'

Alex glanced at the windowsill, where a framed photograph of Chloe and her boyfriend Scott stood. The photo had been taken sometime during the summer; Chloe was wearing a strappy dress and Scott was looking at her as though she was the only person in the world. No one had ever looked at Alex in that way, or if they had, it had happened too long ago for her to be able to recall.

'How long before he moves in, then?' she asked with a smile.

Chloe rolled her eyes. 'Bit soon for that. I don't think he could cope with some of my bad habits. You can warn him if the time ever comes.'

'Must be nice to have your own space back.'

'Yeah, definitely.' Chloe shot Alex a look, embarrassed. 'I didn't mean …'

Alex smiled. She knew what Chloe meant. The young detective constable had worked and lived with her for the previous eight months, but Alex took no offence at her appreciating her own space back. Chloe was twenty-seven; she needed her independence. Alex had thought she would feel the same, yet Chloe's moving out had only served to highlight an emptiness that she feared she would never be able to fill alone.

'Handy for work, too.'

Chloe was living now only five minutes from the police station, an easy walk into work. The terraced house overlooked the river and stood in an area far more built up than the flat in which she had previously lived before moving in with Alex. It seemed she had made the decision to surround herself with life, and placing herself near the safety of the station seemed no coincidence either.

'Yeah, I have wondered about that, though. Bit too easy, maybe.'

Alex finished her tea and stood. 'You're still welcome to come over whenever you want, you know that, don't you? I'm already missing your veggie lasagne.'

'Charming,' Chloe said, taking the empty mug from her. 'You just miss me for my cooking.'

Alex shrugged. 'At least I'm honest.'

'I'll bring some food parcels to the station for you.'

Alex left Chloe's house and drove home to her own. It was already dark, the nights now drawing in early, and only the string of headlights that ran along the A470 gave away the fact that it was still rush hour and not the depths of night-time. Less than fifteen minutes later, she pulled up outside her house and cut the engine. She lived in the imposing semi that had once been her marital home, and it seemed bigger now she lived there alone once again. In the first couple of months on her own, she had lost count of the number of times she'd felt this way upon returning to the place: not wanting to go inside; dreading the long hours that stretched between night and morning, dragging her along amid their quietness.

She took her bag from the passenger seat beside her and got out of the car, slinging it over her shoulder. Chloe had had the right idea, she thought. Leaving everything behind and starting again seemed an increasingly appealing option. She wondered whether she might be able to do the same. Would she be brave enough? She didn't need all this space to herself, and besides, there were too many ghosts in this place. Even from the pavement she could almost feel them waiting there, watching her. If she left, would they follow?

Pushing her bag further onto her shoulder, she fumbled with her keys as she tried to find the one for the front door. Before making her way up the steps, she could already feel something was wrong. An unsettling sense of unease fell over her and she couldn't shake the feeling that someone had invaded her private space. The feeling was quickly justified. Streaked across the front door, in lurid red letters that had run in bloody tears like something from a horror film, was the word 'WHORE', spray-painted in angry capitals that seemed to scream at her.

She stopped on the path, halted by the assault on her home. She turned to look behind her, as though the person responsible might still be there, then hurried back down the steps and looked up and down the street. She knew doing so was pointless – whoever had done this was now long gone – but the wave of unease that had swelled in her chest at the sight of the graffiti made her feel in that moment that she was no longer alone, that someone might still be there, waiting to witness her reaction. The irony of her thoughts struck her: hadn't she just been lamenting her recent isolation?

She returned to the house and went inside. She turned on the hallway light before closing the front door and double-checking the lock was firmly fixed in place behind her. She hadn't wanted to be alone, yet the thought of someone else being inside the house with her now filled her with an unsettling doubt.

Be careful what you wish for, she thought.

CHAPTER TWO

Mahira Hassan muted the television when she heard a noise at the front door. It was late – much later than she had planned to stay up that night – but her sons' non-appearance by 11 p.m. had triggered a familiar anxiety that she was unable to rid herself of. Late nights inevitably meant trouble, at least where her oldest son Syed was concerned.

She stood from the sofa at the sound of stumbling in the hallway. One of the boys slammed the door shut behind him and Mahira hoped they hadn't woken Faadi, who was upstairs in bed. Padding across the living room in a pair of slippers, she went to the doorway and watched her sons as they removed their shoes in the hallway, neither of them noticing her standing there. Syed shoved Jameel, laughing unreservedly as his brother fell against the radiator.

'You'll wake Faadi.'

Syed turned, surprised to see his mother still up so late. 'Very sorry, Mother.'

There was no apology in the words and Mahira tried to ignore the sarcasm with which they were spoken. Behind Syed, Jameel straightened himself, still fighting to remove the shoe from his right foot. When he turned to look at her, he made no attempt to hide the bruising that patterned his left eye, angry and swollen.

'What's happened now?'

'Nothing.'

'It doesn't look like nothing.'

Syed sighed and stepped past his mother, heading into the living room. He scanned the room for the remote control before unmuting the television and sinking back into the sofa, apparently without a care in the world.

'Jameel?'

'It was nothing,' he repeated with a shrug. 'No big deal.'

'Let me take a look at it at least.'

Reluctantly Jameel followed his mother through to the kitchen. He sat at the table while she searched the freezer for a bag of peas, wrapping it in a clean tea towel and handing it to him. 'It'll take down the swelling.'

He pressed the bag to his face, but it wasn't enough to conceal his reddened, bloodshot eyes or the watery glaze that was fixed upon them. Mahira had seen those dilated pupils before; knew all too well what they meant.

'Are you going to tell me what happened now?'

Jameel ran his free hand across his closely shaved head. His mother hated this look on him. It made him appear to be someone she knew he wasn't, not really.

'It was just some idiot.'

'Who?'

'You wouldn't know him.'

'I might.'

With a sigh, Jameel moved his hand from his face and put the bag of peas down on the table. 'Gavin Jones. They call him Spider.'

Mahira knew him: he used the shop fairly regularly, mainly for cans and cigarettes. He had a tattoo of a spider's web that circled his elbow. He had never given her any problems. 'Are you going to report it?'

Jameel shook his head. 'Don't make a big deal about it.'

'If he did this to you, then you need to report it.'

It occurred to Mahira that Jameel's reluctance to report the incident to police was perhaps a suggestion that Gavin Jones wasn't entirely to blame for whatever had happened that evening.

'Fights don't start themselves,' she said.

'Bloody hell.' With a scrape that echoed around the kitchen, Jameel pushed his chair back and stood. 'He said something, all right?'

'Said what?'

'Something racist.'

'Okay. What did he say?'

'I don't know, Syed heard him. Now just leave it, will you?'

She watched him stride to the living room, wondering when her middle son had become so much like his older brother. It was unfair of her, she thought; he had a way to go before he really became like Syed. How long would it be, though, before the gradual changes in his attitude and behaviour amounted to the whole: a new, different son to the one she had known these past nineteen years?

Jameel had always looked up to Syed, always wanting to be just like him. For his own sake, and for all their sakes, Mahira hoped it wasn't going to happen.

CHAPTER THREE

'Jesus Christ.' DC Chloe Lane put a hand to her mouth: an ineffectual attempt to hide her reaction to the horror that awaited them in one of the former hospital wards. It hardly resembled a person. What had once been human was now reduced to a charred and blackened mess of rags and barely identifiable remains. The scene-of-crime officers were going to have their work cut out for them, as were the fire-scene investigators who were on their way.

'What was he doing up here?' Alex wondered, thinking aloud.

The room was bleaker than the bulk of black night sky that stretched beyond the building, the fire having spread rapidly. Fire crew had responded quickly to the 999 call that had been made, with the station being just a few streets away. Alex hoped this would mean that evidence had been preserved. Lifting forensic evidence from fire scenes was always a laborious process, with a myriad of complications. Those complications would be passed on to the incident room, where they would be felt by the rest of the team.

She leaned closer to what remained of the body, her capacity for the brutalities of murder having broadened during her years as a detective. Each time she thought she had seen it all, someone else proved that evil knew no boundaries.

'How could anyone do this to someone?' Chloe said quietly.

Alex left the question unanswered. Chloe had seen enough evil in her life to know that sometimes there was no explanation for it, no matter how much they might seek one. In many ways, the senselessness was the most difficult thing to accept.

The abandoned hospital was in Llwynypia, just a few streets from the main road that linked Tonypandy with the smaller villages that stood between it and the top of the Rhondda valleys. Despite its central location, the trees and shrubs that lined its boundaries kept the derelict buildings fairly secluded. This particular room – still bearing evidence of its former use as a ward – was located at the back of the main hospital building, used now as little more than a brick canvas for spray-painted names and lewd graffitied drawings.

Despite the ravages of the fire, the remnants of messages sprayed and scrawled upon the peeling paintwork could still be seen on the far wall. Alex wondered for a moment whether whoever had been responsible for this person's death had been brazen enough to leave behind a signature. Whatever else they might find here, this was going to prove to be no accident.

Her thoughts roamed for a moment back to her own front door. She hadn't mentioned the graffiti to Chloe. What was the point? How many people had thrown verbal slurs and insults at her during the duration of her career, and much worse besides? The call from the station about the fire had come in not long after she had arrived home, so she hadn't yet had time to speak to any of her neighbours. She doubted anyone would have seen anything. Her front door was pretty secluded from the street and it was nearing the end of October, already dark by 5.30.

Returning her focus to the scene, Alex took in the details of what lay before her. A pile of burned wooden planks and an array of charred debris covered the body, forming a human bonfire. The scene was gruesome and macabre, like something from a horror film. Its structure had held surprisingly well against the force of the flames that had consumed it.

'What's that?' She gestured to the doorway through which they had entered the scene. By the wall, at the edge of the fire's reach, there was a single trainer. She picked her way through the debris and lifted the shoe with a gloved hand. It was a brand she recognised from years back and wouldn't have thought was still in production. The single shoe looked battered and worn, as though the owner had been wearing it all these years.

'Remember these?' she asked, nodding at the trainer.

Chloe shook her head. Alex had thought it unlikely; she hadn't seen a pair of trainers of this make since she was a teenager, before Chloe had even been thought of. If the shoe belonged to the victim then it was likely this wasn't a young person, although at that moment it was impossible to tell anything for sure. She had made the assumption that it was a man, though even that wasn't certain.

There were three scene-of-crime officers in the room, all kitted out in protective white overalls. They roamed the room like ghosts, their silence only adding to the eeriness of the place. Alex gave one of them the trainer and it was placed into a clear plastic bag. She and Chloe moved aside, giving the SOCOs space to work closer to the victim.

'Know how long this place has been left derelict?' Chloe asked.

'Ex-husband's niece was born here. How old would she be now … twenty-eight? Twenty-nine? It closed not long after that.'

'You heard from him at all recently?'

'No, and he'd better keep it that way.'

A near reunion with her ex-husband almost a year earlier had led to disaster, leaving Alex suspecting she might be better off single for the rest of her life. Most days, the prospect didn't seem too bad, but the attack on her home had made living alone less appealing.

They went back out into the corridor. It was a mess: loose wiring hanging in a tangled web from the ceiling, broken plastic panelling lying in sharp shards underfoot; an abandoned trolley still laden with medical paraphernalia resting beside an open doorway into what had once been another ward, sitting there as though waiting for the ghost of a nurse to retrieve it.

'Place gives me the creeps,' Chloe said.

'Fascinating, though, don't you think? As though time's just stopped here.'

Chloe pulled a face. 'If you say so.' There was a noise at the end of the corridor that made her start.

'That'll be the fire-scene investigators.' Alex picked her way across the debris to meet the men who had entered the corridor, all dressed in full protective clothing and armed with an expansive collection of equipment.

'Detective Inspector King. This is Detective Constable Chloe Lane.'

One of the men introduced himself in reply and shook the hand Alex offered him. 'Suspected arson?'

Alex nodded. 'One victim, gender as yet unknown.'

'It's not the first fire we've had up here,' the man told her. 'I don't know how many times we've said this place needs to be pulled down. It's become a magnet for trouble.'

Alex led the investigators through to the room where the body lay, then turned her attention back to Chloe. 'We need to find out if there are any cameras on any of the streets nearby,' she said. 'The call came in from a telephone box about two minutes from here – perhaps there's CCTV somewhere. Let's do a door-to-door, speak to the residents in the nearest houses. It's a long shot, but if there's regular trouble up here perhaps someone's kept enough of an eye out to have seen something suspicious.'

'I still don't get why anyone would choose to come into this place.'

'Curiosity, I suppose. Some people love derelict places.' She watched for a moment as the fire-scene investigators set about their work. Until the pathologist arrived, they would have no details regarding their victim. 'The call that came in was anonymous,' she continued, thinking aloud. Something wasn't sitting right with her. The fire hadn't had time to spread beyond this room, meaning that whoever had placed that call had done so soon after the blaze had been started.

'Think whoever it was might know more?' Chloe asked.

'They certainly knew about the fire quickly enough. And why else would you withhold your name? Whoever it was, they ended the call as quickly as they'd made it.'

One of the SOCOs had crouched beside the burned body and was using a gloved hand to retrieve something from amid the charred remains. Alex understood Chloe's reaction to the place: there was an eerie, haunting atmosphere that was static in the air around them. It seemed an ironic place to die: a building where healing had happened; a place where lives had begun and been saved. It was almost impossible to imagine it now as it might have been then, clean and sterile, bustling with life.

'DI King.'

Alex turned at her name. The SOCO was holding something up with a gloved hand, beckoning her to take a closer look.

'Looks like part of a sleeping bag,' he said.

Alex looked again at the remains that lay beneath the stack of blackened debris. Had the victim been sleeping rough in the hospital building? The circumstances of this person's death now seemed all the more tragic. Had they sought shelter here; been killed in the place they'd considered the closest thing to a home?

Who had ended a life so brutally and callously here, and why had they done it?

CHAPTER FOUR

Mahira Hassan couldn't sleep. She lay in bed – the right-hand side of the mattress always hers – unable to drift off as she tried to fight back the barrage of thoughts that thundered through her brain. There was usually the incessant rumble of her husband's snoring in the bed beside her, and his being away with work again should have meant a much-needed night of uninterrupted peace. For twenty-six years Mahira had been able to count on her fingers the number of nights she had spent without her husband sleeping by her side, but the last year had seen him away with work more often. Rather than missing him, she more often than not these days found herself glad of the break.

She wondered whether he was asleep in his hotel room, imagining that he would be. Youssef always slept soundly. How could he sleep so deeply, she wondered, knowing everything that had happened? How would he react to the news of what had happened again that evening?

She heard a noise on the landing; the soft padding of feet descending the staircase. Slipping from beneath the duvet, she slid her bare feet into the slippers that waited at the bedside and reached for the dressing gown draped over a chair. Edging around the bed, she left the room and headed downstairs.

In the kitchen, Syed was standing at the fridge, illuminated in the darkness by its strip light. He was wearing a dressing gown and his bare feet were exposed, showing a shock of thick dark hair at his ankles. Her eldest son had once been such a source of pride – a good child, hard-working and respectful – but age had changed him. Sometimes Mahira would experience thoughts as she was looking at him – strange, unwelcome ideas that she didn't think it natural for a mother to feel. She loved her son, but she didn't like the person he had become. The thought felt dirty, sinful.

She was his mother. Surely anything he had become was in some way her doing?

Syed turned slowly, sensing someone behind him.

'How many times?' Mahira said, gesturing to the orange juice carton in his hand. 'Use a glass.'

She moved to the cupboard, took a glass from one of the shelves and put it on the worktop in front of him, banging it down with a force greater than she had intended. Her son took the glass and half-filled it.

'This has to stop, Syed.'

He glanced at his mother over the rim of the glass as he drank. 'It's just orange juice,' he said, his lips curling into a smirk. He shook his head, flicking a wave of dishevelled hair from his face.

He had been such a handsome boy growing up, Mahira thought. He had known it, but it hadn't spoiled him. Now, his arrogance and anger were making him ugly. Exasperated, her hands moved to her hips. Where had this insolence come from? This wasn't how they had raised their sons. 'You know exactly what I mean.'

'Speak to Jameel in the morning,' Syed told her, before draining the last of the juice. He wiped the back of his hand over his mouth. 'It's nothing to do with me.'

Mahira tutted. Her hands slid from her hips and slipped into the pockets of her dressing gown. 'It's always something to do with you, Syed. Every time there's a fight, you're there in the background somewhere.'

Syed went to the sink, turned on the tap and briefly held his used glass beneath the flow of cold water before standing it upside down on the draining board. 'Defending my brother's honour.'

'Rubbish,' Mahira said with a sigh. 'Goading him, more like. Don't you think this family has been through enough without you making things worse?'

When her son stepped towards her, she felt a ripple of fear that began in her stomach and raced up to her throat. She suspected it was foolish of her, yet there was always an element of doubt; a nagging thought that ticked at the back of her brain, reminding her not to be complacent. Syed was not to be trusted, not completely. She had seen the results of his anger. She had seen the way his silences could fester over time, manifesting themselves in outbursts of violent rage. Who was to say they wouldn't one day be directed at his own family?

'When are you going to see things as they really are?' he challenged. 'If people left us alone, we wouldn't need to fight. As it is, there's hardly a day we go out without some idiot insulting us. You want us to avoid people, is that it? What would you have us do – stay locked up in this place forever?'

He eyed the room with contempt, as though 'this place' had become unrecognisable as home. The truth, she knew, was that it never had been home. Their home had been back in Cardiff, where the children had grown up. Uprooting their lives had been done with the best of intentions, but it was already proving to be a mistake; one she knew there was no going back from. Where had she gone wrong? Mahira wondered. She had done everything she could, given them everything she had, yet it never seemed to be enough. No matter how hard she had tried to keep her boys on the right path, Syed had been intent on dragging himself elsewhere, taking the rest of them with him.

'You can't control how other people behave,' she told him, 'but you can control how you react to it. You don't have to fight, Syed. You don't have to encourage Jameel to fight. You have the choice to walk away.'

With a roll of his eyes, Syed stepped past her and headed back to the hallway. 'No we don't.'

She sat at the kitchen table and listened to her son go back upstairs. She wouldn't go back to bed now; there was no point. She wouldn't sleep, not after this. She waited, lost within her worry, the ticking of the clock on the far wall and the whirring of the fridge the only sounds to break through her thoughts. When those thoughts threatened to take her to places she didn't want to visit, she got up and went to the sink to wash properly the glass that her son had left unclean.

From the worktop where she had left her mobile charging before she had headed up to bed earlier that evening, the phone began to ring. Mahira crossed the room quickly, not wanting the noise to disturb the house. She wondered who might be calling her, knowing that at this time of night it was only likely to signal bad news.

No number. She answered, and her fears were substantiated.

CHAPTER FIVE

Faadi Hassan sat on the edge of his bed and stared at the calendar that hung on his bedroom wall. It was something he did almost every day, always with the same thought: that time would pass and nothing would last forever. He pulled his school jumper over his head, disappearing for a moment within its itchy confines. If he could have stayed there all day, hidden from the rest of the world, he would have.

The following week was the half-term holiday. The thought of a week off would be enough to get him through that last day at school, just as every half-term he spent counting down the days until the next holiday. He heard a noise on the landing outside his room, then Jameel banging a fist on the bathroom door, telling Syed to get a move on and get out of there. Faadi reassessed his wish for the week to be over. At least at school he was free of his brothers.

He heaved his bag onto his shoulder and went out onto the landing. Jameel was standing outside the bathroom, drumming a slow, repetitive beat on the door.

'Off to school, Fatty?'

Faadi winced. He hated the nickname his brothers had given him. The more he hated it, the more pleasure they took in calling him it, and try as he might, he couldn't help but react every time he heard it. He had never been any good at hiding his feelings. If he was upset, tears would catch at the corners of his eyes no matter how hard he tried to fight them back. If he was happy, his face couldn't help but show it; his thin lips would stretch into a surprisingly wide smile and there was a sparkle in his eyes that his mother never failed to miss.

He could just about remember how it felt to be happy, but the feeling was one that already seemed so distant.

'What happened to your face?' he asked his brother.

Jameel had a split lip. There was dried blood at the corner of his mouth and his left cheek was swollen and bruised. If he was ashamed of or embarrassed by his injuries there was no evidence of either.

'Never you mind,' he said, waving a hand in Faadi's direction as though swatting away a fly. 'You just run along like a good boy and enjoy your day at school.'

There was a click at the bathroom door as Syed undid the lock on the other side. He appeared in the doorway with a white towel wrapped around his waist and his bare chest still damp from the shower. Faadi felt his face flush at seeing his brother's body; at the sight of the thick mass of dark hairs that covered his chest and the taut skin that clung to his narrow waist. He felt his arm move instinctively in front of him, concealing the bulk of his own stomach.

'What are you staring at?' Syed clicked his fingers, ushering Faadi away as though he were a disobedient dog. 'Go on … get yourself to school.'

Faadi went downstairs to the kitchen, where his mother was loading clothes into the washing machine. Her long dark hair was pulled back from her face into a ponytail that swept the length of her spine. From behind, she looked like a much younger woman, but her face had grown older in the past couple of years, with a collection of worry lines now revealing her age.

He spoke to her, but when she didn't acknowledge him, he repeated his hello, wondering if she had heard him. Eventually she turned and looked at him, giving him a smile that didn't reach her eyes. Then she stood and arched her back, placing a hand at the base of her spine and steadying herself against the kitchen unit. She had been crying. There had been a time when she had once hidden any tears she might have shed, but during those past few days it seemed she was now past caring who might be witness to them.

'Are you okay?'

She nodded and ran the back of her hand hastily across each eye in turn. 'No,' she said. Tears followed, thick and fast; awkward for them both.

'What's happened now?' Faadi asked. He didn't know what to do. He wasn't used to outbursts of feeling such as this and he stood fixed to the spot, unsettled by his mother's sadness and not knowing what to do with his hands. He wasn't very good with other people's emotions. He never knew how to deal with his own.

His mother shook her head. 'Never you mind. You just concentrate on school.' She stepped towards him and ran a hand across his thick, short-cut hair. He never minded when she did this at home – if anything, there was something in the gesture that made him feel safe – but she would occasionally do it in public, when each time Faadi would feel his cheeks grow hot and wish the ground would swallow him up.

'Mum ...' he began.

'The shop,' Mahira said, knowing that keeping anything from him was pointless. He was thirteen years old now; she couldn't wrap him up and keep him safe forever, despite how much she wanted to. If he didn't hear it from her, he would hear it from someone else. 'There's been a fire at the shop.'

Faadi pulled a face. 'I don't understand. When?'

'During the night. Look ... it's nothing for you to worry about, okay?'

'But what happened? Why didn't you wake me up?'

His mother gave another sad smile. 'What could you have done, eh? No point in us all being tired this morning, was there?'

'Do Syed and Jameel know?'

Her face changed again, a darkness falling over her. 'No, not yet. Please … don't say anything to them. Let me do it.'

Faadi shifted the weight of his rucksack from one shoulder to the other. 'You're not going to be there today then?'

'I've got to wait to hear from the police. I might be able to go there later today.'

'Dad going with you?'

Mahira shrugged. 'He may not be back from work today.'

'I'll come with you,' Faadi said hurriedly. 'After school … if you've not already been.'

His mother smiled, and for the briefest moment there was light in her eyes. 'You're a good boy, Faadi, you know that? Don't ever change.' She looked away for a moment. 'Go on,' she said, returning her attention to the washing in an attempt to hide her sadness. 'Get yourself off to school now.'

'Promise you'll call me to let me know,' Faadi insisted.

Mahira looked back at him, her best smile fixed firmly in place. 'I promise. Now go … you don't want to be late.'

CHAPTER SIX

Alex and Chloe stood in the stifling heat of the terraced house's front room, assaulted by the heat being pumped out by the five-bar gas fire that was fixed to the wall. Alex remembered her own parents having a similar fire, decades earlier when she had been a teenager, before they'd had central heating installed. The smell of it evoked a number of memories, all of which she was loath to return to in the aftermath of everything the last year had thrown at her. That single fire in the living room had been relied upon to heat the whole house, yet she couldn't remember ever having felt cold as a child. Sliding two fingers beneath the collar of her shirt in an attempt to peel the cotton from her sweating neck, it was obvious why not.

'Cup of tea for either of you?'

The woman who lived there must have been at least eighty years old, though she had the energy of someone far younger. Chloe watched with a mixture of disbelief and admiration as she bustled about between them, clearing her teacup from the side table and plumping the floral cushions on the sofa as though welcoming long-awaited guests. She wondered whether the ringing of the bell that morning had signalled the first signs of human life beyond the house the woman had experienced for a while, and the thought filled her with a curious sadness that managed to make the oppressive heat of the small room even more unbearable.

'Not for me,' Alex said. 'Thank you, Mrs …'

'Adams,' the woman told her. 'Doris Adams, but please, just call me Doris.'

Doris gestured to the sofa and Alex and Chloe took a seat at either end, their mirrored positions with legs crossed and elbows on the armrests making them look for a moment like a couple of misplaced bookends. Alex noted the crocheted furniture protectors beneath her sleeve and behind her head and felt another twinge of nostalgia that tugged at her stomach. An approaching birthday was signalling fresh fears of ageing; fears she knew were futile, but that she was unable to shake off.

'We're speaking to everyone on the street,' Alex explained. 'Did you see or hear anything over at the hospital last night?'

Doris shook her white-haired head. 'I didn't hear anything until the sirens came screaming past. Fire again, was it? Been quite a few up there over the past couple of months.'

Alex nodded. 'So there are trespassers over there regularly, you think?'

'Places like that are always going to attract them. Drug addicts, kids messing about … Such a shame when you think of what the place used to be like.'

'Have you always lived here?' Chloe asked, slipping the sleeves of her jacket from her arms. If she left it on any longer she was at risk of melting inside it.

'Sixty-four years,' Doris said proudly. 'Moved here when I got married, but I only came from just up the road. I was a nurse over at the hospital, you know. C2 ward sister.'

She got up from her chair and went to an old-fashioned sideboard, where she opened the top drawer. She pulled out a photograph album, velvet-covered and frayed at the corners, and crossed the room to sit between the two detectives on the sofa.

'There,' she said, turning a few pages and pointing to a photo-graph that was protected behind a thin page of clear plastic. 'That's me.' The black-and-white image showed a row of female nurses standing for a photograph, all in full uniform. Doris was second from the right, little more than in her early twenties. Her hat was tilted on her head and she was smiling proudly for the camera. She was quite striking, Alex thought, the sparkle behind the old lady's eyes making her still recognisable as the young woman in the picture.

'It's a lovely photograph,' Chloe told her.

Alex stood and turned to the window, though little could be seen through the net curtains that kept the room hidden from the world beyond. The only view from this room would be the houses on the other side of the street, but she wondered whether the hospital's derelict buildings were visible from the bedrooms upstairs. She doubted anything useful could be seen from this distance anyway. Most of the street had now been spoken to and it already seemed they were wasting their time. It appeared that at this time of year everyone was inside with the television on and their curtains drawn by six o'clock in the evening.

'You must have been very sorry to see the hospital close,' she said.

It seemed a dreary prospect: to have lived in the same house for all those years and to watch the places around you – the things that had once formed the shape of your life – crumble and disintegrate, left to go to ruin. The small town a mile or so further along the main road was evidence of the area's decline: shops stood empty, buildings boasted boarded-up doorways and windows; the air above each street seemed to hang dreary and grey, as though even the sky had given up on what lay beneath it.

'Well now,' Doris said, closing the album and smoothing the front of her pale blue skirt over her knees. 'Everything must come to an end, mustn't it?'

'Sadly true,' Alex said, turning back to the room. 'Thank you for your time, Mrs Adams. If you do think of anything, no matter how small it might seem, please let us know.'

Doris stood and followed the two women back out into the narrow hallway and to the front door. The detectives thanked her and stepped out into the October air. Out on the street, Chloe breathed in a cold lungful, grateful to have escaped the heat of the house.

'What a lovely woman.' She slipped her coat back on. 'She doesn't seem to know about the death at the hospital. Everyone else on the street appeared to have heard about it.'

'She might not have left the house for days. Come on,' Alex said, unlocking her car. 'I think we're wasting our time here. Let's go and find out how Dan's getting on with the missing persons database.'

Back at the station, they found DC Daniel Mason at his desk in the incident room, lost in the pages of the database. It never failed to surprise and sadden Alex that so many missing persons cases existed; even now, with so much technology and so many resources available that it seemed impossible anyone should be able to just disappear.

'Any joy with the hostels?'

The remains of the sleeping bag found among the burned remains suggested that someone – presumably their victim – had been using the hospital for shelter. There were few facilities for homeless people in the Rhondda valleys, but in recent years a couple of hostels had been opened that offered free beds for those who might find themselves having to sleep rough.

Dan shook his head. The flecks of silver in his hair were beginning to compete for dominance and he was wearing the look well. 'Homelessness is still Cardiff's problem, by all accounts.'

'Missing persons?' Chloe asked.

'I don't know what I'm looking for,' Dan said despondently as Alex and Chloe sat either side of him. 'I think we need to wait until we get the post-mortem report back … I don't even know if I'm looking for a man or woman at the moment, do I?'

Alex had realised that morning when she had assigned Dan the task of checking the database that doing so at this stage would probably prove fruitless, but patience had never been her strong point. With little else to go on, she had to try to cover any possible angles. DC Jake Sullivan had been helping with house calls on the street behind the hospital, while the rest of the team was looking into details of any CCTV footage in the area. So far, they were drawing a blank on all fronts. Alex hoped the pathologist would be true to her word and would get the post-mortem report to her by the end of the day.

She was SIO on the case, but she would be expected to report back to Detective Chief Inspector Thompson later that afternoon, and she needed something to offer him. No permanent appointment had been made since Superintendent Blake had retired during the summer, and in his absence Thompson had temporarily transferred from Bridgend. The man seemed decent enough, but it was obvious he resented being taken away from his own team.

'The fire at Llwynypia Stores last night,' Alex said, perching on the edge of Dan's desk. 'Also arson?'

Dan nodded. 'Window at the side of the building was smashed – petrol-soaked rag thrown in.'

'No CCTV?'

'No tape. Camera was put there just to act as a deterrent.'

Alex rolled her eyes.

'Think they're linked?' Chloe asked. 'The residents we spoke with this morning said fires at the hospital aren't unusual, though. Fire investigation team said the same.'

'Fires aren't that uncommon round our way either,' Dan said, turning in his swivel chair and scratching his head. 'Starting mountain fires is like a sport during the summer.'

Dan lived in Pentre, just up the valley from Llwynypia. He had been born in the valleys, had grown up there and was raising his own two daughters there. He was well known locally, and despite him being with the police, even the regular offenders had a respect for him that was rarely extended to his fellow officers. There had been occasions when he had been involved in the arrest of members of his own family, yet there never seemed to be any lasting resentment towards him.

Yet again, Alex's thoughts were drawn back to her own house and to the graffiti sprayed across it. If only she had Dan's personable nature, she thought. Clearly someone still had a lasting resentment where she was concerned. She knew she could just choose to ignore it, but a nagging doubt had been gnawing away at her all day. It was obviously not a random slur, and for someone to put themselves to the trouble of finding out where she lived and then going to the house meant that they were intent on unsettling her at the very least.

At worst, she didn't like to consider what they might wish upon her.

'We'll have to wait for the fire report,' she said. 'Have the owners been back to the shop yet?'

Dan shrugged. 'Don't know.'

'Find out. And if not, I'd like you two to go with them. We need as many details as possible – who was the last person there before the fire broke out, what security measures they've got in place, if any, who had access to the shop … get as much as you can. They'll have been asked all this already, but perhaps the fire at the hospital changes things. If there is a connection between the two, we don't want to miss it.'

They needed details of the victim whose body had been burned at the hospital, but Alex realised that this might prove difficult. The corpse had been so badly burned that identification would be a challenging process. She would call the pathology lab at the hospital in Cardiff and arrange to visit the place later that day.

Speaking face to face with the pathologist often proved far more useful than simply reading the report.

She couldn't see any reason for the two fires to be connected, but that didn't mean they should be ruling out the possibility. The shop had been empty when the fire had been started, but had whoever was responsible for the blaze been aware of that?

In Alex's experience, it was always worth assuming the worst.

CHAPTER SEVEN

'You can't see them.'

Julie Morris stood in the doorway of the terraced house with her arms folded across her chest. She smelled of cheap hairspray, and the curls that hung about her shoulders suggested she wasn't planning on spending her evening in front of the television.

'Why not?'

'I'm going out.'

'So let me look after them while you're out then.' Gavin Jones raised an eyebrow expectantly, knowing that Julie was going to find any excuse she could to prevent him from seeing his sons. She'd always hated him, and when the boys' mother had died five years earlier, she had seemed to blame him for it, as though he'd been the one behind the wheel of that car.

'No,' she said flatly. 'Look at the state of you.'

She was referring to the black eye Gavin was sporting that evening; actually less of a black eye and more of a green swelling that had yet to develop to its full glory. How many times had Julie seen this particular look on him over the years? She had lost count. She didn't know what her daughter had ever seen in him.

'It's nothing,' Gavin said with a shrug. 'I got jumped.'

Julie rolled her eyes. She had heard it all before. Gavin was always the victim, always in the wrong place at the wrong time. Nothing was ever his fault. Being caught red-handed with enough drugs to keep an addict satisfied for a fortnight hadn't been his fault either, and his attempts to fob off the jury with a claim of personal use had been swiftly quashed by the judge, who had handed down an eighteen-month sentence. Six years after his release, he was still making claims of getting his life back together, never quite able to answer the question of when he was actually intending on finalising those plans.

Her daughter might have fallen for the fake charm, but Julie was no fool.

'So who's looking after the boys if you're swanning off out?' Gavin wanted to know.

Julie narrowed her eyes. 'I'm not "swanning" anywhere – I haven't had a night out in God knows how long. You might not have noticed, but I've had my hands full looking after your kids.'

'Exactly. So let me give you a break.'

Behind his grandmother, Gavin's younger son appeared in the hallway. He was dressed in a pair of blue and red Spider-Man pyjamas that were too small for him now – the ankles halfway up his shins and the sleeves stretching at his elbows – and he was carrying an iPad that tinkled with the repetitive music of the game he was engrossed in.

'Curtis! Come here, son!'

Gavin leaned forward, his bulky arms outstretched towards the boy, who looked up from the iPad briefly before turning his attention back to its screen, oblivious to his father's attentions.

'There we go,' Julie said smugly, her lips curling into a triumphant sneer. 'Hardly knows who you are. You can't just turn up once every few months when you've got nothing better to do.'

Gavin's jaw tensed. 'Where's Tyler, then? Let me guess … he's doing your babysitting tonight, is he?'

With a loud sigh, Julie slid the safety chain back in place. She was too slow to shut it: Gavin slammed his shoulder against the door, using his weight to hold it open against her.

'Tyler!' he shouted.

'Gavin, do yourself a favour before I call the police, and just fuck off.'

Julie gave Curtis a tap on the bottom with her bare foot, directing him back into the living room, while Gavin continued to attempt to push his way into the house, his bulk making it impossible for Julie to get the door shut.

'Tyler!'

God, she hated him. He turned up when he felt like it, always managing to throw their lives off balance in the process. He hadn't cared about them too much after their mother had died, and he had missed most of their birthdays since. They got a visit every now and then; a visit that inevitably made Tyler upset and left Julie having to answer a succession of questions she didn't really want to have to address. They were doing fine without him. They had always been better off without him.

She heard Tyler trudging down the staircase behind her, his skinny frame as always managing to make the noise of half a dozen elephants. He was still wearing his school uniform, too lazy to have bothered to change into anything more comfortable. She'd asked him how his day was, but all she'd got was a grunt in return. It was just a phase, she told herself. He was thirteen: they were all the same.

'Fancy going for some food, son?' Gavin asked, speaking over Julie's shoulder.

'He's eaten already.'

'He's a growing boy. Needs to keep his strength up, don't you, son?'

Tyler, tousle-haired and nonchalant, shrugged his skinny shoulders.

'Tyler ...' Julie began.

'There's that new pizza place down the road just opened. We could try there, what d'you reckon? Come on,' Gavin coaxed, shooting his son a smile. 'I'll throw in dessert as well, if you think you can manage it.'

Julie watched resignedly as Tyler reached for his coat from the row of pegs that lined the hallway wall. She had spent the past five years trying to dissuade him from seeing his father, but the boy was a teenager now and anything she tried to keep him from would only become more appealing, Gavin included. She was getting too old for all this, she thought. She'd done her time with her own kids; she hadn't ever thought she would end up having to raise her daughter's as well. They weren't bad boys – she'd known a lot worse – but Tyler was getting to that awkward age when he'd argue with anything she said, and if stopping him seeing his father meant things in the house would get worse, then she really didn't have the energy to resist. It wouldn't take him long to see Gavin for what he really was. Let Gavin hang himself, she thought.

'Better phone your friends,' Gavin said, pulling a feigned expression of disappointment. 'Can't leave Curtis on his own, can you? Social would be round like a shot.'

Julie turned to him, keeping her face hidden from sight of her grandson. 'Fuck you,' she mouthed.

Gavin gave her a smile.

CHAPTER EIGHT

They followed the police officers into the shop, where strips of crime-scene tape hung from the doorway and flapped about in the breeze. Faadi hadn't heard the man's name when he had introduced himself; he had been too distracted by the young woman with the blonde-tipped hair who had smiled at him kindly and in doing so made his face flush with a heat he suspected might be visible. She didn't look like a detective. For a start, she seemed too young – around the same age as his brothers, he guessed – and she was far too pretty. Then there was the fact that she seemed just too … well, just too nice. Not like the detectives he had seen on TV shows, who were mostly old and grumpy.

He watched his mother fight back tears as she studied the burnt-out carcass of the shop. An acrid, dirty smell lingered in the air – air that still looked grey – and the skeletons of what had once formed their livelihood lined the walls: charred shelving units, blackened cans and shrivelled plastic; the dusty ashes of piles of newspapers and magazines.

'This was definitely arson?' Mahira asked, her voice unsteady as it tripped over the question.

The female detective – Chloe Lane, Faadi remembered; he had been paying enough attention to catch her name – nodded. 'I'm sorry. This must be very difficult for you.'

There was a single window in the storeroom at the side of the building. It had been smashed with a house brick that had been found beneath a set of shelving, and a burning rag had been used to start the fire. The rag had been taken to the lab for testing.

Faadi watched his mother take a tentative step into the blackened depths of the room, carefully picking her way through the debris of what remained of her business. 'We've reported so many things,' she said, her voice tinged with both sadness and anger. 'Theft, vandalism … verbal assaults. You've seen the abuse scrawled on the walls out the back. No one has listened to us. I thought the police were supposed to take a zero-tolerance approach towards hate crime?'

It was a phrase that had been used a lot recently in the Hassan household, particularly by Faadi's two older brothers. This was the first time he had heard his mother use it, though. Every time Syed and Jameel got into yet another argument or fight, the words would reappear, staining the air like the mention of a relative no one wanted to be reminded of. It seemed to Faadi a strange phrase. If someone stole something from somebody, they must have hated that person in some way, if only during the act of stealing. If they hadn't hated them, even if only for a split second, would they have been able to take something from them? If someone fought with another person, that must mean they hated them in some way or another. You had to hate someone to hurt them, didn't you? No matter what crime Faadi imagined, each one involved a perpetrator who, if only for the briefest of moments, had been capable of hate. It seemed to him that every crime was a hate crime.

He had said so once. The idea had been met with a slap to the head from Syed, accompanied by the suggestion that he keep his fat nose out of things he was too young and too stupid to understand.

'Your complaints have all been logged,' DC Chloe Lane was saying. 'But this is the second fire to take place overnight in the area … We've no reason at the moment to believe it is a race-related matter.'

'The fire up at the hospital, you mean?' Mahira asked. 'You think that what happened here might be linked to that?'

'We don't know yet,' the male officer told her. 'Forensics are still looking at the cause of the other fire.'

A cold shiver swept the length of Faadi's body. He had heard about the fire in the old hospital; everyone had been talking about it in school that day. Bad news and gossip spread much like fire did: thick and fast, leaving nothing in their way unharmed. He knew a dead body had been found there, and that the person had been set on fire. It didn't quite seem real. Things like that only happened in films and on TV, not right here on their doorstep.

Another thought occurred to him. If the person who had started the fire at the hospital was the same person who had set fire to the shop, had that person been hoping somebody might still be inside there too?

Were they trying to kill someone?

He didn't want to think about it. The person most often inside the shop was his mother. His father had another job – he was a sales representative for a stationery company – and though his brothers were supposedly employed by his parents to help out at the shop and give his mother some time off at weekends, the reality was that they tended to turn up for a couple of hours before making their excuses about needing to leave. They were always going to interviews for other, more permanent full-time jobs, but the interviews never seemed to go their way.

What if his mother had still been inside the building when the fire had been started? Had someone wanted to hurt her? The thought filled Faadi with sickness and he swallowed nervously, his focus still fixed on the shop floor.

'Are you okay?'

He was snapped from his thoughts by Chloe's voice, calm and soothing. She was looking at him with kind brown eyes, her lips turned up in a half-smile that Faadi realised was intended to make him feel better. He nodded, finding himself tongue-tied. There was a smear of foundation lining the young woman's jaw, and he wondered why the policeman with her hadn't told her about it.

'People are saying that the fire at the hospital was started deliberately,' Mahira said, 'and not that the person just happened to be inside and got caught up in it.' She glanced at her son warily, but Faadi knew exactly what she meant. The victim at the hospital had been set on fire purposely. The thought horrified him, making his own body flare with a sudden and uncomfortable heat.

The male officer looked at him with caution, as though he was deliberating over his choice of words before he spoke them. 'We can't say anything for certain yet.'

Faadi looked around the room, following his mother's eyes as they continued to absorb the mess that had been made of the place. The family had moved here for a new life; a fresh start. Now, looking at the ruins of her business, Mahira knew it had been their biggest mistake. They should have faced their problems in Cardiff – no matter what that had meant for Syed. Sometimes it really was a case of better the devil you knew.

'As soon as we find out more,' the male detective continued, 'we'll let you know. In the meantime, have you been in contact with your insurance company?'

Mahira nodded. It was the last thing she wanted to think about having to deal with, but she had already contacted them and they were in the process of establishing their investigation. From what she knew of insurance companies, she assumed that meant they would be assessing the ways in which they might be able to avoid a payout.

'You have my number if you need anything, Mrs Hassan,' Chloe said. She reached out and put a hand on Mahira's arm, leaving it there for just a moment. 'If there's anything you need or anything you think of that might help the investigation, please contact us.'

Faadi watched his mother nod. She was unable to make eye contact with the other woman, as though doing so might unleash the tears she had been struggling so hard to hold back. 'Thank you,' she muttered.

Faadi didn't really know what she was thanking her for.

CHAPTER NINE

Helen Collier, head pathologist at the University Hospital of Wales in Cardiff, ushered Alex into the sterile lab. What remained of the fire victim was laid out on the steel examination table beneath a clinical white sheet that temporarily hid the horrors of what had once been a living, breathing human being. Alex had mentally prepared herself for the sights and smells that awaited her at the lab, though she knew nothing could ever really ready her. In her eighteen-year career with the police, she had been exposed to the most brutal effects of the most heinous of crimes: she had seen bodies bruised and battered; stabbed, drowned and tortured. She had seen burns victims before, although nothing quite like this one. It had been barely recognisable as a corpse at all, and she assumed dental records would prove the only method of identifying it.

'You don't need me to tell you,' Helen said, 'but this isn't pretty.'

Helen was small and bird-like, and her soft voice contrasted with everything the room represented. Alex had wondered previously why the woman had chosen this particular career path, although she assumed the same question could be asked about her own choice of job. There was a quiet life waiting somewhere for her, she was sure of it, but it didn't look set to ever find her. Perhaps she would only choose to shun it if it did.

'The fire was started post mortem,' Helen said. 'I suppose we can be thankful that he wasn't burned alive.'

'He?'

Helen nodded. 'You ready?'

She pulled the sheet back from the body. The victim looked gruesomely recognisable in his prone position upon the steel table. His chest had been cut open and his internal organs removed; his blackened flesh cracked and fallen away like ashes.

'Bodies tend to assume a certain position when they're burned prior to death, but it was evident at the scene that this wasn't the case here. He was lying flat, outstretched, his arms by his sides rather than lifted in the way that might be expected if he'd been burned while still alive. In those cases, victims tend to adopt a pugilistic stance, with the arms raised and fists clenched.'

Alex waited to hear where Helen's explanation was leading. She was still trying to block out the awful smell that emanated from the remains of the victim.

'The blood test determined a low carboxyhaemoglobin level.'

'He didn't breathe anything in?'

Helen shook her head. 'I'd say categorically that he died before the fire was started. He had sustained a number of injuries before death – fractured collarbone, broken wrist, several cracked ribs.'

'Any of them old injuries,' Alex asked, 'or are we talking shortly before death?'

'I'd say he endured a prolonged and vicious assault not long before he died.'

Alex forced herself to look again at the nameless body laid bare before her. Had this man gone to the hospital alone and been followed there, or had someone gone with him? Had the fire been started in an attempt to conceal the crime?

'His face,' she said. 'Injuries there too?'

Helen nodded. 'Definitely, although the fire has made it difficult to differentiate between the inflicted injuries and the cracking of the skin caused by the extreme heat.'

'So what are we looking at?' Alex asked, thinking out loud. 'He was beaten to death before his body was set on fire?'

'Not necessarily beaten to death.' Helen moved to the table and pulled the sheet back over the body, seemingly in an attempt to spare Alex any further gruesome details. The effort was made in vain: once she had seen something, it stayed with her indefinitely. Until the person responsible was identified and made to face justice for their crime, she wouldn't allow the images to leave her. Even then, she always knew she would never truly be free of them.

'Analysis of the lung tissue found that the man suffered from restrictive lung disease,' Helen continued. 'There was considerable scarring to the tissue. In basic terms, he would have struggled to get enough air into his lungs during times of stress or exertion. His liver shows evidence of long-term alcohol abuse. It's all in the report,' she said, gesturing to a file waiting on the far worktop near the lab's computer. 'I've emailed you a copy as well. My estimation would be that the assault brought on a panic attack and the victim struggled to inhale sufficient oxygen to survive it.'

Alex's mind was running into overdrive. She would need the report from the fire-scene investigators before drawing any conclusions, but a picture of their victim and the moments leading up to the start of the fire was beginning to emerge.

'Any idea of his age?' she asked, thinking back to the trainer that had been found at the scene.

'It's quite difficult to establish an age in this case,' Helen admitted, 'but the condition of the lungs and heart would suggest somewhere between forty and sixty. I'm sorry I can't be more specific.'

Alex shook her head, acknowledging the apology but dismissing it as unnecessary. At least they now had somewhere to start looking on the missing persons database, although the faster her brain worked, the more she suspected any attempt to identify their victim in this way would still prove fruitless. There were too many missing people and the description they had so far was too broad.

And perhaps their man wasn't on the system. Not everyone who went missing was reported as such. Some people were just lost.

CHAPTER TEN

Gavin Jones and his son Tyler sat in the far corner of the room, staring in awe at the shared pizza they had ordered. It was so big it took up half the table, but Tyler was hungry enough that he reckoned he could probably have given the majority of it a good go by himself. He reached for the crust and tore off a slice, dropping it onto his plate as the hot cheese burned his fingertips.

'Steady,' Gavin said, giving the boy a smile. It wasn't reciprocated, but Gavin hadn't expected it to be. It was going to take more than a pizza to win Tyler back over. During these past five years Julie had had plenty of time to fill the boy's ears with poison against him. He had probably heard all sorts, most of it lies.

'So how's school going?'

It was a lame question, but he didn't have much else to start with. He didn't really know anything about his own son, but it had been obvious years earlier that things were going to go that way. Besides Julie doing her best to keep the boy from him, there was Tyler himself. Studying his son as he chewed a mouthful of pizza, Gavin realised not for the first time that the two of them had nothing in common. Tyler was nothing like him. In fact, Gavin had wondered years earlier whether the boy was even his. A DNA test reluctantly agreed to by Tyler's mother had years ago proved he was, yet Gavin still found it hard to believe.

'Fine. Yeah ... it's fine.'

Tyler was at the start of Year 9; Gavin at least knew that much. He couldn't remember much about Year 9 at school – he hadn't been there most of the time, and when he had bothered to turn up, his mind was always somewhere else – and he could already feel the conversation drying up before it had even begun. He wondered whether his son got bullied. He was a prime target, what with the shoulder-length hair and the pale skin, although apparently that sort of look was back in fashion. Maybe elsewhere, Gavin thought, but he couldn't see it catching on round these parts.

'Not long left,' he said. 'Couple of years and you won't have to go any more.'

'I like school,' Tyler said flatly.

'Oh.'

Tyler took another bite of pizza, while Gavin aimlessly prodded with a knife at the slice on his own plate. He wasn't particularly hungry, and the tomato base that had been added too liberally was spilling from the edges of the melted cheese, oozing onto the plate like fresh blood on an operating table.

'Look,' he said, knowing he couldn't spend much longer submerged in this uncomfortable silence. 'Your nan's probably said a lot of stuff about me. She's poisoning you against me, that's what she's trying to do. She doesn't want us to be friends, I don't know why. Don't believe her lies, okay, Tyler?'

Tyler looked blankly at him across the slice of pizza he was holding near his chin. There was a thin string of cheese caught at the corner of his mouth. 'You've been to prison,' he said. 'That's not a lie.'

'I know,' Gavin said, leaning across the table. 'But it was years ago and I never did anything to hurt anyone, Tyler. Only myself. You believe that, don't you?' It wasn't strictly true, but he figured that what the kid didn't know wouldn't hurt him. It was all a long time ago now and a lot had happened since then. He had served his time: didn't that mean he was entitled to a fresh start?

Tyler was looking at him sceptically. That was another reason why Gavin had doubted his paternity: the green eyes. They were almost too green, unnaturally so, as though the boy was wearing contact lenses. Tyler leaned back in his seat and reached both arms behind his head, gripping his hair in his hands and pulling it into a knot. To Gavin's horror, his son pulled an elastic band from around his wrist and used it to tie his hair back into a bun.

'What about your face? You've been in a fight.'

Gavin had wondered how long it would take before the bruises were brought up. He had already prepared his answer, which mostly involved telling Tyler the truth. He could afford it on this one. 'I got jumped, that's all.' It wasn't entirely a lie. Those Hassan brothers had been looking for trouble – everyone knew they were both always ready for a fight wherever they could find one – and he had only given them what they were after.

'It wasn't your fault, you mean? That's what Nan says you always say.'

Gavin forced himself to bite his tongue, something he'd always had trouble doing. He was going to have to play the long game here, he thought; chip away at Tyler bit by bit until he realised that his nan wasn't exactly a saint either. It was okay: Gavin wasn't in a rush.

In fact, he thought, as he watched his son take another slice of pizza, he had all the time in the world.

CHAPTER ELEVEN

She strikes a match and watches it burn right down to her fingertips, feeling the heat assault her skin before she drops it to the ground. She watches the flame die at her feet. It is cold in the yard, just days now from the end of October, and the sky is already ablaze with the sparks and sounds of fireworks. It has been like this for weeks. She listens to the screeches, the hisses and bangs as she lies in her bed at night, wishing the month away, wishing November and then Christmas away, always hopeful for the start of a new year despite the disappointment that each inevitably brings.

She has to have hope for something else, something better. Something more. Without it, what does she have to look forward to?

A rocket flares skywards, released from the back garden of one of the terraces in the streets behind her house. She tilts her head and follows its ascent, keeping watch as it explodes in a kaleidoscope of shapes and colours. She loves oranges, yellows, reds. The colour of flames. She loves the heat that seems to radiate from them, their warmth so close she can almost touch it.

There has always been a fascination with fire. As a child, she loved to watch the bonfires that would be lit at the park every 5 November. Left alone, she could watch a single flame as though hypnotised by it, lost in every flicker and every curl of heat. She liked to arrive early and watch as the bonfire was assembled, her favourite part always being the moment when the floppy-limbed guy was added to the dried-out stack of wood.

It wasn't real; she knew that. It was just pretend, and everything was different when it was just pretend.

She moves a foot to the burned-out blackened match on the ground and brushes it to one side with a sweep of her slipper. She tilts her head and follows a stream of colour as it screams across the sky.

She wonders for a moment how it might feel to burn.

CHAPTER TWELVE

The following morning, Alex, Chloe and the rest of the team gathered in the station's incident room for a briefing. Alex now had both the post-mortem report from the pathologist and the South Wales Fire and Rescue Service investigators' report, and put together, they made some of the suspicions she had begun to develop at the mortuary the previous day seem more than a possibility. She had stayed up late reading the reports, and the two sugared coffees she'd already drunk since arriving at the station that morning had done little to deter the tiredness she now felt tugging at her temples.

'Okay,' she said, bringing the low-level chatter that had passed around the team to a close, 'we've now received both the post-mortem and fire-scene investigation reports and quite a few things have come to light. As we already know, the victim was male, aged between forty and sixty. He suffered from restrictive lung disease and is believed to have died as a result of restricted lung capacity either shortly following or during a brutal and sustained assault. The attack took place in the room where his body was recovered and he was set alight after death. Petrol was used as an accelerant.'

'Someone set fire to the body in an attempt to conceal their crime?' DC Daniel Mason asked.

'Perhaps,' Alex said. 'Although I'm not convinced.' She reached to the computer keyboard on the desk beside her and clicked on one of the already opened windows. A voice recording was paused, waiting to be replayed. 'The 999 call came in at just after nine forty in the evening. It was made from a phone box on Station Road.

We now know there are no CCTV cameras anywhere in the area, and I'd guess that whoever made the call was already aware of this.' She clicked the recording.

'*Hello, you've requested the fire service ... What is your emergency please?*'

'*Fire ...*'

'*Sorry, sir?*'

'*Fire. Old Llwynypia hospital.*'

'*There's a fire at the old Llwynypia hospital?*'

The line was bad, made worse by the muffled noises that disturbed the sound of the voice making the call. It sounded as though the mouthpiece might have been purposely obstructed.

'*Could you tell me your name, please, caller?*'

'*Now ... please ...*'

'*Are you inside the building? Is there anyone else with you?*'

At that point, the line went dead.

Alex minimised the window on the screen and returned her focus to the team. 'Why end the call so abruptly if there was nothing to hide?' she asked. 'Why not answer the questions? My guess is that whoever made this call knows how the fire started.'

'So that would ruin Dan's theory that it was started to conceal the assault?' Chloe said. 'If you think we're listening to the murderer?'

'Not necessarily. But why set a fire in order to conceal a crime and then alert the authorities to it? Makes no sense.'

'Why call then?' The question came from DC Jake Sullivan, who was sitting on a desk at the back of the room, one leg crossed over the other.

'I don't know,' Alex admitted. 'Could be a number of reasons. Panic. Guilt. That's something we may be able to work out a bit further down the line, once we've established who our victim was and why he was attacked. The fire-scene report holds a few possible clues about who he might have been, or at the very least some details about his life. He was lying on a sleeping bag at the time the fire was started. There were a couple of items of clothing found elsewhere in the room, along with empty beer cans. It's highly likely our victim was homeless and was using the hospital for shelter.'

There were a few murmurs among the team.

'Not many people sleeping rough up that way, are there?'

The question came from DCI Thompson, who was standing at the back of the room. He had always struck Alex as a curious figure, slight in frame and aloof in demeanour, and she had trouble imagining him out on the beat as a younger officer. He must have been eaten alive, she thought, although perhaps he had come to the job straight from university and been fast-tracked towards CID as a result.

'Not according to recent figures,' she admitted, 'but they're at least eighteen months old now.'

'It might explain why no one has reported him missing,' Dan said.

'Perhaps. Now, if we work on the theory that this man was homeless, then either someone knew he was using the old hospital as a base, or someone happened to find him there by chance. Let's say for a moment it was chance. Did he interrupt something? Might it be the case that he wasn't expected there and was beaten to keep him silent?'

'Silent about what, though?' queried Chloe.

Alex raised her hands, surrendering to the lack of information. 'These are the things we need to find out. I think going public with the known details of our victim needs to be our next step. Homeless or not, someone must know who this man is. We know there have been other fires up at the hospital, so maybe someone unconnected to this incident was aware it was being used as a shelter. I'm giving a statement to the press this afternoon. In the meantime, we need to speak to as many people in the local area as we can, in particular, shop owners, bar staff – anyone who may at some point have come into contact with the victim, who was also suffering from liver disease associated with years of heavy drinking. If we can get a possible ID, we may be able to find him on our database if he's got previous. It's a small community; people tend to know each other. If anything comes up, I want to know about it straight away, please.'

There was further chatter as the team dispersed, but Alex called Dan over, asking him to wait behind. 'I think we should hold off before returning to the missing persons database,' she told him. 'If we do manage to get an ID today, it'll save you a lot of time. You don't fancy doing this statement for me, do you?' It was asked with a roll of the eyes.

'Go on,' Dan said with a smile. 'You know you love it.'

Alex made no secret of her dislike of press statements and TV appeals. On previous cases she had often been known to pass them over to Superintendent Blake, but she didn't think DCI Thompson would appreciate the request.

'Thanks for nothing. Well you'd better be around after it, so I've got someone to slag the press off to once I'm done. I'd usually bend Chloe's ear, but she's going to canvass local businesses with Jake.'

Dan smiled again. 'I didn't know you weren't a fan of the press. You never mentioned it.' He glanced over his shoulder at DC Jake Sullivan, who was standing at the doorway. 'Still on thin ice?'

It was no secret that Alex wasn't keen on DC Jake Sullivan. There was nothing specific he had done that had annoyed her, but maybe that was the problem: she wasn't that sure what it was he actually did.

She rolled her eyes again. 'He could be worse, I suppose. It'd be a good start if he lost the bravado.'

'The ignorance of youth.'

'I wouldn't know … I can't remember that far back.' She glanced at her watch and sighed. 'Wish me luck, then.'

CHAPTER THIRTEEN

Sian Foster was nearing the end of a long eight-hour shift. With every bleep of the scanner and every item that was passed along the checkout, she felt herself become more and more distant, until eventually the motion became hypnotic. She glanced at the screen that showed the bill total and recited the amount as though it had been programmed into her tiring brain.

'Seventeen pounds forty-two, please.'

'And I'm not even going to get a hello?'

She looked up from the screen. Gavin Jones had bagged up the items she had scanned and was waiting with a raised eyebrow. She hadn't noticed him there; he could have been anyone.

'Sorry,' she said, giving him a half-smile. She pushed her short hair behind her ear and fought back the flush she could feel developing at the base of her throat. 'Long day.'

'You were miles away. Anywhere nice?'

'Anywhere but here,' Sian said, taking the twenty-pound note he offered her. She shoved it into the till and counted out his change.

'What time are you finishing?'

She looked over at the clock on the far wall. Every hour that passed felt more like four. 'Twenty minutes.'

'Right,' Gavin said, taking the carrier bag of shopping from the checkout and hooking the plastic handles over his wrist. 'I'm taking you for a drink. No excuses,' he added quickly, sensing her imminent refusal. He had asked her out a couple of times previously and each time she'd either turned him down or had a last-minute reason why she couldn't make it. 'I'll wait over in the café for you, all right? Don't stand me up in Asda … I'll never live it down.'

As she began to scan the next customer's shopping, Sian wondered why he was still pursuing her despite everything. Plain old Sian, nothing much to look at; nothing much going for her really. Hadn't her ex-husband reminded her enough times that no one else would look twice at her? So why Gavin Jones – notoriously popular despite being a renowned troublemaker – would be interested in her was a mystery. There was only one way to find out, but it was something she had promised herself she wouldn't do. Men like Gavin were bad news, and she had known bad news before, too many times. She was a magnet for it.

Twenty minutes later, Sian clocked out, collected her things from her locker in the staffroom and headed towards the main doors of the supermarket. Rain lashed down against the windows of the store and she zipped her jacket up to the neck, preparing herself for the walk home.

'You've broken my heart, Sian Foster,' she heard a voice say behind her as she passed the flower stand, its buckets bursting with colour against the drab car park that lay beyond it.

She turned, feeling a burst of her very own shade of red flood her face. 'You're very persistent, aren't you?'

'Thanks.'

'It's borderline stalking.'

'Do you mind, though?'

'If I did, would you stop?'

Gavin hurried to keep up with her as she left the building. She was keen to keep the exchange from the prying eyes and ears of anyone she worked with. It was a cliché, but it was true that round their way everyone seemed to know everyone else's business, and if they didn't, they made a point of finding someone who did. She had been the source of enough gossip over the years; she didn't want to create any more.

Rain hammered down in noisy thuds on car roofs, turning the concrete ground to a shimmering sheet. Sian pulled her hood up over her head and held it in place in an attempt to keep the rain from her face.

'So you don't mind then,' Gavin said, taking her arm and turning her to face him. 'Sorry,' he said, when he saw the look she gave him. He pulled his hand away quickly. 'I'm sorry, I shouldn't have grabbed you. I was only messing.'

'I know,' Sian said, glancing back to the supermarket entrance to make sure no one had seen them.

'I didn't mean—'

'It's fine,' she said quickly, cutting his explanation short. She grimaced as the rain lashed at her face, its icy bite pinching her skin. 'Look … can we just get out of here, please.'

She accepted his offer of a lift, not wanting to attempt the ten-minute walk back to her house. Accepting the lift would mean taking him up on the drink he had mentioned earlier, but she couldn't let him drop her home, not with Keeley there. Like so many other things, that was something that could wait. She would only feel the need to explain herself, not that there was really anything to explain.

And then there would be the inevitable conversation about Nathan.

Gavin pulled into the pub car park and cut the engine. The rain was already beginning to ease; from here, Sian thought, she could be home in less than five minutes. 'Wait a minute,' she said, putting a hand out as Gavin reached for the door. Her hand rested on his arm for a moment and she retracted it quickly. 'Sorry … I just … I don't know if this is right.'

She could feel his eyes on her, the weight of his stare making her feel uncomfortable. She had wondered on several occasions why she liked him when she knew he was so obviously wrong for her, but it had always been the same. There hadn't been many men in her life, but they had all been wrong. At the age of thirty-five, she still hadn't learned.

'I just don't think Keeley and Tyler would be too happy about it, do you?'

Gavin shrugged. 'What's the problem?'

'They've been seeing each other a while now. I'm not sure they're going to be too happy about their parents … you know …'

'Their parents what?' Gavin asked, turning in the driver's seat. 'This doesn't have to be a big deal, Sian. It's up to you. I know you've said before about things with your ex and everything, and I get all that. I'm not looking for anything heavy either. And the kids … they're thirteen, for God's sake. They're just kids – it won't last. You can't let your daughter rule your life.'

'She doesn't,' Sian snapped defensively.

'Whoa,' Gavin said, raising both hands in mock surrender. 'Easy. I was just saying, that's all.' He shifted towards her and ran his hands along the length of her arms, stopping at her shoulders. 'You know what your problem is, don't you?' he continued, squeezing gently. 'You need to learn to relax.'

Sian closed her eyes as she felt his breath against her skin. It was a nice thought, in theory. She couldn't really remember what relaxing felt like, it had been so long since she'd last allowed herself to do it. Keeping herself knotted was the only way she knew how to survive. Her whole body was a coiled spring, taut and tightly wound, waiting for life's next problem to ricochet off her: work, Keeley, Nathan, Christian. Her ex-husband was recently released from prison and it would only be a matter of time before their paths crossed. He wouldn't do the decent thing by moving somewhere else. Being decent was something that had never occurred to Christian.

When Gavin kissed her, Sian kissed him back. The kiss felt nice, though she knew what she was doing was wrong. Gavin Jones had a reputation – the kind that preceded the man himself – but just for that moment it was cast to one side. The moment was short-lived.

'I can't do this,' she said, pushing him away.

Gavin nodded and sat back. 'So you keep saying.'

'I need to get home,' she said, opening the car door. 'Sorry.'

She slammed the door behind her and Gavin watched as she hurried across the car park and back to the main road. Sian Foster was a challenge, he thought, but it was nothing that deterred him. He liked a challenge.

CHAPTER FOURTEEN

Alex glanced down at the buttons on her shirt before putting on her jacket. It was always the last thing she checked before addressing the press. Nothing would help skew attention from the case in hand like the unintentional flash of a detective's bra. It was a sad fact that journalists' attention could be so easily swayed, and that nothing was more enjoyable to them than finding ways in which to undermine or bring embarrassment to the police. And any scandal would be jumped upon; in Alex's experience, they actively searched for it. Years earlier, she had naively assumed that the press would work alongside the police, with a mutual interest in the pursuit of justice. Now, older and wiser, she realised that nothing was allowed to get in the way of a good story, least of all the truth.

She had joined the police service eighteen years earlier and during that time had experienced multiple cases in which journalists had been responsible for misrepresentation. At their worst, she had seen them jeopardise convictions, unwittingly empowering guilty men to walk free. Almost a year earlier, they had been responsible for bringing shame to Chloe, tarnishing her with a reputation she was still having to work hard to banish. As far as Alex was concerned, any form of relationship she might have previously had with the press was now dead.

She resented what she was about to face, as brief as this statement would inevitably be. The cameras that would be pointed accusingly towards her, questioning why more hadn't yet been done; the microphones that would be shoved in her face as soon as she was finished speaking; the inane questions that would pour from the mouths of local journalists, despite her standard closing sentence that she had no further information to offer. The statement she was about to give that day was to be a short one – there was little at this stage that they were able to disclose – but she hoped that in making public at least a few details of their victim, someone might come forward to identify him. Surely someone must have known this man and missed him in the time that had passed since Thursday night.

She addressed the waiting press outside the police station in Pontypridd.

'There have been a number of cases of arson in the Rhondda valleys over the previous few months, but this latest incident sadly involves loss of life. On Thursday night, a fire was started in one of the buildings that formerly made up the hospital in Llwynypia. At this stage we can give very few details about the victim other than that he was male and aged between forty and sixty. We have reason to believe he may have been homeless and using the hospital building for shelter, and are therefore keen to speak to anyone with links to the homeless community who may be able to offer identification of the victim or his family.'

She paused, deliberating over her next words: words that had been carefully prepared in advance. Poor phrasing could easily lead to misinterpretation, and that was something the press would inevitably jump upon. She didn't want to create fear among the public with any suggestion of murder, though there was no doubt that murder was what they were dealing with. Had the man's attacker known that he was already dead before the fire was started?

'If anyone has any information regarding the fire, or any details regarding a missing person that may help us identify the victim of this incident, please contact the number shown on the screen below.'

Alex moved away from her audience, but the questions that were thrown at her came too quickly for her to escape them. A young man with an oversized beard that looked as though something might have recently been living in it thrust a microphone towards her.

'DI King, do we know how the fire was started?'

'I'm sorry,' she said, turning sharply back to the press and avoiding eye contact with the man. 'That's really all we have for you at the moment.'

She headed back into the station and closed the door on the babble of chatter and gossip that swelled behind her. A sigh of relief involuntarily escaped her.

'Well?' asked Dan, meeting Alex in the corridor on the first floor. 'How did it go?'

'Let's hope for the best, as always. Likely a waste of time, but we'll have to wait and see.'

She feared the statement would lead to an inevitable stream of calls from time-wasters, as seemed to be the case with every television appeal they put out. Occasionally there would be a scrap of something useful among them – something that would make the countless dead ends worthwhile – but the occasions on which this happened were few and far between, though they were enough to merit putting themselves out there and hoping for something that might move an investigation forward.

'Guess what I've just heard,' Dan said, lowering his voice conspiratorially.

Alex pulled a face. 'Christmas is coming early this year? Jake just worked out how to use the coffee machine without breaking it?'

Dan laughed. 'Slow down ... we're not quite there yet. You remember Christian Coleman?'

'As if I could forget.'

Christian Coleman had been well known to South Wales Police for over a decade, having made more visits to Pontypridd station's cells over the years than a duty solicitor. His police record ran longer than the River Taff and had only been brought to an end when his son had attempted to kill him by lacing a takeaway curry with antifreeze.

'He's been released.'

'Already?' Alex held the door open for Dan and followed him through to the incident room.

'I know. Makes a mockery of the whole bloody system, doesn't it?'

Despite the fact that Christian Coleman had been a wife-beater and all-round thug, he'd been sentenced to just five years in prison. That had been little more than two years earlier.

'I wonder what the family make of it.'

'His ex-wife had a restraining order against him, didn't she? Don't know whether that still stands.'

Alex's eyes scanned the room, though she took in none of the details of the team at work. Her thoughts were elsewhere, back at home: back on the hateful graffiti that had been sprayed across her front door.

She was the one who had interviewed and charged Christian Coleman following the brutal assault that had left the mother of his two children hospitalised. She had also appeared in court to give evidence against him, as had his ex-wife. He had tried to break Sian Foster during their years of marriage, but an underlying streak of determination saw her take the stand to make sure the man who had wrought such cruelty on her family was finally brought to justice.

And what had been the last thing Christian Coleman had said to Alex before he'd been sent down? *I'll fucking kill you, you ugly whore. Whore.*

She shook herself from her thoughts. There were plenty of people who had called her all sorts of things over the past two decades. It was just a word; it didn't mean anything. Focusing her attention on the evidence board at the back of the incident room, she resolved not to waste any further time thinking about it.

CHAPTER FIFTEEN

Jameel and Syed Hassan sat in the corner of the supermarket café, neither of them touching the coffees they had ordered. Syed looked as though he hadn't had much sleep; his eyes were heavy and his focus shifted uneasily, not knowing where to rest. He ripped open a sachet of sugar and tipped it into his coffee before staring at the surface of the drink, lost for a moment in the direction of his thoughts. 'Gavin Jones,' he said eventually.

'What about him?'

'Well, what are we going to do about him?'

Jameel's delayed response was met with his brother's trademark impatience. Syed leaned forward in his chair and rested his elbows on the table. 'The fire,' he said slowly, as though Jameel had somehow managed to forget about it. 'Obvious who started it, don't you think?'

'Gavin?'

Syed rolled his eyes. 'You two get into a fight and a few hours later the shop is torched. I wouldn't call that a coincidence, would you?' He sat back and looked around, making sure no one was near enough to overhear the conversation. 'So what are we going to do?'

It was meant to sound like a challenge; they both knew it. For a long time now Jameel had needed to start sticking up for himself, and with Syed's help that was exactly what he was now beginning to do. He was getting better, but he still had a long way to go. Gavin Jones seemed as good a place as any to start.

'We don't have any proof, though.'

In his lap, Syed's hands curled into fists. 'Who else would have done it, eh?'

Jameel, tall and slim, stretched his long legs from beneath the table, shifting uncomfortably as Syed's focus bore upon him. 'Well … like you keep saying … we're not exactly popular round here.'

He watched his brother's jawline tense. 'Don't be an idiot, Jameel. If you're not man enough to deal with the problem, I will.'

'I didn't say that, did I? Okay … let's deal with it. What are you suggesting?'

Syed stirred his cooling coffee aimlessly and glanced down at the shoppers moving around like ants on the ground floor of the supermarket. 'Hallowe'en coming up,' he said, not meeting his brother's eye. 'And what does everyone love to do for Hallowe'en?'

Jameel stared at him vacantly and shrugged. 'Eat sweets?'

Syed ground his teeth. Sometimes he wondered whether Jameel really was this stupid. That was why he needed help and guidance. He could look after himself when he had to, but he never had the foresight to realise when he needed to put his guard up. He needed to learn when to stop a situation before it became one. That was where Syed was happy to step in. His mother saw it as goading. Syed preferred to call it the teaching of self-preservation.

'Dress up,' he said, expelling the words through gritted teeth. 'People like to dress up at Hallowe'en.'

Jameel's dark eyes widened as the possibility of what his brother might be suggesting began to sink in. 'So what do we do?' He looked at the shop below. 'You want to get some outfits today?'

'Not from here,' Syed said, rolling his eyes. 'You want a hundred witnesses to be able to say they saw us leaving this place with them?'

For a moment Jameel fell silent, burned by the scathing tone of his brother's criticism. Syed was always putting him down, trying to make him look stupid. He was sick of it. It was about time he showed him just what he was made of.

'Okay,' he said finally. 'Tell me what you think we should do.'

CHAPTER SIXTEEN

'A long shot,' Chloe said to the woman behind the counter, 'but we're trying to identify a man who may have been sleeping rough around here.'

DC Jake Sullivan was standing behind Chloe, his attention momentarily distracted by one of the betting shop's televisions. Like the couple of elderly men who were seated on high stools to the side of him, he was transfixed by the race that was playing out on the screen: mesmerised by the stampede of hooves, the blur of colour, the manic tones of the commentator as the horses reached the home straight. Chloe couldn't abide any form of sport that involved animals. Horse racing in particular seemed unnecessarily cruel.

'Is this about that fire up at the hospital?' the woman asked. She leaned forward across the counter, bringing with her a cloud of sickly-smelling perfume.

Chloe nodded. 'How did you hear about it?'

The woman shrugged and picked at a purple-painted nail. 'One of the regulars was in earlier talking about it. News travels fast round here, like. Specially bad news. You don't know who he was then?'

'Not yet.'

'Fuck it!'

Chloe turned. One of the old men had stood from his stool and was pulling his raincoat on, continuing to curse as his companion stared at the television open-mouthed as though willing the race results to somehow alter.

'Stupid animal. They should put the lazy bugger down.'

An uncharitable response flitted through Chloe's brain and she held back the temptation to share it. Where was the appeal in this? she wondered. A few minutes of anticipation that resulted in inevitable disappointment and certain financial loss. She would rather give her money away than help further line the pockets of a betting shop owner.

Perhaps she was being unfair, she thought. Hadn't she once known what desperation felt like? There had been a time when she would have done anything for money. And she had. She wasn't really in a position to judge.

'You must get quite a few regulars in,' Jake said, breaking Chloe's train of thought. 'Anyone you might usually see who's not been in over the past couple of days?'

The woman sat back and pulled her jet-black hair back from her face, knotting it in a bun with the elastic band she wore around her wrist. 'We get plenty of regulars, but only a few you could set your watch by. The others are in and out all over the place. I can't think of anyone I've noticed who's not been in recently.'

Chloe retrieved her mobile phone from her pocket and showed the woman an image from it. It was a photograph of the trainers the victim had been wearing; not the pair retrieved from the hospital, but an internet image of the same style.

'Ever noticed anyone wearing these?'

She wasn't surprised by the perplexed look the question received. Expecting this woman to have noticed the shoes of every customer who walked through the doors of the betting shop was more than a long shot.

'They're quite distinctive,' she added hopefully.

The woman shook her head. 'Sorry.'

Chloe thanked her and left, with Jake following behind. They stepped out into the afternoon air and scanned the street for the places they had not yet been. There wasn't that much to work with: a café that appeared to have no customers, a boarded-up TV repair shop that looked as though it hadn't been in business since the nineties; a women's clothing shop that bore a forlorn-looking 'CLOSING DOWN SALE' sign on its front window. The busiest place was the Spar, but the staff there hadn't had anything of use to share.

'Never seen any homeless people round here,' Jake said as they headed back to the car. 'Think the DI has got it wrong?'

'Just because you haven't seen them doesn't mean they don't exist.' Chloe folded her arms across her chest in an attempt to stave off the cold. It wasn't yet November, but it already felt as though winter had taken a grip. Being homeless at any time of year must be a miserable experience, she thought, but during winter and with the approach of Christmas it must be especially desolate.

Jake had a point, though. She had never seen anyone sleeping rough this side of Cardiff. There were shelters with emergency beds, and a recent rise in food banks meant that those who were in need were able to eat, but where were these people the rest of the time? Homelessness was on the increase in the capital; to think that it wasn't spreading elsewhere would be naïve. And yet, somehow, the homeless managed to make themselves invisible. Or maybe everyone else was responsible for making them so.

CHAPTER SEVENTEEN

Youssef Hassan had spent the past year looking tired, but that evening he looked more weary than his wife could ever remember having seen before. He sat at the dining room table and stared at the meal Mahira had cooked, having barely touched it. It was his favourite curry and she had made it especially for him. Even during the preparation, she had known she was likely wasting her time. She was trying to recreate something – a past family life she longed for, though she knew they had long left it behind; that things were never going to be the same again. Watching her sons across the table, she knew in her heart which of them was to blame, though she still couldn't bring herself to speak the words aloud.

'We need a reminder of some house rules,' Youssef said, sitting back in his seat and trying to assume an air of authority. 'Have you heard what people are saying about you? My own sons, discussed in the street like common thugs.'

The arguing had started as soon as he'd returned home. First he had been told about the fight and then Mahira had had to tell him about what had happened to the shop. She had listened to the raised voices, wondering when all this would finally come to an end. It was always the same – Youssef would shout for a while, lay down his set of rules, but by the time morning arrived, things would all be swept under the rug again, ignored as though nothing had happened.

She had once thought her husband a strong man, but in recent months she had begun to question whether the act was greater than the reality.

Youssef caught Jameel's eye. The bruising on his son's face remained livid, broadcasting the fight he had got himself embroiled in on Thursday night. 'You're not to go out again until those bruises are gone.'

Across the table, Syed laughed. It was subdued, subtle, but there nonetheless.

'Do you have something to say about it?' Youssef challenged.

The words said one thing, but the tone with which they were spoken said another. Mahira studied her husband with sadness. He was a broken man. He didn't have the strength to go through this again, not now, after everything else.

'He's nineteen,' Syed said with a shrug. 'You can't tell him what to do.'

In his lap and hidden beneath the table, Youssef's hands clenched into fists. Syed was always doing this. Always challenging; always disobeying. He was the reason they'd been forced to leave their old life behind, yet here he was trying to sabotage what might become of their new one.

'He lives in my house,' Youssef said, the words now sounding more like those of the man he had once been. 'He eats my food. If either of you don't like the way we tell you to do things, then you are free to move out and fend for yourselves.'

Jameel hadn't spoken. He was staring glassy-eyed into his curry, having eaten even less than his father. Beside him, at the end of the table, Faadi sat eating silently, his head bowed over his plate in an attempt to shut out the sounds of what everyone knew would escalate into an argument. He didn't really have the stomach for food either, but with no one else eating he didn't want his mother to feel that her efforts that afternoon had all been for nothing.

'I thought we were going to talk about the fire.'

Youssef glanced at Jameel, his jaw tensed and dark eyes narrowed. 'We are.'

'What is there to talk about, though, really?' asked Syed. 'It was only a matter of time. People round here hate us.'

Mahira sighed and dropped her fork into her bowl. 'Not everyone hates us, Syed. There are plenty of nice people around if you bothered to look for them.'

'Where?'

'I speak to nice people every day of the week. You know, if you stopped being so angry and confrontational all the time, perhaps people might start being nice to you too.'

Syed gave a bitter laugh. 'How long are you going to keep up this pretence, eh? How much more abuse do we have to listen to? How many more insults do we have to have smeared across the shop walls before you open your eyes and see things for what they are? You know, it's all well and good wanting to see the best in people, but sometimes it's just burying your head in the sand.'

'They're a minority, Syed,' Mahira argued. 'Ignorant people are everywhere, or do you know of somewhere they can be avoided completely?'

Syed shook his head, his mouth turned up at the corner in an angry smirk. 'You're deluded, you know that?'

'Enough!' Youssef slammed his fists on the table, sending water slopping from the rim of his glass. At the far end of the table, Faadi winced in his seat. A lump of chicken lodged for a moment in his throat.

'You will apologise to your mother for speaking to her in this way.'

When Syed said nothing, Youssef rose from his chair. Father and son glared at one another, each refusing to back down.

'Say you're sorry.'

Syed pushed his chair back from the table and stood. 'No. I'm not sorry. Unlike you, I'm not scared to speak the truth.'

As he walked to the door of the dining room, Youssef followed. He grabbed his son by the arm, and Syed responded by shoving him away. 'If you walk out of here without apologising to your mother, then don't you dare think about coming back to this house.'

'Youssef—'

'No,' he said, turning to his wife and cutting her short. 'Enough. You've defended him and made excuses for him and where has it got us? We moved here for him, to keep him safe, to keep him out of trouble, yet here we are still mopping up his mess and still pretending we can make a better man out of him.' He was shouting now, and Mahira caught sight of tears spiking at the corners of his eyes. He had always been a proud man; he had never let his family see him reduced to tears before. 'Our whole lives have been turned upside down for that boy, and for what? So we can watch everything we've worked for be ruined? You can stand by him if you want, Mahira, but think carefully if you choose to. It's me or him.'

Mahira hoped it was an idle threat, but when she looked at Youssef she realised he meant every word. 'Youssef,' she said, keeping her voice low and steady. 'You're tired and upset. The fire … your job … you've taken too much on. You need to rest. You don't mean what you're saying.'

Youssef turned back to Syed, who was hovering at the doorway. 'Why are you still here?' he asked flatly.

His eldest son looked to Jameel, widening his eyes, conveying a secret message that no one else could decipher. Jameel nodded before looking away. Their father might be prepared to ignore the real problem, but that didn't mean they had to.

CHAPTER EIGHTEEN

When Sian got home, Keeley was in the living room watching television. She was dressed in a pair of pyjamas, and the sight made Sian's heart sink a little. She had hoped that her daughter might be going out that evening and that she would have the house to herself for just a few hours, but the pyjamas meant that Keeley would be staying put. Sian was going to have to tell her about Nathan, though she had been hoping to put it off for as long as possible. If she didn't do it tonight, Keeley would end up hearing it from someone else.

'Not seeing Tyler tonight then?'

Keeley's eyes remained fixed to the TV screen as she answered. 'No.'

Sian walked through to the kitchen and flicked on the kettle. Then she turned it off again. She needed something stronger; something that might take the edge off the day that lay behind her and the evening that stretched ahead. In the back of the cupboard above the washing machine she found a half-empty bottle of vodka.

She took a glass from one of the cupboards and poured in a large measure of the spirit before topping it up with Coke from the fridge. Gulping down half the glass, she leaned against the back door and closed her eyes. The letter was at the bottom of her bag, where she had stuffed it early that morning. It had been waiting for her on the hallway floor when she'd got home from work the previous day, and it had taken her until Keeley had gone to bed to summon the courage to open it and read its contents. She had already known the news it would hold, but knowing hadn't made seeing the words any easier.

She finished the drink and mixed herself another before taking it to the living room. Keeley was still sprawled on the sofa, her attention fixed on the television screen, where a young couple were arguing over a sex text the man had sent to the woman's sister.

'Keeley?'

'Yep.'

'Can we talk for a minute?'

'Yep.'

Sian waited for her daughter to turn off or mute the television, but she did neither. The voices of the shouting couple continued to fill the room. When Sian said nothing more, Keeley glanced up at her. 'What is it?'

Sian sat down and sipped her drink. The flood of warmth the alcohol had momentarily sent racing through her body had already passed and in its place a chill had seeped into her bones. She felt a heaviness settle in the pit of her stomach.

'I've had a letter about your brother from the Criminal Appeals Court.'

For the first time, Keeley turned to look at her mother. Her face, pale and for once make-up-free, was difficult to read. This was nothing new. She would be fourteen the following month. Nathan had been exactly the same at that age, aloof and unresponsive. Yet Sian knew just how close her son and daughter had been, as thick as thieves throughout their childhood. Her body tensed in anticipation of Keeley's reaction.

'Nathan's appeal?'

Sian nodded. She wasn't sure she would even need to say anything; she knew her face was already giving away the contents of the letter.

Reading her mother's thoughts and understanding what she wasn't able to say, Keeley stood hurriedly from the sofa. The glass of Coke that had been at her feet was knocked over, spilling in a dark puddle across the laminate flooring. 'Why?' she wailed. She stood over Sian, fighting back tears as she tried to comprehend the news. 'You said he stood a good chance this time.'

Sian shook her head. She might have said that, but she had never really believed it. Nathan's sentence of twelve years had already been lenient in comparison to other similar cases. His defence lawyer claimed he had done as much as he could to press for mitigating circumstances, but they had all known it wouldn't be enough. Nathan was still guilty, and he had pleaded so.

'Listen,' she said, trying to keep her voice steady and hold her own sadness in check. 'This isn't forever, okay? If he keeps his head down and carries on doing what he's doing, he could be home in a few years.'

Keeley's eyes narrowed, disbelieving. 'How many years?'

Sian hesitated. Nathan had been in prison now for just short of two years. He would probably have to serve at least half his sentence before he was even considered for early release. He would be twenty-two by then, no longer a boy.

'I don't know,' she said, guessing it a better answer than the truth.

Keeley looked suddenly so young, standing on the living room rug in her pyjamas, her mousy hair dishevelled. Her face bore a confused expression of dejection and anger. Like Nathan, the child in Keeley had quickly disappeared. Sian could just about remember the days when she had wrapped her little girl in a blanket and held her close when the nightmares had come, but those memories were fading faster by the day. She had tried her best to forget them.

'I hate him,' Keeley said quietly, the words almost lost to the room.

Sian wondered if Keeley somehow knew that her father had been released from prison. Had someone already told her? She lingered on the words, chewing over them before swallowing them down. Things were hard enough already.

As her daughter's face twisted into a grimace and her body began to shake with anger, Sian looked down at the drink in her hand. She wished she had a bigger glass, one she could sink right to the bottom of and drown in.

She flinched as Keeley hurried past, slamming the door as she left the room, then downed the remainder of her drink and leaned back into the sofa, trying not to think about what might come next. He would come to the house, she knew he would. The restraining order meant nothing to him, and she knew that the temptation to cause trouble would prove too much for him to resist.

And if he did, then what?

She sighed. Like so many other things, it was easier not to think too much about it. Thinking had proved to be a dangerous and compulsive pastime. She leaned her head back, and tried to fight the vision of Christian's face that greeted her when she closed her eyes. It was only a matter of time before she would come face to face with him again.

CHAPTER NINETEEN

Alex sat in her living room with the curtains pulled shut to block out the darkness of the evening. She had been able to find a local handyman who had painted the front door for her that afternoon, successfully concealing most of the insult that had been sprayed there. The beginning of the letter W and half an E were still evident on either side of the door, still staining the paintwork of the house, but it would need a proper clean to get rid of them. She would get around to it at some point, but for now it wasn't a priority.

Sipping a cup of coffee and pulling her legs up on to the sofa beneath her, she opened the second web page on the list that had been thrown up by the search engine. It was a newspaper article that dated back over two years. *Poisoned Father Guilty of Domestic Abuse*, read the headline.

> A father of two from the Rhondda valleys has been sentenced to five years' imprisonment for GBH against the mother of his two children. Christian Coleman, 37, was sentenced at Cardiff Crown Court, where photographs of the injuries inflicted upon Sian Coleman were shown to the jury. The family made newspaper headlines earlier this year when Christian Coleman was poisoned with antifreeze at the family home by his sixteen-year-old son, Nathan, who was later sentenced to twelve years in prison for attempted murder.

Alex didn't need reminding of the details of the case. She had been responsible for charging Nathan Coleman with attempted murder, and later she had questioned the sentence that had been passed down to the boy. It seemed unjust that Christian – a notorious thug whose reign of terror over his partner and children had been documented in distressing detail in court – had been given such a lenient sentence while his son was set to lose the best years of his young life.

Not for the first time, she pondered the question of what would have been right in this case. She hadn't envied the judge the decision he had been faced with making. Regardless of what Christian Coleman had done, it hadn't given Nathan the right to take matters into his own hands. Many people had applauded him – in some corners of the town in which Christian had made himself notorious, people had actively celebrated Nathan as some sort of hero – but that didn't make the boy's retaliation acceptable in the eyes of the law. If everyone took revenge in such a way, the world would exist in chaos.

But if the criminal justice system had been more efficient, Alex thought, Christian Coleman would have been behind bars long before his son had had a chance to try to kill him.

She left the web page and ran a Google Image search on Christian Coleman. She found him instantly: a broad-shouldered bull of a man with a scar that ran from his left temple to his nose; a souvenir of a fight he had lost as a teenager. He had a face that looked permanently angry, scrunched up and wrinkled like a bulldog's. Alex had wondered what Sian Foster, Christian's ex-partner, had ever seen in the man, though it was obvious fear had kept her in the relationship long after she had wanted to leave. It had been impossible not to feel sympathy for Nathan. He had watched his mother endure years of suffering at the hands of his violent father, and evidence in court proved that this violence had extended to the boy and his sister too. Perhaps he had seen no other way out for them.

Looking up from the screen of her laptop, Alex thought back on Christian Coleman's trial. As well as charging Nathan with the attempted murder of his father, she had also been responsible for Christian's arrest. She had questioned him at his hospital bed, where he was being treated for irreparable kidney damage following the poisoning.

Those last words he had spoken to her on the day he was finally sent down repeated yet again in her head.

She pushed the laptop to one side and got up to go the kitchen, taking her empty coffee cup with her. She needed something stronger. From the fridge she took a screw-top bottle of white wine, half finished the previous evening. Since Chloe had moved out of the house and into her own place the occasional glass had become something of a nightly habit, but the alcohol helped soften the edges of Alex's loneliness.

Whore.

She was being neurotic, she thought as she poured the wine. Yet the word was so specific – so memorable as his. *Bitch* could have belonged to anyone. But *whore* was different. Alex couldn't recall anyone else having referred to her using that word.

Throwing back half the glass, she attempted to straighten out and organise her thoughts. Not for the first time, she was overthinking things. Besides, graffiti hardly seemed Christian's style. He was more likely to send a couple of heavies to her house to frighten the life out of her rather than resort to idle insults, and if he had been intent on carrying out his threat of killing her, then he was hardly like to achieve it through paint fumes.

But what if this was just the start of something more?

Shaking herself from her musings, Alex took the wine to the living room and returned her focus to the laptop. Concentrating on work allowed her to distract herself from thoughts that plagued her: her mother's recent death, her estranged ex-husband; the silence that surrounded her, filling the house she had hoped would be a family home. Images of the beaten and burned victim found in the abandoned hospital building took hold, all the more harrowing for the detail in which she was able to recall the scene. There was hardly time to waste on Christian bloody Coleman when they had a killer to find.

She pushed the laptop to one side and went to the front window, checking past the curtains and out into the front garden. The shadow cast by the hedge to the left boundary threw darkness over the small stretch of steps that led down to the pavement, and the breeze caught the tree that stood at her gate, sending its branches flailing.

There was nothing out there, she told herself, letting the curtain fall. But in spite of herself, she went back out into the hallway to check the lock on the front door one last time.

CHAPTER TWENTY

Julie Morris arrived home late from a twelve-hour shift to find her older grandson Tyler sprawled on the sofa, flicking the television remote between music channels. She wanted nothing more than to have a warm shower and change into a pair of pyjamas, but she needed to talk to Tyler about his dad and there seemed no time like the present. He and Gavin seemed to be growing closer; something Julie wasn't happy about. She wasn't entirely sure that Gavin really wanted to be involved more in his son's life or whether he was simply making the sudden effort just to get under her skin.

'Curtis in bed?' she asked, pushing her shoes from her feet and kicking them against the skirting board.

Tyler nodded, not taking his eyes from the television screen, where a young man dressed in a leather jacket writhed against a guitar in a way that looked both uncomfortable and obscene. This recent phase her grandson seemed to be going through involved long hair and a depressing soundtrack, and though Julie hoped it would prove a brief transition into something else, it was a phase Tyler had been stuck in for a while now.

'I've been trying to call you.'

'Left my phone at Keeley's.'

Julie rolled her eyes and sighed. 'You're useless with that bloody phone. Start looking after your things. So you've not seen your dad today?'

He shook his head.

'Listen, Tyler … about your dad. Can you turn that down for five?'

Tyler muted the television and turned to face her. Even in the low light of the table lamp beside the sofa, Julie could see the start of facial hair appearing at her grandson's top lip and shadowing his jawline. She had blinked, and in that moment Tyler had grown from a baby into a young man. The five years since his mother had died had passed by in a blur, yet in so many ways they had been the longest of Julie's life.

Gavin had missed so much of his sons' childhood; even the parts when he hadn't been serving time and had simply chosen to be an absent father. He'd been happy to let Julie and her daughter do the hard work, and he didn't deserve to have Tyler or Curtis back now.

'I know you're getting on well and everything,' she said, sitting down on the sofa beside him, 'but just don't expect too much, okay?'

'Like what?'

'Like anything. It's just …' She stopped, realising she had been about to sugar-coat what she really wanted to say. There she'd been, pondering how the hell he'd grown up so quickly, and now she was about to patronise him as though he were still a little kid. 'You know about your dad's drug dealing,' she said. 'You know that's why he went to prison.'

Tyler nodded, watching her as though waiting for something else; something new and previously unknown. There was always something new where Gavin was concerned.

'He's probably told you he's changed. Has he said that yet?'

'He said something about wanting a fresh start.'

Julie rolled her eyes. 'People don't change, love, not really. They'll say they want to or they'll try to prove they have or they can, but you know the expression "a leopard never changes its spots"? Well there's a reason for it. Your father's a chancer – he always has been.'

'Why did Mam get involved with him then?'

It was a reasonable question, Julie thought: one she had repeatedly asked herself both before and after her daughter's death. She'd been a smart kid, a pretty girl who could have had her pick of anyone, but she'd chosen Gavin and she'd paid the price for it. The evening she was killed in the hit-and-run she'd been over to Gavin's parents' house, trying to get him to take responsibility for his sons. Julie shrugged. 'Honestly? I don't know.'

She stood from the sofa. 'Look ... you want to see the best in people. That's fine. That's exactly what your mother was like when she was younger. That's why she stayed with your dad, always hoping things would be different one day. But he can't change, love, even if he thinks he wants to. He'll be back to his old ways in no time. I just don't want you to be disappointed when it happens.'

She went to the living room door. 'Have you eaten anything? Shall I put some toast on?'

Tyler nodded. 'Nan?'

'Yeah.'

'What would it have taken for her to stay with Dad? If he'd had to prove himself, like ... what would he have had to do?'

Julie put a hand on her hip as she pondered the question. 'Been the person she wanted him to be, I suppose. He'd have had to be something he wasn't.'

She watched her grandson for a moment as he unmuted the television and turned his attention back to the screen. Then she headed to the kitchen to make him some toast.

CHAPTER TWENTY-ONE

The skies are ablaze with colour. She sits on the wall in the garden, her head tilted to the heavens, emptiness filling the space in which her anger only recently resided. Her anger has so often felt like a separate person, as though it doesn't belong to her. When it builds beyond her control – when the desire to break something becomes so strong that it seems it might instead break her – it feels as though she is being held by some greater force that is able to move her and make her do as it pleases.

She could try to resist it, but she doesn't want to.

She checks her phone, still waiting to hear from him. There is nothing. If it didn't cost so much to replace, she would throw the thing at the garden wall; watch it smash into pieces across the patio slabs. There is satisfaction in watching something break and in knowing her own hands are responsible for something that no one else can ever undo.

And now she has discovered a new way to sate her appetite. It is like a drug, overpowering and addictive.

She was angry at first. She listened for the sirens, hearing their screams fill the streets, and the sound filled her with a secondary rage so different to any she had experienced before; so unlike the first anger: the one that makes her do the things she does.

Fear doesn't come into it. Like so many other parts of her brain, the piece that senses fear has failed her. It is missing.

And one day soon she will go missing with it.

CHAPTER TWENTY-TWO

The smell of Chinese food that wafted from the carrier bag was making the man's mouth water; he hadn't eaten anything since that morning and had waited for his girlfriend to finish work before ordering the takeaway. He was still in her bad books. She had left him a list of chores the length of his arm while she'd been away with a couple of friends during the week, and had come home the day before to find none of them had been done. He wasn't intentionally lazy; he just found it difficult to be organised. He was hoping that a house special chow mein and the bottle of red he had waiting back at the flat would win her round. She couldn't stay mad at him forever, although some days it felt as though she was determined to give it her best effort.

The man cut down a path that divided a row of terraces and turned left towards the park. It was dark behind the houses, without the glow of street lights to soften the blackness of the evening, and every footstep he took seemed to echo around him, bouncing from the doors of the garages. He wondered whether they might watch a film later, depending on his girlfriend's mood when she got home.

There was a hiss and a screech and the man looked up to see a lone firework scream upwards to the sky before it exploded in an umbrella of colour. Reaching the end of the lane, he turned towards the path that ran alongside the park and quickened his step, wanting to get home before the food needed reheating in the microwave. As his eyes adjusted to the shadows thrown across the footpath by the overhanging trees that lined the park, he saw a figure ahead. It staggered in the middle of the path as though drunk, but as he got closer he realised it wasn't one person, but two.

He stopped and narrowed his eyes to gain better vision in the darkness. As the outlines of the figures sharpened, it became clear that they were fighting.

'Oi!'

The man hurried forward, oblivious to the potential threat ahead. The figures came into focus: one dressed in Hallowe'en costume, the black and white of the skeleton making him harder to distinguish in the darkness; the other just a boy. It was the boy the man had seen staggering, falling back as a flurry of punches had rained down upon him.

'Leave him alone!' the man shouted.

Then he heard something else: the splash of liquid as it was slopped from a can and thrown across the cowering boy, who tripped on something and fell with an echoing thud to the ground.

Dropping the takeaway bag, the man charged at the skeleton, throwing himself at the figure whose face was hidden behind a mask of bones and darkened eyes. The skeleton stumbled before regaining his balance. With a shove, he sent the man staggering before fleeing into the darkness of the path. The man might have chased him, but the pitiful whimpering that sounded from the ground near his feet kept him fixed where he was.

'Come on,' he said, offering the boy a hand. He couldn't have been more than sixteen, he thought. Just a kid. The boy stayed cowering on the ground, reluctant to accept help from a stranger, clearly terrified by what had happened, and what might have happened had the attacker not been intercepted.

Then the smell hit the man, stronger now than the waft of chow mein that drifted from the fallen takeaway splattered across the concrete path feet behind them. He reached down and put a hand to the boy's arm, touching the wet sleeve of his jacket.

The boy had been doused in petrol.

CHAPTER TWENTY-THREE

Alex was dozing when she got the call. She hadn't been able to settle in bed that night, turning beneath the duvet in a sleep-starved state before admitting defeat and getting up to instead set up camp beneath a blanket on the sofa. It occurred to her that this was how Chloe must have spent the past nine months, and that this was the reason she had been reluctant to live alone. Yet she knew that Chloe's fear had existed on a scale she couldn't comprehend. This feeling of anxiety took hold quickly and without reprieve, and she could only imagine how difficult it must have been for Chloe to attempt a normal existence after her attack. Not for the first time, she felt an increasing respect for her young colleague.

The officer who called her reported that a fifteen-year-old boy had been attacked in a lane just a few streets from his home. Petrol had been thrown at him, but the attacker had been interrupted by a passer-by before he had been able to ignite it, if that had been the intention. Given recent events, Alex feared it a certainty. The account given to her over the phone – a call that had been made much later than she was happy with – suggested that the boy was refusing to speak to anyone, least of all the police, but that was hardly surprising. The trauma of what had happened to him was likely to have stunned him into temporary silence.

Pulling on a pair of trousers, Alex wondered what the hell was happening to the world. Attacks such as this seemed to be on the rise, but the news reports that filled the TV and radio with an ever-increasing sense of bleakness at the state of mankind always consisted of stories plucked from other places: the big cities that lay miles from the supposedly sleeping hills of the South Wales valleys. People didn't expect incidents such as this to occur on their doorsteps, and when they did, they were all the more shocking for it.

Fifteen, Alex thought as she searched her jacket pockets for her car keys. Just a kid. Why would anyone attack a kid like that?

Making sure she had her mobile phone with her, she pulled the front door shut behind her, locked it and made her way out into the night. Recent temperatures had been unusually mild for the time of year, but during the past few days a chill had kicked in and winter seemed to be making its first appearance. Beneath the glow of a street lamp, Alex unlocked her car and got inside, turning the heater up as soon as she started the engine. Her thoughts strayed once again to the homeless man found in the derelict hospital, murdered and still to be identified. Had he been sleeping rough for some time, or had he only just been made homeless? Someone must have known him well enough to have missed him at some point.

As she pulled the car from the kerbside, she mulled over the recent incidents. The fire at the Hassan shop. The blaze at the old hospital in which a man had been killed. And now the teenage boy doused in petrol. Were the three linked? The use of petrol made it too coincidental – the time between the incidents too brief – for the events not to be connected in some way.

The boy had been taken by ambulance to the Royal Glamorgan Hospital in Llantrisant, where uniformed officers had spoken with his mother. His physical injures included a fractured wrist and bruising, but Alex knew the psychological impact of the incident would stay with him for much longer. The officer she had spoken with had told her the boy was autistic, although few further details had been given. She wondered the extent to which he was affected; she knew little about autism, but assumed it would inevitably impact upon the boy's ability to comprehend and cope with the assault.

As she approached the end of her street, Alex put her foot to the brake. Nothing happened. She wasn't doing much of a speed, but it was night-time, the street was quiet and the hospital was a half-hour's drive away, so she was going faster than she usually would. She tried the brake again, pushing the pedal flatter to the floor in an attempt to slow the car. The end of the street neared and she felt herself begin to panic. She pumped the brake with her foot, but still nothing happened.

As she closed upon the junction that connected the end of her street with the main road that snaked up the side of Caerphilly Mountain, Alex yanked the handbrake. It slowed the car, but not enough to stop it pulling out onto the main road. She swung the steering wheel in the hope of getting out of the path of any oncoming traffic, but the glare of lights from a car racing up the mountain road told her she was too late.

The other car was going too fast to stop. Alex pushed herself back against the driver's seat, bracing herself for the inevitable collision. There was a screech of tyres and a crunch of metal against metal as the back of her Audi was smashed into and the car careered into the front wall of one of the gardens opposite.

CHAPTER TWENTY-FOUR

Keeley had gone over to Tyler's house that morning, and Sian was grateful for it. The atmosphere at home had been even more fraught than usual and Keeley had spent much of the previous evening slamming doors and playing music too loudly in her room. Sian might have tried to talk to her, but she didn't want to, not yet. She had learned over the years that with Keeley it was best just to let her vent her frustrations in her own way and she would come round when she was finally ready.

She hadn't bothered to get dressed. The news of the rejection of Nathan's appeal had hit her hard. She wasn't going anywhere, not today. After abandoning the idea of breakfast, she went into the living room and curled up on the sofa beneath a blanket. She didn't want to put the heating on, not if she could avoid it. It was all she could manage to keep food in the fridge these days. The more she worked, the more expensive the bills became. It was a never-ending cycle, one she couldn't see herself ever breaking free of.

Turning the television up in an attempt to drown her thoughts, she sank further into the sofa. So many tears had been shed the previous night that she didn't think there could possibly be any more to spare. She was wondering whether she might be able to catch up on some sleep when there was a knock at the front door. She sighed; she didn't want to face anyone this morning. She waited a moment. The doorbell was pressed before a second knock came, this one more insistent. With another sigh, Sian got up from the sofa and went to the window. Pushing aside the curtains, her heart skipped a beat at the sight of her ex standing at the front door. She hadn't seen Christian in over two years, but little had changed in that time. He was still repulsive.

What was he doing there? She'd taken out a restraining order against him before he had been sentenced, and as far as she knew, it was still applicable. She let the curtain fall and leaned against the window frame, breathing deeply to try to slow her heart rate. The last time she had seen Christian had been the day he was sentenced; before that, it had been the day he'd left her hospitalised. She could still remember it so clearly now: waking in hospital to the muffled sound of nurses' voices somewhere along the corridor as the memories of the previous evening collapsed on her like a landslide, burying her.

The pounding of his fist on the front door snapped her back to the present.

'I know you're in there, Sian! I'm not going anywhere until you speak to me.'

She scanned the room for her mobile phone and caught a glimpse of it on the arm of the sofa where she'd left it earlier. The threat of the police would surely be enough to deter him, unless he had some sort of wish to end up back inside prison so soon after leaving.

'Sian!'

She crossed the room and retrieved the phone from the sofa. She wouldn't even threaten him with it, she thought as she tapped in her mobile's password; she'd just call them and let them turn up without warning him.

'Police, please,' she said to the female voice that answered the 999 emergency call. Once she was transferred, she explained the situation. Someone would be round to the house as soon as possible, she was told. In the meantime, Christian had continued to bang his fist against the front door, now in a rhythmic beat that Sian assumed was intended to drive her mad until she relented and answered.

'Sian,' she heard again, his voice different this time, softer. 'I'm not here to cause trouble.' She realised he was speaking through the letter box now, his voice clearer than it had been. 'I just want to talk about Nathan.'

The sound of her son's name momentarily eased Sian's anger, replacing it with a sadness she knew would keep her trapped in its grip for the rest of the day; for every day until he was released. What did he want to talk about Nathan for? There was nothing for him to say. He was responsible for everything Nathan had done, regardless of what the judge who had passed down his sentence might have said.

She left the living room and went into the hallway, keeping her mobile phone clutched in her hand.

'Just piss off, Christian. You're not supposed to be here.'

'I heard about the appeal.'

Sian leaned against the wall and closed her eyes for a moment. She wondered where everything had gone so wrong. It wasn't so hard to work out: nineteen years earlier, when she'd met Christian at a party at a friend's house. That was the moment her life had gone from could-be-something to everything-ruined. She had fallen pregnant within months of meeting him, much to the dismay of her parents. No matter what they had said back then, Christian had been nothing like he was now, or at least she hadn't thought so at the time. Evil had a clever way of concealing itself sometimes.

'Look,' he said through the letter box. 'I'm not here to argue, okay. I heard about the appeal and … I'm sorry, all right? Prison's no place for a boy like him. I don't blame him for what he did, not any more. I've had plenty of time to think, Sian.'

In the hallway, Sian rolled her eyes. She'd heard it all before: he'd learned his lesson, he'd changed, he was sorry. All of it meaningless.

'You're not supposed to come anywhere near me.'

'I know that, but I just want to talk. I don't want any trouble. Please, Sian.'

She stood her ground and waited. Eventually he'd get the message, she thought.

'Come on, Sian. I don't expect you to ever forgive me, okay, but let's try to be civil, shall we? For the kids?'

'Civil?' Sian's composure left her and she strode down the hallway and snatched at the letter-box cover, snapping it up from where his fingers pushed it open. 'You should have thought about civil when you were smashing my head through the back door.'

A pair of eyes appeared in the gap; the same pair of eyes she had once let fool her with their false kindness. 'I know, and I'm sorry. I can keep saying sorry but it won't make any difference will it? Look, I don't want to talk about this and you don't want to talk about this, right? I'm here about Nathan.'

Sian kept the letter box lifted, standing to one side of the door so that Christian was unable to see her. Once again, Nathan's name filled her heart with a sadness that overwhelmed her. Every time she went to visit him, it seemed another small piece of her son had been lost. Since his move from the young offenders' prison to the central prison in Cardiff, things had only got worse. Another few years and all those small pieces would eventually amount to the whole.

'Sian,' Christian tried again, his voice still soft and persuasive. 'I just want to talk about Nathan, I promise. I know a way we might be able to get him home.'

Sian unlocked the door and opened it slightly. 'Five minutes.'

Christian raised his hands in mock surrender. 'Five minutes.'

She glanced along the street as he entered the house, checking that none of the neighbours had seen him there.

'This place hasn't changed much,' he said, looking down the hallway and into the kitchen. He stepped into the living room.

'Well?' Sian prompted.

'Well what?'

She watched helplessly as Christian sat down on the sofa, leaned back and looked around him as though taking a trip down memory lane. Her heart raced as she realised she had made a mistake by letting him in. 'This plan.'

'What plan?' He turned to her and gave her a smile. 'Put the kettle on, would you, love?'

With the phone still clutched in her hand, Sian felt herself begin to shake. There was no plan to get Nathan home at all; it had been a cruel way of Christian getting himself inside the house.

'I've called the police,' she told him.

'You might want to get a few extra cups ready then.'

CHAPTER TWENTY-FIVE

The boy's mother stood in an empty hospital room with Dan and Chloe beside her. In her early forties, she was pencil-thin, her narrow hips protruding in the skinny jeans she was wearing. They had already met her son, Corey, a slight boy who looked younger than his fifteen years and was reluctant to make eye contact with anyone. He was lying in bed in the room next door and had refused to speak to either Chloe or Dan. According to his mother, Leanne, he hadn't yet said a word to her either.

'I encouraged him to go out,' she said through gritted teeth. 'This is my fault.'

'It isn't your fault,' Chloe tried to reassure her. 'You mentioned earlier that Corey struggles with social situations?'

Leanne Davies sank onto a plastic chair and rested her elbows on her knees and her chin in her hands. She wouldn't make eye contact with either officer, as though too ashamed to look at them. 'Corey is different. He always has been. He's in a world of his own half the time, and when he does decide to join this one for a while, he doesn't make an effort to fit in. He can't go through his whole life like that. I just want him to try to be—' She cut herself short. A flush of colour rose to her cheeks.

Normal, Chloe thought. That was the word she'd been about to use.

'Where did Corey go yesterday afternoon?' Dan asked.

Leanne sat back. 'Only over to someone's house. There's a new boy not long ago started at his school, he's been trying to get to know people. Why he'd choose to latch onto Corey I don't know. Maybe no one else would have him.'

Dan glanced at Chloe.

'Sorry,' Leanne said quickly, seeming to sense the exchange without having witnessed it. 'I love my son, I really do. I'm just tired, that's all.'

'Do you know what time Corey left this other boy's house?' asked Chloe. 'We'll need his name and contact details if you have them.'

Leanne nodded. 'I don't know what time he left there, though. I don't know anything.' Her tears were sudden and explosive, and they left Dan shifting uncomfortably from foot to foot. 'Petrol,' she said between sobs. 'Who the hell would want to hurt him like that? He's just a kid.'

Chloe looked to Dan. 'Could you go and find us some tissues?'

It was more a reason to get him out of the room. Leanne Davies had been through enough already; having Dan looking as though he'd rather be anywhere else wasn't going to help. Dan was useless around tears. He never knew where to look or what to say. He was so infamously inept in that area that the job of informing relatives of a victim's death was no longer assigned to him. Perhaps that was what he'd been aiming for.

'I sound like a terrible mother,' Leanne said once Dan had left the room.

Chloe pulled up a chair and sat down next to her. 'No you don't.'

'I don't understand Corey, see, and the problem is he knows it. He can't talk to me about things ... he can't talk to anyone.' She used the heel of her hand to rub her eye, and a smear of yesterday's fading make-up smudged across her cheek.

'Is Corey's dad around?' Chloe asked.

Leanne nodded. 'He's in the RAF, though, so he's away from home quite a bit. At least he gets a break.' She bit her bottom lip. 'I'm sorry. I get so frustrated sometimes.' She looked to Chloe, making direct eye contact now. 'When Corey was little, he used to say and do the most annoying things, weird things, but he was never a bad kid, not like some of them you see about. He would never hurt anyone.' She stopped for a moment to catch her breath. 'What if he'd been set alight?'

Chloe placed a hand on the other woman's arm as the tears escalated again. 'There's nothing about this to suggest Corey was a chosen victim. It looks like a random attack. I know it won't make what's happened any easier, but there's no one to blame here other than the person responsible, okay?'

Leanne nodded, though she didn't look convinced. She was still blaming herself for encouraging her son to go out. She looked up as Dan came back into the room, gratefully accepting the box of tissues he handed her. 'Do you think the samples are going to be any use?'

She was referring to the fingernail scrapings that had been taken from Corey and the man who had intervened during the attack. Both had come into direct physical contact with the attacker, so there was a chance that they might have carried evidence in the form of DNA from the man's skin cells. Chloe realised it was a long shot; evidence rarely came about that way. The man had also told police that the attacker was wearing an outfit that had covered much of his body, making the chances of any DNA being transferred even slimmer.

'We hope so,' she said, neither wanting to raise the woman's hopes nor leave her with no hope at all. 'It might take a couple of days to get any results back from the lab, though.'

Leanne nodded, wiped the back of a hand across her eyes and stood from her chair. 'Can I go back to see him now?'

Chloe nodded. 'The boy Corey was with yesterday,' she reminded her.

'Oh yeah. Faadi Hassan.'

Chloe shot Dan a look.

'You know him?' Leanne asked, acknowledging the exchange.

'We know of the family.' Chloe stood. 'When Corey does start talking, please let us know. Anything he might remember, no matter how small, might be a help to us.'

Once Leanne had left the room, Chloe turned to Dan. 'Faadi Hassan. Small world, isn't it?'

As they made their way out of the hospital, she retrieved her mobile phone from her pocket and turned it back on.

'Have you heard from Alex?' Dan asked.

'Only to say what happened. She said she was fine, but she sounded a bit shaken up to me.'

Dan pushed open the double doors, holding one open for Chloe. 'Car been looked at yet?'

'Don't know.' Chloe waited for any messages or missed calls to come through, but there was nothing from Alex. 'She'll probably be at the station when we get back.'

'Wonder why the brakes just went like that?' Dan said, thinking out loud.

'Don't know. She'll probably get rid of that car now, though. She's never liked it anyway.'

They stepped out into the fresh morning air and headed across the bridge to the overflow car park. Chloe's thoughts strayed from Alex to the boy they had left lying mute in his hospital bed. There was the obvious link of the petrol – and now that of Faadi Hassan – but other than that, what were the similarities between the recent cases involving fire, or an attempt at it? Was there a link between the victims?

She shuddered at the thought of what might have happened to Corey Davies. Someone had targeted him with the intention of setting him alight. The viciousness of the crime was difficult to comprehend. When she'd told Leanne that her son had just been unfortunate enough to be in the wrong place at the wrong time, was she right?

The mobile phone still in her hand started ringing, breaking her chain of thought.

'DC Lane.'

Dan stopped at the car, waiting as Chloe took the call.

'The station,' Chloe said, returning the phone to her pocket. 'Sounds like someone might have CCTV footage of our victim.'

CHAPTER TWENTY-SIX

Sian flinched at the sound of the front door, even though she had been expecting Gavin's arrival since she'd called him twenty minutes earlier. Christian had gone just over an hour ago, only leaving when the police had finally turned up. He'd mentioned Nathan knowing he was Sian's weakness. She would do anything for her son, even if it involved having to speak to Christian.

She had deliberated over calling Gavin. She didn't want him to think she was falling back on him in a moment of weakness, despite the fact that that was exactly what she was doing. She just didn't want to be on her own in that house any more.

'What's he done to you?' Gavin asked, closing the front door behind him.

'Nothing,' Sian said, heading down the passage and into the kitchen. 'He just came to wind me up and it worked. Do you want a drink?'

Gavin followed her. 'I thought you had a restraining order or something?'

'I do. The police took their time turning up, though.'

'Did he hurt you?'

Sian reached up to the cupboard above the microwave and took out two mugs. 'No.' She moved to the kettle, lifted it from its base and filled it with water.

'You could probably do with something stronger than tea,' Gavin suggested. 'Where's Keeley?'

'With your Tyler.' Sian opened the fridge and scanned its shelves. There was barely anything inside. The irony of working in a supermarket yet having empty cupboards didn't escape her. 'Nothing left here.'

Gavin leaned against the kitchen worktop. 'I'll pop to the shop in a bit. You haven't told her yet, then? About us.'

'Is there an us?' Sian returned to the kettle and set about making tea.

'Do you want there to be?'

'I don't know,' she admitted, keeping her back turned to him. 'I don't know anything any more.'

'I like you, Sian,' Gavin said hurriedly. 'You know that. I know I'm not perfect and I know you'll have heard plenty of stuff about me, but most of it's not true, okay? I want to make a fresh start, put everything behind me.'

With her back still turned, Sian rested her hands on the kitchen worktop and took a deep breath, as though the words that were about to leave her required her full energy. 'Nathan's appeal has been rejected.'

For a moment, Gavin said nothing. Everyone knew what had happened within Sian's family a couple of years earlier: it had spread through the valley like a virus, picking up embellishments and false details on its way. Christian Coleman had a history that could rival any of the inmates Gavin had met during his own stint in prison. News of his poisoning had mostly been met with applause.

'Shit,' he said finally, knowing there was little else he could offer. 'I'm sorry.'

Sian poured milk into two cups and passed Gavin his tea. 'It's just so unfair. Nathan was protecting us, yet he's the one stuck in that bloody place while that bastard walks around without a care in the world. I should have left him years ago, then none of this would have happened.'

'Hey,' Gavin said, setting his tea down and stepping closer to her. 'None of this is your fault, okay?'

He put an arm around her and Sian rested her head against his broad chest. He ran a hand over her hair and held her close to him. She looked up and kissed him. She didn't care any more. She didn't care whether he was the wrong type, or whether her daughter was seeing his son. Why did her happiness always have to come second to everyone else's?

She kissed him again. His hands ran over her waist and slipped beneath her top. Remembering why she couldn't let this happen, Sian grabbed his wrists. It was too late. He had already looked down. He had already seen enough exposed flesh to know what she'd been trying to keep hidden.

'Did he do that?'

Sian pulled her top down over the waist of her jeans and turned back to the cupboards. 'There's some biscuits in here somewhere.'

Behind her, Gavin sighed. 'Sian. Did he do that to you?'

She had studied the stain of purple and black bruising in the bathroom mirror that morning, ashamed to see herself in the reflection. It made her look like a victim, and she was tired of being a victim. 'It's nothing.'

'Doesn't look like nothing to me. Why'd you let him in here anyway?'

She turned back to him, anger streaking her face. 'He's only just been here,' she snapped. 'You think they'd be this colour that quickly?'

'So he's been here before, then. Are you still seeing him? You need your head looking at.'

Sian swiped a hand across the worktop, sending the sugar tin flying across the room. The lid bounced across the tiled floor as a shower of sugar fell at Gavin's feet. 'I can't do this,' she shouted, her body shaking with a sudden and uncontrollable rage. 'I can't go back to having someone questioning my every move, making me explain myself all the time.'

Gavin looked stunned for a moment, taken aback by her burst of anger. 'Fine. Then don't.' He turned to leave.

She didn't want him to go, not really, but she knew he couldn't stay either. 'Gavin …'

'No, it's fine, Sian. Forget it. I don't need this either. I've got enough drama of my own without taking on yours.' He stopped in the kitchen doorway and turned back to her. 'Why are still protecting him?'

'I'm not.'

He rolled his eyes, shook his head and left. At the sound of the front door closing behind him, Sian turned and lashed out, knocking her mug from the worktop and sending the tea splashing to the floor, scalding her bare feet.

CHAPTER TWENTY-SEVEN

'Are you sure you're up to this?'

Alex unclipped her seat belt and opened the passenger-side door. She was too shaken up from the crash the previous night to drive and had been spared admitting so when Chloe had made the offer. She had planned to tell her colleagues as little as possible, but as soon as she'd mentioned the brake failure she knew she'd made a mistake. She didn't want to discuss it any further, but Chloe was unlikely to let the matter drop.

'I'm fine,' she said.

She wasn't fine, but sitting at home feeling sorry for herself wasn't going to achieve anything. She kept telling herself that whatever had happened the previous evening had been nothing more than an accident, but the more she tried to convince herself, the more unlikely the scenario seemed. It was very rare that accidents just happened. More often than not, there was someone to blame.

Alex and Chloe waited at the front door before following Mahira Hassan into the house and through to the living room. The woman was clearly house-proud: there was not a single cushion out of place on the sofa and the room was so spotlessly clean and minimalist that Chloe felt as though they had entered a show home. Mahira gestured to the sofa and offered them a cup of tea. Alex declined, but Chloe accepted. Mahira went to call Faadi before making her way to the kitchen. She told the officers he was upstairs in his bedroom and had barely left there since hearing about what had happened to Corey the night before.

'Bit weird all this, don't you think?' Chloe said once Mahira had left the room. She perched on the edge of the sofa, too uneasy to sit back and disturb the arrangement of the cushions. It was a wonder anyone could ever relax when surrounded with such order. The place was so tidy it made Chloe's own minimalist home seem cluttered in comparison. 'I was only with them a few days back at the shop, and now this. Seems a bit coincidental.'

She stood and crossed the room to the fireplace, looking at the family photograph that hung in a thick gold frame above it. She guessed it had been taken several years earlier: Faadi, the boy she had met at the shop, looked no more than eight years old, and Mahira seemed much younger than the woman who had just left the room. In the photograph, she was standing next to her husband, whose arm was draped around her shoulder. There were two other boys, older than Faadi, who Chloe assumed were his brothers.

She turned to the door at the sound of voices in the corridor: Mahira Hassan cajoling her youngest son into entering the living room and speaking with the two officers waiting for him there. When he finally did come in, he kept his head lowered and his eyes fixed to the carpet. He was wearing tracksuit bottoms that were a size too small for him and stretched around his middle, and a T-shirt that looked as though it was part of a pyjama set. He didn't know what to do with his hands, first shoving them into his pockets and then pulling down his T-shirt, awkwardness radiating from him with an intensity that quickly became uncomfortable for everyone else in the room.

'You're not in any trouble, Faadi,' Chloe told him with a smile.

He didn't respond, but sat down at the end of the sofa, still keeping his focus away from the two officers.

'We just want to ask you a couple of questions about yesterday evening. Is that okay?'

'Is Corey all right?' Faadi asked, his voice barely audible.

'He's fine,' Alex said. 'He's back home already.'

The tension in Faadi's shoulders eased slightly, his body relaxing at the news that his friend was okay. His mother stood at his side, a reassuring hand placed on his back. 'There we are,' she said, rubbing her palm up and down his spine. 'I told you he'd be all right, didn't I?'

Chloe sat on the sofa, making sure to keep a distance between herself and Faadi. From what she had already seen of him at the shop on Friday, he seemed a shy boy, younger than his thirteen years. It had been impossible to get anything from Corey; perhaps speaking with Faadi was going to prove just as challenging.

'Have you and Corey been friends long?'

Faadi shook his head. 'I don't really know him,' he mumbled.

'Faadi,' Mahira said gently, 'try to speak up a bit so the officers can hear you.'

The boy looked embarrassed by his mum's words and shifted uncomfortably on the sofa. 'We talk online, on the Xbox. I don't really know him, but Mum says I should try to make some friends and Corey's the person I've spoken to the most.'

'So you invited him over to play computer games with you?' Chloe asked. 'Sounds fun.'

'Not really,' Faadi said, his brief confidence already lost and his voice lowered to a mutter once again. 'I mean, it was okay.'

'I'll go and make that tea,' Mahira said. She didn't look as though she wanted to leave the room and glanced nervously at her son as though doubting he would cope without her there. Chloe felt sorry for the boy: he didn't know where to look, and she wondered if he went about his life like this, seemingly nervous of his own shadow. He was slightly overweight, and she suspected that along with his nervousness it probably made him an easy target for bullies.

'Faadi,' Alex said, 'did Corey say anything to you about meeting anyone on Saturday?'

'No. He just said he was going home. Mum doesn't drive and Dad wasn't here, but he said he was fine to walk. It isn't far.'

There was a sound out in the hallway, the closing of the front door, and moments later the living room door was opened and a young man appeared, his hands buried in the pockets of his jacket and his sullen face set in a scowl. He had chiselled features and thick black hair that fell over his face. 'Who are you?' he asked, looking from Chloe to Alex. The question had the tone of a challenge.

Chloe recognised the young man from the photograph she'd been looking at above the fireplace: the oldest of the three Hassan brothers.

'DC Chloe Lane,' she said, standing from the sofa. 'This is DI Alex King.'

Syed glanced down at his brother before putting a hand on his shoulder. 'Fatty,' he said, dragging the word out in a drawl. 'You been in trouble with the police again, eh?' He laughed at his own joke, and Chloe noticed the fingers he held clasped on Faadi's shoulder tightening. By the looks of things, the boy didn't need to go to school to get bullied.

'I expect you've heard about the attack on Corey Davies that took place last night,' Alex said, having also noted the way in which Syed Hassan manhandled his brother. 'We're just here to ask Faadi a few questions.'

'Why?' Syed snapped. 'It's nothing to do with him.'

Mahira appeared in the doorway behind him, a mug of tea in her hand. 'Syed ... now isn't a good time. You're not supposed to be here.'

He glanced back at her. 'Who's the tea for? They're not stopping.'

'Actually,' Chloe said, accepting the drink, 'we're in the middle of speaking with Faadi, so if you wouldn't mind leaving us to it ...' She held his gaze, unprovoked by his attempts to unsettle her. It was clear Syed Hassan had little respect for the police, and it seemed he had even less for women.

'Found out who torched our shop yet?' he asked, raising an eyebrow and turning his attention to Alex.

'The investigation is ongoing.'

Syed laughed. 'So no, then. But, you know,' he said, turning back to his mother, 'let them do their job, isn't it, Mother?'

Mahira moved past him, avoiding any physical contact. 'Please go, Syed,' she said, her voice fraught with exhaustion. 'I'll call you later.'

He opened his mouth to speak, but finding himself outnumbered thought better of it and left, slamming the front door behind him.

'I'm sorry,' Mahira said quietly.

'No need,' Chloe said, sipping her tea as she moved to the sofa. 'Okay, Faadi, we're almost done. You were telling us about Corey leaving here yesterday. What time was that?'

'About eight o'clock. He texted his mum to say he was leaving.'

'These games you play on the Xbox,' Alex said. 'Do they involve you speaking to other people online? People you don't know?'

Although the incident involving Corey Davies appeared at first to be random, they had to consider the possibility that the boy might have known his attacker. He was vulnerable – more so than most boys of his age – and it was this that made him an easy target. Had his attacker chosen him, he had done so knowing that Corey would be unlikely to fight back.

Mahira shook her head and looked at her son, concern etched on her tired face. 'We don't allow him to do any of that,' she told Alex. 'He's too young. It's not safe.'

'Faadi,' Chloe said, knowing that even the most attentive of parents couldn't possibly be aware of their child's every movement. 'You're not going to be in any trouble, okay?' She looked to Mahira and gave her a nod. It was difficult for parents to hear that their child might have been involved in something they had known nothing about, particularly in cases that involved potential danger. 'Did you or Corey speak to anyone online yesterday?'

Faadi's head remained lowered, but Chloe could see a tear escape the corner of his left eye. 'No,' he said finally. 'We didn't speak to anyone.'

Chloe stood. 'Thank you, Mrs Hassan, that'll be all for now. Thank you, Faadi.' She paused for a moment, wondering whether the boy might offer anything else. When he didn't, they left.

'What do you think?' Chloe asked when they were back at the car.

'Which part?'

'Faadi. Poor kid seems scared of his own shadow.'

'That might well be,' said Alex, doing up her seat belt, 'but he's probably a lot more scared of that brother of his.'

Chloe started the engine and pulled away from the kerb, casting a parting glance at the Hassan house. For whatever reason, Faadi was withholding something, and she was determined to find out what and why.

CHAPTER TWENTY-EIGHT

The team gathered in the incident room, forming a semicircle around the evidence board, which now included the incident involving Corey Davies. Alex headed the meeting. She was physically fine, although the events of the previous evening had left her feeling more than a little paranoid. She couldn't shake off the feeling that had gripped her when she had found herself unable to stop the car. It hadn't even been the prospect of an accident that had unsettled her: it was the thought that someone was responsible for it. The car had only recently been in for an MOT. There had been nothing wrong with it.

It was her suspicions about who might have been responsible that were making her feel so unsettled.

'Right,' she said, bringing the chatter around her to a close. 'You're all aware of the attack on fifteen-year-old Corey Davies that occurred yesterday evening in the park next to Ystrad sports centre. He was kept in hospital overnight but has already been discharged. Corey has autism,' she said, pointing to the photograph of the boy that had been added to the evidence board that morning. 'Dan and Chloe have met his mother and by all accounts he struggles with social situations and is quite reclusive. As things stand, he still hasn't said a word to anyone. As you know, the attack was interrupted, but the perpetrator managed to throw petrol at Corey before he fled.'

She turned to the board and ran a finger from the photograph of the interior of the Hassans' burned-out shop to the horrific image of the charred remains found in the derelict Llwynypia hospital.

'We've no link between these cases at the moment other than the occurrence of fire, but the proximity of the incidents time-wise suggests that they may be somehow connected. Following the TV appeal, we've received a call from a café owner in Tonypandy who recognised the description of our victim. Last Tuesday he asked a man to leave the premises – he claims the man was drunk and was making a nuisance of himself.'

She stopped for a moment and leaned across the desk in front of her, clicking a few keys on the laptop that lay open there. No one said anything. Alex's tone was abrupt, her words clipped, and rumours about the circumstances surrounding her accident had circulated around the station quickly that morning. The car had been taken into a local garage she had managed to find open on a Sunday, and she was waiting to hear back from them. Until she did, she knew she should avoid speculation. The thought was easier than the deed. One name kept repeating itself.

If she achieved little else that day, she had resolved to find out where Christian Coleman had been the previous evening.

On the whiteboard behind Alex was projected a still taken from the CCTV footage that had been passed on by the café owner. The image was surprisingly good, the man's face turned so that the camera was able to capture a clear picture. He was wearing a dark coat and a thin beanie hat. The bottom half of his body was out of shot, meaning they were unable to see what he was wearing on his feet.

'Obviously the image is black and white, but the café owner has given a description of the man's clothing that matches items found at the hospital.'

'So it seems more likely now that he was sleeping rough there?' Chloe asked.

Alex nodded. 'The image is going to run on this evening's news. Dan, I'd like you to get it up on social media, see what comes back from it. Hopefully someone will be able to identify him.'

Moving from the desk, she returned to the evidence board. 'Before he was attacked last night, Corey had been with Faadi Hassan, the youngest son of the couple who own the Llwynypia Stores. Chloe and I visited the family's house this morning. Chloe.'

'The two boys played computer games in Faadi's bedroom before Corey left at around eight o'clock,' Chloe told the team. 'Faadi didn't say much more than that. Trying to get anything from him was like pulling teeth. If this morning was anything to go by, the two boys probably didn't speak to each other while they were together yesterday.'

'His brother made up for it, though,' Alex said.

'What do you mean?' Dan asked.

'Syed Hassan seems to have a bit of a chip on each shoulder, put it that way. It could still be a reaction to the arson at the shop, perhaps. Do we have a link between Corey and Faadi here, or is it just coincidence? A petrol can was found a couple of streets away from last night's attack – it had been thrown over a garden wall. It's with forensics at the moment. Ideally we'll be able to retrieve fingerprints, but the contents have also been sent for testing. Once we know the brand of petrol, we may be able to find out where it was purchased.'

'So what do you want us doing in the meantime?' DC Jake Sullivan asked.

Alex shot him a frosty look. Not for the first time, Sullivan seemed to want spoon-feeding and she didn't have the patience or the time for team members who couldn't use a bit of initiative. 'Your job,' she suggested. She could feel Chloe's eyes on the side of her face, judging her reaction. She turned back to the board. 'What do these victims have in common?'

When no one responded, she found her impatience growing. 'A Muslim family relatively new to the area who have already reported a series of racially motivated incidents, most of which are connected to their shop. A man we believe to have been living homeless whose post-mortem report shows evidence of substance abuse and who was likely to have been under the influence when he was attacked. A fifteen-year-old boy with severe autism ... do I need to spell it out for you?'

The atmosphere had chilled even further, the temperature in the room challenging that of outside. No one spoke for a moment, taken aback by the uncharacteristic anger that emanated from Alex.

'All vulnerable victims,' Chloe said, breaking the uncomfortable silence.

'Thank you,' Alex said, exasperation still lacing her tone. 'There was no victim in the physical sense at the Hassans' shop, but we don't know whether that was intentional. The fire was started at around one thirty in the morning, so it's unlikely that the person responsible would have believed anyone to be inside at that time. So what are we looking at, if in fact the same person is responsible for all three incidents?'

'Are we expecting another incident, given the time frame between these?' DCI Thompson asked.

'I'd say it's likely. Let's not forget the timing, either. We're in the lead-up to Bonfire Night. Perfect time of year for a pyromaniac.'

'You think something else might happen then?' Chloe said.

'I just think we should prepare ourselves for the possibility.'

'Looks as though you'd better get a move on then, Detective Inspector King.'

Alex glanced at DCI Thompson, who was assuming his usual nonchalant stance next to the doorway, ready to leave as soon as he was able. She swallowed a response, though doing so nearly choked her.

'Okay – Dan, if you could get things moving on social media, get this image out there and we'll see if anything comes back. Chloe, I'd like you to come with me to Ystrad sports centre. Something might have been picked up on CCTV there. Jake, I need some background checks done on the Hassan family. I'm not expecting to hear anything from forensics today, but as soon as anything comes in I want it shared with everyone, please. Let's find some solid connections between these incidents.'

As the team dispersed, Chloe lingered. 'You sure you're okay?' she asked.

'Yeah, fine.'

'What's his problem?' she asked, giving a nod in the DCI's direction.

Alex rolled her eyes. 'Missing the home comforts of HQ, I'd imagine.'

'Any news about the car yet?'

Alex shook her head.

'You seem uptight.'

'Chloe,' Alex said abruptly, gathering her things from the desk in front of her. 'I said I'm fine.'

She swept past her and left the room, leaving Chloe wondering just what had happened the previous evening. One thing was certain: Alex was far from fine.

CHAPTER TWENTY-NINE

Alex and Chloe waited in the sports centre's reception area for the staff member they had spoken with to return with the assistant manager. Alex realised they were hoping for a miracle: the path on which Corey Davies had been attacked was at least fifty metres from the building, and the security cameras would only have captured an image of the suspect if he had entered the park from a particular direction and if the sports centre's cameras were located in the right spot.

The assistant manager was young, in his mid thirties, and was wearing a tracksuit. The sheen of sweat across his forehead suggested he'd just come from the gym, and when he saw the two women waiting for him at the front desk he self-consciously ran a hand through his hair in an attempt to make himself more presentable. Alex didn't miss the double-take that Chloe received, though she imagined that, as always, the look had passed Chloe by unnoticed.

'Is this about the attack on that kid last night?' he said.

Alex nodded. 'We're hoping one of your security cameras might have picked something up. Can you show us where they are?'

They followed him through the centre's main doors and out into the car park. Chloe shot Alex a look that she pretended not to notice. The atmosphere between them had been strained since they'd left the station, with Chloe still smarting from the way Alex had spoken to her earlier. Using the sports centre manager's looks as a way to break the ice was going to fail before it even started. Ever since she'd moved out of Alex's house, Chloe seemed to have been on some sort of mission to get Alex back into the world of dating. It wasn't going to happen. It definitely wasn't going to happen with a man a decade younger than her.

'We've got three,' the assistant manager said, pointing up at the far-left corner of the sports centre's roof. 'One up there that overlooks the car park, one at the main doors and the other one round the back.'

Alex looked across the car park and back to the security camera on the roof, assessing the angle at which it was pointed. They were going to need more than a miracle, she thought. 'We'll need a copy of the recordings from yesterday evening,' she told him, knowing they would probably prove fruitless.

They followed the man back inside the centre and waited at reception as he went to retrieve the recordings.

'You're not hopeful,' Chloe said, having read the reaction Alex had given in the car park.

Alex shook her head. 'Too far away and too bloody dark.'

'What did you think of him?' Chloe asked with a smile.

Alex rolled her eyes. 'You don't give up, do you?'

'What?' she said with mock innocence. 'He seemed nice.'

'Yeah, lovely. We could go on double dates. He and Scott could talk training routines ... that'd be fun.'

Chloe smiled at Alex's sarcasm. Whatever was going on, she was confident her friend would confide in her when she was ready.

After the assistant manager returned with copies of the recordings, the two women left the centre and headed towards the park, frustration quickening Alex's steps. The attacker could only have left the park in one of two directions: either along the street that ran parallel with a local primary school, or up a narrow path between two end-of-terrace houses and out onto the main road. She stopped at the path's end, assessing the options. Had he planned the route he would take when fleeing the scene, or had he made an impulsive decision when faced with the choice?

'He went this way,' she said, gesturing to her left and speaking more to herself than to Chloe.

'How come?'

'The primary school is likely to have CCTV as well,' she said. 'I'm not so sure this was a random attack. He knows the area. If he's managed to avoid being picked up on CCTV at the sports centre, he'd have known to avoid the school.'

The two women headed up to the main road. Sunday afternoon meant the area was fairly quiet, and the sky was already beginning to grow dark though it was not yet four o'clock. They stopped outside a terraced house that was decorated for Hallowe'en, a fat pumpkin staring at them with blackened hollowed eyes from the living room windowsill.

Alex scanned the street. She knew what she was looking for, and if her hopes were realised then there was a chance their attacker had been captured elsewhere.

'Bingo,' she muttered.

Chloe followed as Alex crossed the road and led them to the bus stop.

'Our witness left the takeaway on Brynglas Terrace at quarter past eight. It would have taken him a couple of minutes to reach the sports centre, so the attacker would have got to this main road at around twenty past eight or just after.' She traced the bus timetable with a finger, stopping at the 20.14 that passed through from Porth to Treorchy. 'They're never on time,' she said, still talking to herself.

'CCTV on the bus? Bus company might be worth a visit then.'

Chloe waited for a response, but none came. Alex hadn't been listening all day, not really. She hadn't been herself, and the accident the previous night was responsible for that. Chloe wondered why she was so reluctant to talk about it.

'I'm leaving the country,' Chloe said. 'I was thinking Asia, maybe. I've heard Thailand is nice.'

'Hmm.'

She narrowed her eyes. Whatever was going on, it was definitely keeping Alex somewhere else. More had happened the night before than she was letting on.

Alex's mobile sounded from her pocket, its ringtone bringing her back from wherever it was her thoughts had strayed. 'Detective Inspector King,' she said, answering the call.

It was the garage. She stepped away from Chloe, keen to keep the details of the conversation to herself. Chloe would only worry, and if Alex's suspicions proved to be correct, there would be too many questions she didn't have the patience to answer.

Pulling her jacket closer around her to stave off the biting cold that nipped the air, she crossed the road and headed back towards the corner that led down to the sports centre.

'Bad news, I'm afraid,' the man at the other end of the call told her. 'If you weren't already with them, I'd be suggesting you call the police. This was no accident. Someone cut your brake fluid line.'

CHAPTER THIRTY

Gavin left the pub in a bad mood. The argument he'd had with Sian had preyed on his mind all afternoon, and when he saw Keeley across the street a part of him wanted to go and speak with her. Though he had never properly met his son's girlfriend, Gavin suspected Keeley knew who he was. Sian was probably right: news that their parents were involved with each other wasn't exactly going to go down well with either Tyler or Keeley. He could remember what it was like to be a teenager, just about. He wouldn't have been too impressed either.

Deciding that speaking to Keeley wasn't the best of ideas, Gavin kept his head low and hoped she hadn't seen him. He didn't need another argument with Sian, and things were going well with Tyler, or at least better than Gavin could have hoped for, all things considered. He didn't want to spoil it. Now that he was a bit older, Tyler could make up his own mind about things and be less influenced by his grandmother. Gavin didn't really mean Julie any harm; he just enjoyed winding her up. When the boys' mother had died, Julie had used the boys as a weapon to punish him with, making sure she did everything she could to keep them from him. Now she was getting a taste of her own medicine. It wouldn't do her any harm.

The thought of what Christian Coleman had done to Sian played over in his mind, the image of those bruises etched on his brain. Gavin had done some bad things in his time, but he had never hit a woman. He and his ex had had some blazing rows on occasions – times during which he might have felt he could quite happily have thrown her from a first-floor window – but he had never carried out any of the sometimes crazy thoughts that flitted through his brain during an argument. Christian Coleman, though, was scum: everyone knew it. News of what he'd done to Sian a few years back had spread quickly, and once it had made the TV news, there were few places he could go in the valleys that would be safe for him. He knew that, so why he'd come back after being released from prison was anyone's guess.

Gavin crossed the main road and cut through the lane that ran behind the row of terraces on which he lived. A sudden optimism for the future coursed through him, warming him against the bite of the late-evening air. It wasn't too late to change. He wanted a clean break, a fresh start; every other cliché used by ex-cons who didn't want to be reacquainted with the inside of a prison. He hadn't meant what he'd said to Sian; it was just bravado. He liked her. Despite her obvious doubts about him, he reckoned if he kept up this good-boy routine for long enough, he might be onto a winner.

He turned the corner at the end of the row of terraces. Perhaps he could take Sian somewhere for a night away, he thought; maybe this side of Christmas if he could scrape together the cash. Sneaking around behind the kids' backs was funny in a way, like some sort of parent/child role-reversal. It'd be quite a turn-on, he thought.

It was the last thought he had before a blow to the head rendered him incapable of any others.

CHAPTER THIRTY-ONE

In her office, Alex sat and read the local news update on her phone, pausing at the CCTV image from the café, which had now been broadcast on the local news and shared on social media in the hope that it might bring them some clue as to who their victim was. She had been listening again to the recording of the 999 call made to police on the night of the fire, but her attention had been distracted by thoughts of the call from the garage. Someone had cut the brake fluid line on her car.

Someone had tried to kill her.

It was late and the rest of the team had long since headed home for the evening. The station had a depressing air on evenings such as this, with everyone's pessimism left behind them, ready to be collected and worn again upon their return the following morning. Alex wished she could do the same – just head home and shut her brain down for the night – but it had never been that easy for her. With no one at home to distract her from the morbidity of her job, just how was she supposed to find any peace away from it?

Paperwork relating to their ongoing cases lay strewn across the desk, serving as a reminder of just how haphazard the current state of things was. The pace of the investigation was frustrating Alex, and though she knew there was nothing more she could do that evening, she didn't want to head home while she was feeling so ineffectual.

She moved from the CCTV image back to the internet web page that showed a photograph of Christian Coleman. His poisoning had been one of the most notorious cases of Alex's career, mainly for the amount of press coverage it had received. She had never forgotten the man. It now appeared that perhaps he hadn't forgotten her either.

Glancing down at the notepad in front of her, she traced a finger across the address she had just been given over the phone. A few calls had put her in touch with Christian's parole officer, who had been able to tell her where Christian had been staying since his release from prison.

As she sipped a coffee that was barely lukewarm, Alex started at a sound outside her door. She exhaled audibly when Dan entered the room. She hadn't realised he was still here. The paranoia that had been born the previous night had grown considerably during the day, morphing into something she could already feel consuming too much of her energy. This wasn't like her, she thought.

'Not going home?' Dan asked, shutting the door behind him.

Alex hurriedly closed the window on her computer. She knew if anyone saw what she had been looking at, they would only think her paranoid. The more she thought about it, the more she suspected the paranoia was in this case justified.

'I could ask you the same.'

Dan smiled. 'You're not fooling anyone, by the way.'

Alex looked back to the home screen of her computer and shrugged in a poor attempt to feign nonchalance. 'This 999 call,' she said, keen to divert attention from herself. She clicked a few keys and retrieved the audio file. 'Listen.'

Dan sat opposite her as she played back the recording. She waited until it had ended before replaying, stopping it midway through. 'Hear that?'

'What?'

'Listen closer.'

She played the recording again, stopping at the same place. *Fire*, the man said. *Old Llwynypia hospital.* She went back and played it again. *Fire.* Stop. Replay. *Fire.* Stop. Replay.

'Hear that?'

Dan pulled the chair around the desk and drew closer to Alex as she replayed the recording once again. 'Is it music?'

'Sounds like it.'

'Can we enhance the sound?'

'Not on here, but we can get it done first thing tomorrow.' She sat back. 'There's something about this call. This person either wanted the fire stopped, or he wanted us to know about it. I just can't work out which.'

'Glory-hunting, you mean?'

'In a sense, I suppose. It's not unheard of. For all we know, he might have been waiting for us to show up, watching the action as it unfolded.'

Her thoughts drew her back to her own home and to the accident that had happened the previous night, an accident she realised could have been so much worse. Had the person responsible for sabotaging her car been there outside her house, waiting to watch her drive away in a car they hoped she would be unable to stop? The thought filled her with unease. Home was supposed to offer a place of safety. Once that idea was broken, there was no going back. Chloe had been proof of that, and her only solution had been to break free of the place.

'You going to tell me what's going on?' Dan asked. 'I thought you might have spoken to Chloe about it.'

'Chloe's got her own things going on,' Alex said, though this wasn't the reason she had chosen not to confide in her. She knew Chloe would listen, but it didn't seem fair. The younger woman was only now beginning to find happiness, and after shedding her own problems, the last thing she needed was to be burdened with Alex's. With her mother's death earlier that year, Alex had already leaned on her colleague too often for support. She sometimes wondered whether she had done the right thing and whether blurring the boundaries between working relationship and friendship might at some point prove to be a mistake. 'Anyway, everything's fine.'

'You're a terrible liar.'

Alex forced a smile. She wanted to confide in someone, but she didn't want everyone at the station knowing what had happened. She would be considered a victim, and the term inevitably brought associations of vulnerability. That was the last thing she needed, especially now, when she was in the middle of such a major investigation.

'Go home,' she told him. 'We should be getting a few results back tomorrow, and if we do, it's going to be a busy day. You'll be needing your beauty sleep.'

'It's a deal,' Dan said, standing from his chair, 'but only if you take your own advice. How are you getting home anyway? You haven't got a car.'

'Taxi, probably.'

Dan whistled through his teeth. 'Won the lottery, have you? Get your things, I'll give you a lift.'

'I live in the opposite direction to you,' Alex said, closing down her computer.

'I'm ignoring you,' Dan said, heading towards the office door. 'I'll meet you downstairs in five. You can tell me what's really going on with your car then.'

He closed the door behind him, leaving Alex in the silence of her office. She listened once more to the 999 call before closing the file. It sounded like music or a mobile phone ringtone. She would get it enhanced tomorrow, she thought. If it was a ringtone, getting a clearer sound might allow them to identify the make and model of phone.

Five minutes later, she met Dan in the station's reception area. The roads were clear, and the journey back to her house took fifteen minutes; long enough for Alex to tell him about the cut brake line. The closer to her home they'd got, the greater her need to talk had become, but despite Dan's generosity in having offered her a lift, she realised he would want to get home to his family. A flicker of envy tripped through her at the thought. For a moment she allowed herself to picture Dan and his wife at the kitchen table together, their two daughters curled up on the sofa watching a film on television.

Stupid, she reprimanded herself. This time of year was always the worst; as soon as Bonfire Night had passed, all the focus would be on Christmas, a time when everyone was supposed to be in high spirits.

Plus it was her birthday tomorrow. Forty-five, Alex thought, as she gazed through the window at the darkened blur of the A470 rushing past her. Had anyone asked her a decade ago where she imagined her life in ten years' time, this wouldn't have been it. She didn't really know what she wanted, but perhaps that had always been her problem.

She hadn't told anyone that her birthday was approaching. She didn't want the fuss, and besides, since turning forty, birthdays had no longer felt like things that needed to be celebrated. She knew that if she had a family, things would be different. But alone, another birthday meant just another day.

She shook herself from her thoughts in order to direct Dan to her street. As they pulled up outside the house, the thought of Christian Coleman lurking somewhere in the shadows of the neighbours' hedgerow filled her with an increasing sense of unease. If she'd had anywhere else to go that evening, she knew she would have headed straight there.

'Let's have a look, then,' Dan said, unlocking his seat belt.

Alex had told him about the graffiti when they'd left the station. 'There's not much left to see,' she said, getting out of the car.

She led him up the front steps.

'I would have said it's probably kids,' Dan said, running a hand across the remainder of the letter E on the wall of the house, 'but the car changes things. You know who did it, don't you?'

'I've got my suspicions.'

'Do you want to tell me?'

Alex shook her head. 'Get yourself home. I'll be fine.'

'I'm sure you will be,' Dan said, 'but that wasn't what I asked. Is there anywhere else you can stay for a few days?'

Alex shook her head. She had contemplated the idea of checking into a hotel temporarily, but what would be the point? She would have to return here at some stage. Running away never solved anything.

'Let me at least check the place over before I go.'

She unlocked the front door and Dan followed her into the hallway. It occurred to Alex that the place was a mess and she wondered how it managed to be so cluttered when she spent hardly any time here. Perhaps that was why. She popped in, she popped back out; she left things where they landed and over time those things had accumulated to a chaos she didn't have the will or the energy to confront. An array of coats and jackets hung from the end of the banister, while a pile of shoes lay abandoned at the foot of the staircase. Unopened post sat in messy piles up the left-hand side of the stairs. The vacuum cleaner – pulled out from the cupboard but not recently put to use – was propped against the wall and the wooden flooring bore the muddy footprints that had been dragged in over a week earlier. The hallway seemed a sad metaphor for her life: chaotic and unloved.

'Do you want a cup of tea? I'd offer you something stronger, but you're driving.'

'Tea's fine.'

Dan checked the living room before following Alex through to the kitchen. 'Nice house.'

'Thanks, though I've been thinking of moving. It's a bit big for just one.'

Dan leaned against the fridge and watched Alex as she checked the back door. 'You can tell me who you think it was, if you want to. Why won't you report it?'

'You know as well as I do that it'll be a waste of time,' she told him, pouring steaming water from the kettle into two mugs. She dribbled milk into the tea and moved one to the worktop beside him. 'How often do reports like that lead to anything?'

'So?'

'So what?'

'Name.'

Alex exhaled loudly and cupped her tea in both hands, allowing its heat to warm her. 'Christian Coleman.'

Dan pulled a face. 'Why do you think it's him?'

She shrugged. 'Just something that was said, that's all. He called me a whore, right after he was sentenced. It's not that common an insult, really.'

She moved to the other side of the kitchen, feeling Dan's eyes watching her. She didn't want sympathy or pity, but she didn't want to be alone with this fear either. She had tried to fool herself into believing she wasn't scared, but she knew only too well what Christian Coleman was capable of.

'Have you chased it up?'

'Not yet.' Alex thought about the address tucked into her jacket pocket. 'He'll have an alibi, no doubt. Doesn't mean he wasn't involved, though, does it?' With a sigh, she put a hand to the back door, pressing on the handle to check that it was locked. 'It was a long time ago now … I'm probably being paranoid.'

Dan drank his tea, watching as Alex pulled down the blind hanging at the window. 'The very reason I sometimes think of quitting. The paranoia can get to you a bit.'

'You're not going anywhere, are you?' Alex said, setting her mug down on the worktop beside the sink. The thought wasn't a pleasant one. Young blood had proven itself worthy in Chloe's case, but in DC Jake Sullivan's it was causing increasing problems. He seemed to require constant supervision, and Alex didn't have the time for babysitting. He needed to prove himself worthy of his place on the team soon, or she would need to start questioning his position. It wasn't in Alex's nature to make things unpleasant for people on her own team, but perhaps this was part of the problem, she thought. She'd always been a team player. She'd been too nice for too long. Nice didn't seem to be getting her anywhere.

'I wouldn't have thought so,' Dan said, draining the last of his tea and crossing the kitchen to place the empty mug beside hers at the sink. 'I'm too old to start anything new now.'

'Exactly. You're stuck going grey with me, I'm afraid. Please don't leave me with the kids.'

Dan smiled. There was a moment between them; something so subtle that it could have been just left to pass had Alex not chosen to cling to it.

'You should get home,' she said.

'I don't really want to leave you like this.'

'I'll be fine.' Even to Alex, the words sounded unconvincing.

He reached for her hand, allowing it to warm his. 'Alex …' He leaned towards her, and when he kissed her, Alex kissed him back.

CHAPTER THIRTY-TWO

On Monday morning, Alex called a taxi to take her to the station in Pontypridd. Her car would be ready by the end of the day, providing the parts arrived at the garage as expected. She knew she should report the crime, but she couldn't see where it would lead. She had no evidence of anything other than the damage to the brake line, and if Christian Coleman was responsible, it was a safe bet that there wouldn't be any fingerprints to be retrieved. He was a thug, but he wasn't an idiot. What good would come from pursuing the matter? If he had been intent on causing her harm, it would only be likely to exacerbate things.

Besides, she had bigger things to worry about that morning.

She had tried to tell herself that it had meant nothing, but the excuse was only intensifying her guilt. Being meaningless made her kiss with Dan somehow even worse. He was her colleague. He was a married man with children. Yet those things had meant nothing the previous evening – not while she was kissing him and not while she was hoping for more – and it was this that made Alex wonder what the hell had happened to her.

The team gathered in the incident room. There had been a few key updates that morning and she was keen to get them shared as quickly as possible. DC Jake Sullivan had been assigned the task of searching the CCTV recordings from the bus that had passed through Llwynypia on Saturday night, and it hadn't taken him long to find something of interest.

'I was hoping a passing bus might have picked up our suspect when he reached the main road from the park,' Alex said, opening a file on the laptop in front of her. 'Unbelievably, we got even better than that.'

There was a flood of chatter among the team as the CCTV footage taken from the 20.14 bus on Saturday evening was played out on the screen behind Alex. The vehicle was near empty, just two people and the driver visible, but at twenty-one minutes past eight, it picked up a person wearing a skeleton fancy dress outfit. The figure could be seen leaving money on the tray that rested beside the driver, then taking a seat near the front.

'Until now, we've been assuming that our suspect had everything well planned and is thorough. This would suggest otherwise.'

'Thick as shit, perhaps?' Jake offered. He laughed at his own contribution, the smile quickly falling from his face at Alex's silent response.

After an uncomfortable moment, she exhaled loudly. 'Obviously it's not a great image in terms of identification. The outfit is hooded and has a mask, so we can't even tell if our suspect is black or white. This person attacked Corey and panicked. He was intercepted, threw the petrol can over a nearby wall and jumped on the nearest passing bus.' She moved from the desk. 'We've had the results back from the lab regarding the petrol used in the attack on Corey Davies. It's a match with that used at the hospital, but not with the fuel used to start the fire at the Hassan shop.'

'Are we reconsidering a link then?' asked Chloe.

'We might have to reconsider a link between all three. I don't think the person responsible for the fire at the hospital is the same person who attacked Corey Davies. I think we might be looking at a copycat. Texaco petrol was used in Corey's attack and to start the fire at the hospital. The closest Texaco petrol station to the incidents is in Llwynypia, with another in Pentre and the next being further down the valley in Porth. Most importantly, a set of prints were lifted from the petrol can.' Alex returned to the desk and clicked a few keys on the laptop in front of her. An image was projected onto the screen behind her. 'They belong to this man. He might be familiar to some of you.'

'Spider,' said Dan. He kept his focus on the screen, avoiding eye contact with her. Alex wondered if anyone else had noticed that neither had acknowledged the other that morning.

'You know him?' asked Jake.

'Know of him. He's got a spider-web tattoo,' Dan explained, gesturing to his own elbow. 'Here.'

'Gavin Jones is thirty-six years old,' Alex said, cutting through the exchange between the two men, 'and lives in Pentre. He's got quite an extensive record that stretches back fifteen years.'

'Any previous for assault?' Chloe asked.

Alex nodded. 'One caution dating back nine years. Bar brawl. At the moment there appears to be no known link to Corey Davies. We do know that Gavin has previously worked as a mechanic and that he rides a motorbike. Chloe, I'd like you to come with me to pay Gavin Jones a visit. Dan, if you could continue updating social media and let me know if anything else comes in. The image of our suspect needs to go public. Jake, I'd like you to speak with the driver of the bus that picked up our suspect on Saturday night, see if he can remember anything else that might be useful to us. The rest of you, we need to find out where that skeleton outfit was purchased. We're still waiting to see whether any DNA was retrieved from Corey's fingernails or from those of the man who intercepted the incident. I'll chase that up today.'

Alex brought the meeting to a close, but the team stayed put, chatting among themselves for a moment. She hadn't noticed that Chloe had sloped off towards the meeting's end, but she returned now, armed with a cake adorned with an array of burning candles.

'*Happy birthday to you, happy birthday to you …*'

The team's attempt at singing came to a staggered and awkward halt as one by one they noticed Alex's response to the obviously unwelcome attention. Her mouth had set in a thin line and her jaw had tightened. She hadn't made eye contact with Chloe.

An uncomfortable silence fell over the room.

'Not really appropriate, is it?' she said after what felt like an age.

The flush that rose in Chloe's face was instant. 'I—' She cut herself short, glancing to Dan for support. Realising the gesture had been misjudged and that Alex's bad mood had not been merely temporary, she lifted the cake board from the desk, letting the candles burn on as she turned away.

'Okay,' Alex said behind her, as though Chloe had already left the room. 'Let's get on with it, please.'

CHAPTER THIRTY-THREE

It was the same process every time: she was searched, and her possessions were removed from her to be stored in a locker, making her feel like a criminal herself. Sian hated the prison. There was a horrible irony about its central position within the heart of Cardiff: Nathan was right in the thick of things – the world moving by in all its vibrancy and colour – yet the high walls and barbed-wire fences that surrounded the ugly grey block buildings meant he was so far removed from life outside the place that he may as well have been living on the moon.

She would wait in line with the other relatives, occasionally recognising a returning face. People rarely looked back. They had all come to look the same to her: all apprehensive; all a little broken in some way. She had thought at first that she might find a certain solace in the other people who came to visit family and friends; that their pain might in some way help to ease her own, but that hadn't been the case. Each visit saw her more removed from other people.

She knew that was why she had been drawn to Gavin. She knew he was wrong, but he'd been kind to her and loneliness wasn't picky. He was there, and that was more than could be said for anyone else.

The guard at the door barely acknowledged her as she entered the visiting hall. Her eyes scanned the room until they found her son. He was sitting with his back to her, hunched forward in his seat; his shoulders slumped as though he was carrying a dead weight, not the mere one hundred and forty pounds that made up his skinny frame.

Her heart broke a little more every time she saw him. Since being moved from the young offenders' prison, he had become even more withdrawn. She had always feared losing him, but had never imagined it might happen like this.

'Nathan.'

He didn't lift his head when she spoke his name, and when she sat opposite him, she realised why. His left eye was a bloodshot burst of green and purple bruising.

'Jesus, Nathan, what the hell's happened?'

It was obvious what had happened. What had Christian said through the letter box the previous day? Something about prison being no place for a boy like Nathan.

Sian felt a sickness lurch in her stomach. She wanted to reach across the table and hold her son, but the prison visiting rules forbade physical contact. Anger coursed through her, sudden and violent. She wanted to find the person who had hurt him and rip his head from his shoulders with her bare hands.

'What are they doing about it, Nathan? You need to report whoever's done this.'

'Don't start, Mam, please.' His eyes pleaded with her. He looked on the edge of tears and she suspected that if they hadn't been sitting in a room filled with his fellow inmates, there would have been nothing that would have stopped them flowing freely. 'My appeal ...' he began.

He couldn't get past the words. He looked down at his lap and picked at the nails on his right hand, searching for anything that would keep him from having to look at his mother's face.

'I'm so sorry.'

The words sounded pathetic. They were meaningless. Sorry wasn't going to change the decision that had been made about Nathan's future. Sorry wasn't going to alter the fact that even when his sentence was finally over, he would still be scarred by the brand of criminal; a sentence that would hang over him for the rest of his life, wherever it took him.

The empty promise his own father had made just to get access to the house and taunt her with her helplessness bounced around Sian's brain, deafening her. Perhaps she should take the anger she felt for the person who had harmed her son and direct it purely at Christian, she thought. There was no one more deserving of her bitterness. The so-called justice system had practically let him get away with what he'd done to her family. Maybe it was time for her to do something about it instead.

'I am not giving up on you,' she said, moving closer to the table between them. 'Nathan. Listen to me. I'm going to speak to another lawyer, get us some better help.'

'There's no point. We can't afford it anyway.'

'It doesn't matter. I'll find the money somehow.'

The buzzer rang for the end of visiting and Sian cursed the noise, as she did on every visit. There was never enough time. Just as she felt they had just got started, he was ripped away from her once again.

'Do me a favour, please, Mam?' Nathan said, standing from his chair.

'Course, love. Anything.'

'Don't come again.'

He turned his back and walked away, before Sian had time to respond.

CHAPTER THIRTY-FOUR

Alex sat in her office and waited for someone to answer her call. She had thought about going to the address she'd been given, but the case required her to be at the station and she couldn't justify popping out for what was currently little more than a nagging suspicion.

'Hello?'

'Is this Mandy Lewis?'

'Who's asking?'

Alex felt her lip curl. Charm evidently ran in the Coleman family. 'Detective Inspector Alex King, South Wales Police,' she told the woman. 'Am I right that your nephew, Christian Coleman, is staying with you at the moment?'

'So what if he is?'

'Can I speak with him?'

The woman started coughing and Alex instinctively moved the phone from her face, as though her germs were going to be sent shooting down the receiver. 'He's not here,' she spluttered eventually.

'When was the last time you saw him?'

'Bloody hell, what is this, twenty questions? I don't know … yesterday afternoon sometime.'

'So he didn't come home last night?'

The woman paused before answering, apparently belatedly realising that whatever she said might in some way incriminate Christian. 'I didn't say that. I said I hadn't seen him … doesn't mean he didn't come home. Why don't you ask him yourself?'

Alex opened her mouth to respond, but the line had gone dead. If she wanted to ask him, she was obviously going to have to do so face to face.

*

Dan was sitting at his computer in the incident room. He hadn't seen Alex since the meeting earlier that morning and for now he was happy for it to remain that way. Trying to prise his thoughts away from what had happened between them the previous evening, he scanned the long list of comments that followed a Facebook status relating to the attack on Corey Davies. The original status had been posted by one of his own relatives; a distant cousin who his wife insisted on writing a Christmas card to every year despite the fact she had never met him:

Whatever bastard assaulted Corey Davies last night better sleep with one eye open. Picking on a disabled kid #scumoftheearth #watchyourback

He felt a hand on the chair behind him as Chloe leaned over his shoulder to take a look at the comments.

'Anything of interest?'

'Not yet. Just the usual vigilantes. Why do people use hashtags on Facebook?'

Chloe shrugged. 'Not sure. Annoying, though. Is autism classed as a disability?'

'Don't know. If it's severe enough, I suppose.'

She pulled up a chair and sat beside him. If she noticed his reaction – the flinch of unease that sparked from him at her proximity – she didn't give anything away. Chloe and Alex had grown close during the past year. If Alex was going to confide in anyone about what had happened the night before, Dan thought, then Chloe would be that person. But surely she wouldn't. There was too much at stake, for both of them. And after this morning's outburst, he suspected that the friendship between the two might be left to cool a little.

The photograph of his wife and two daughters stared at Dan from the side of his desk. Their eyes, usually a source of such comfort in a place that was a constant reminder of the darkness of the world, now seemed to glare at him accusingly. He had been with his wife for almost twenty years. They had been married for fifteen. In all those years he had never been unfaithful to her. He had never wanted to be.

'What about the image from the bus?'

He clicked a second window and brought up the comments section that followed the post appealing for anyone who might recognise the fancy dress costume worn by the suspect. It hadn't yet been online an hour, but already a stream of comments was strung beneath it. Most were expressing anger at the attack, but there were the inevitable jokers who thought it appropriate to make wisecracks at the expense of a victim of crime.

The kid got battered by Funny Bones, someone had posted. *#fail*

'There's always a comedian,' Chloe observed. 'Some of these people need to get a job – they've got too much time on their hands. Dan. Dan …' She waved a hand in front of his face. 'Don't let me keep you here,' she said.

'Sorry,' he said, returning his gaze to the computer screen. 'Have we found out where the outfit might have been bought yet?'

'There are three possible shops north of Pontypridd. One in Porth, one in Tonypandy and the third in Treorchy. Alex and I are going to pay them a visit after we track down Gavin Jones. He's conveniently nowhere to be found.' She glanced behind her, checking Alex hadn't returned. 'She hasn't said anything to you, has she?'

'About what?'

He realised his response was too abrupt, his defensive tone too apparent. He'd tried to tell himself it was only a kiss, but it hadn't done anything to ease his guilt. If his wife had kissed another man, he knew exactly how he'd react.

'Her car. I've tried to speak to her, but she won't talk about it. She was in a bad enough mood yesterday, but this morning was something else. I don't know what I've done to upset her.'

Dan shook his head. He had promised Alex he wouldn't mention the cut brake fluid line to anyone and he certainly wasn't going to go back on that promise now. 'She shouldn't have spoken to you like that this morning. She was out of order.'

Chloe shrugged. 'Doesn't matter.'

Her expression suggested it clearly did matter. Dan knew she looked up to Alex, and being berated like that in front of the team would have hurt her more than she was letting on.

'Chloe.'

She turned at the sound of her name, feeling her face flush at the sight of Alex standing behind them. She hoped Alex hadn't overheard any of the conversation that had just passed between her and Dan.

'Just got another call in,' Alex told her. 'We might have the name of our dead man.'

CHAPTER THIRTY-FIVE

Faadi sat on the top step of the staircase and listened to the argument that was escalating in the living room below. Syed had returned again to the house, bringing with him his usual torrent of bad feeling. He knew he wasn't supposed to think it about his own brother, but Faadi sometimes wished that Syed had stayed in Cardiff when the rest of the family had moved to the Rhondda valleys. Their mother and father had hoped that moving from the city would keep Syed away from the gangs he had got involved with as a teenager, but from what Faadi knew of his brother, Syed didn't need to find the company of trouble: it was in him anyway.

Things had been pretty miserable for Faadi in Cardiff, but at least there he'd been familiar with the misery. Here there were new faces to avoid in the school corridors, new rooms in which to feel lost, new things to worry himself sick about. And now Corey had been attacked, he felt even worse. He had invited him over to the house to play computer games, so it was his fault. If Corey had stayed at home on Saturday, he'd have been okay.

As awkward as it had been, the family meal on Saturday night had at least given Faadi an excuse to get Corey to leave. Inviting him over had been a stupid idea. He didn't know what to talk to Corey about, and Corey hadn't spoken for much of the time he'd been at the house other than when the subject of the weather arose. Weirdly enough, as soon as the mild temperatures for this time of year had been mentioned – a subject even Faadi had thought it odd for a boy of his age to bring up – he hadn't shut up, going off on a tangent about current temperatures in far-flung places

Faadi had never even heard of. In a way, it was reassuring. Faadi had spent much of his life feeling that he didn't fit in. Corey had at least proved that he wasn't the only one.

As the volume of the voices from the living room grew louder, Faadi wondered if this was why Corey took such an interest in the climate of foreign lands he probably wouldn't ever get the opportunity to see. At that moment – as in so many others – Faadi wished he was anywhere but there.

'Everything has been for you and this is how you repay us,' he could hear his mother saying.

'I never asked you for it,' Syed replied.

'He's unwell,' Mahira said, her voice trembling and broken. 'Can't you see what all this is doing to him?'

'We were fine where we were. If you want to blame anyone for this, blame him. Coming here … it was his idea.'

'For you!'

Faadi had never heard his mother shouting. Even when the police had turned up at their doorstep years earlier – with a teenage Syed who had been cautioned for antisocial behaviour – Mahira had kept a quiet and controlled calm about her, dealing with things in her own patient way. Now Faadi was a little older, things were beginning to look different. All his life he had depended on her to be the strong one, the reliable and consistent presence in his life, but it had occurred to him recently that maybe she wasn't in control at all.

He was beginning to wonder if that was why she liked to keep him close.

'That's how much he thinks of this family,' she continued. 'All the hours he works in a job he hates, all the comments he has to let pass over his head. He's estranged from his parents because of you, Syed – because of what you've done. And this is how you repay him. And now you're blaming him for saying enough's enough?'

'We could have stayed in Cardiff,' Syed argued.

'And then what? If we'd stayed, what would have happened next? How many more cautions were you going to get away with before you started facing charges? How much longer would it have been before you ended up in prison like the rest of them?'

'You're overreacting. All of this – moving us up here – it was an overreaction. I was just a kid. It was nothing until you two made a big deal of it.'

'Nothing? Just like the other night with Jameel, eh? Was that nothing too?'

'What Jameel does is his business.'

Mahira laughed, but there was no joy in the sound. 'He's always looked up to you, you know that. Ever since you were little it was Syed this and Syed that, and now you're making him just like you. Your father's right. You shouldn't come back here ... not until something changes.'

There was silence for a moment.

'I don't have anywhere to go.' Syed's voice was changed now, quiet and vulnerable. Out on the landing, even Faadi could tell what he was trying to do. And why not? Playing the victim had worked for him so many times before.

'I'm sorry. That's a problem you're going to have to work out for yourself this time.'

'But—'

'Syed, you're a man, not a little boy any more. You are to blame for this. Stop searching for excuses.'

The conversation was punctuated by the slam of the living room door. Syed appeared in the hallway, his face contorted with anger. He glanced at the staircase and caught a glimpse of Faadi as he disappeared onto the landing at the top, too slow to escape without being seen by his older brother.

Faadi hurried into his bedroom and closed the door behind him. Not for the first time, he wished he could just disappear.

CHAPTER THIRTY-SIX

Alex and Chloe sat outside the home of Gavin Jones. They had knocked on the door but there had been no answer, so they returned to the car to wait. The journey there had passed with the bare minimum of communication exchanged along the way, the attention of both women focused on the case and neither wishing to return to what had happened at the end of the meeting earlier.

'The man who called in this morning,' Chloe said. 'Richard Peters. When are we expecting him at the station?'

'This afternoon. He claims the man might be his brother, but the fire has probably ruined our chances of a DNA test. We'll have to seek out his dental records. Peters says he hasn't spoken to his brother for a couple of years, but he seemed pretty sure it's him in the footage taken from the café.'

There followed a silence that was uncomfortable for them both.

'Look,' Alex said, finally breaking it. 'I'm sorry about this morning. I shouldn't have reacted like that.'

'It's okay,' Chloe said, still keeping watch out of the passenger window in case a returning Gavin Jones should make an appearance.

'Put it down to getting old.'

'I never guessed an innocent Victoria sponge might cause so much offence.'

She turned to Alex with a smile, but it wasn't returned. Alex's eyes remained focused on the street ahead, concentration etched in the lines of her furrowed brow.

'You can talk to me if you want,' Chloe said.

Alex turned sharply. 'Talk about what?'

'Saturday night. The car. It wasn't an accident, was it?'

She turned back to face the windscreen. 'Someone cut my brake fluid line.' There was no point in keeping it from her; if Chloe suspected something untoward, then she wouldn't stop pestering Alex until she had the truth. Alex knew she should be grateful for the concern, but in her current frame of mind it was difficult to find it anything but annoying.

'Have you reported it? Who would do that?'

'I don't know. Well, I think I might know, but I can't prove anything so what's the point.' She took the keys from the engine and nodded at the windscreen. 'Break time's over.'

Gavin Jones was walking along the front of the terrace a hundred metres or so along the street, the hood of his jacket pulled up over his head, oblivious to the greeting that would be awaiting him at his front door.

'Hold that thought,' Chloe said, getting from the car. 'You're not escaping this conversation that easily.'

They approached Jones as he was searching for his front door key. He had his head lowered, cursing beneath his breath as he scrabbled in his pockets.

'Gavin Jones?'

'Yep.'

Alex pulled her ID from her pocket. 'Detective Inspector Alex King. This is DC Chloe Lane.'

'News travels fast,' Gavin said as he unlocked the front door and left it open behind him for the women to follow him inside.

Alex glanced at Chloe. It was hardly the reception they had been expecting. 'Meaning?'

Gavin unzipped his jacket and threw it over the end of the stairs. 'Well I assume you're here about this,' he said, pointing to his head. He turned to the side, giving them a view of the dried blood that matted his thinning hair.

'What happened?'

'Got jumped, didn't I? How did you know about it anyway?'

'We didn't,' Alex told him. 'Have you reported it?'

Gavin shook his head and went through to the living room. They followed him in, having to pick their path between furniture stacked in piles and cardboard boxes overflowing with clutter. 'Only just moved in,' he said, by way of explanation of the chaos. 'No, I haven't reported it. We don't grass round here.' He gestured at the sofa, but neither Chloe nor Alex accepted the offer of a seat. 'I'll deal with it in my own way.'

'Where were you on Saturday evening between the hours of eight and nine o'clock?' asked Alex.

Gavin narrowed his eyes and moved his focus from Alex to Chloe. 'Why?'

'Just answer the question, please.'

He folded his arms across his chest. 'You already know I've done time, right? Jesus Christ, give me a break. You lot just can't wait to trip people up, can you?'

'There's an easy answer to that,' Alex quipped. 'Don't break the law.'

Gavin smiled, yet there was nothing pleasant in the expression. 'I was in Wetherspoons in Ponty on Saturday night. Got there about seven o'clock, left about ten thirty. There should be a few witnesses – the place was packed.'

'I'm guessing you've heard about the petrol attack on a teenage boy?' Chloe said. 'Happened not far from here.'

Gavin's arms dropped to his sides. 'Hang on a sec. You're here about that? I don't know nothing about that.'

'A petrol can was found in a nearby garden,' Alex told him. 'Can you explain how your fingerprints came to be on it?'

For a moment, the colour drained from Gavin's face. 'Actually, yes,' he said, heading to the kitchen door. Alex thought for a moment he was going to attempt to make a run for it, but instead he turned back to them. 'You coming, or what?'

They followed him through to the kitchen, where yet more boxes were waiting to be unpacked. He unlocked the back door. The outside space was minimal, just a small square of grass that had been left to grow wild, but it backed onto a garage that separated the house from a lane at the back of the row of terraces.

'Got broken into last week,' he said, shoving the door open. 'Look.'

He pushed his way through the junk that filled the garage and went to the main door, gesturing to its broken lock. It looked as though it had been forced open with a bolt cutter. 'Bastards took a load of stuff,' he said. 'Half my tools ... God knows what else. They must have had the petrol can along with it.'

'You reported this?' Chloe asked, knowing what the answer would be.

'What's the fucking point? You lot don't do nothing anyway.'

'So we've just got your word for it,' Alex said flatly.

'Listen,' Gavin said, turning sharply and colliding with a box of paperwork, which fell to the ground and spilled envelopes across the garage floor. 'I don't care what you want to believe, I told you where I was on Saturday night. I didn't attack that kid – what the hell would I do that for?' He stopped to catch his breath. 'Look, I moved into this place for a fresh start, right? I don't want no more trouble. I didn't hurt that kid. I've never even seen the lad, all right? It's not me that goes around attacking people. You want to talk to anyone about that, you should be talking to those fucking Hassan brothers.'

'The Hassans?' Alex glanced at Chloe. 'Why would we want to talk to them?'

Gavin jabbed at his head with an index finger. 'They attacked me last night. Knocked me out cold, right.'

'You saw them?'

He rolled his eyes, exasperated. 'I didn't need to see them.'

'So you don't know it was them, then.'

'Jesus fucking Christ. I didn't need to see them. We had a bust-up last week. It was nothing. One of them thought I said something racist, so the other one just went for me. And I didn't say nothing racist, by the way, they were just playing the Paki card.' He paused for breath again, the colour having risen in his cheeks. 'I know it was them, okay.'

The Hassan brothers' names kept recurring, but there was as yet no apparent reason for it. Alex had asked Jake Sullivan to research the family; by the time they returned to the station later something useful would hopefully have arisen.

'You need to come to the station to make a statement,' she told Gavin. 'Unless,' she added, as he began his objection, 'you'd prefer to do things the more complicated way.'

'What does that mean?'

'It means we've got your prints on a petrol can and at the moment only your word that you were somewhere else. Meaning we can arrest you and do things that way.'

Admitting defeat, Gavin sighed and led them back to the house. Alex wanted out of there, and the sooner the better. It was time she met both older Hassan brothers for herself.

CHAPTER THIRTY-SEVEN

Back at the office, Alex and Dan sat at his desk in the incident room. The 999 call that had been received on Thursday night had been enhanced so that the music Alex had picked up on in the background could now be heard more distinctly. Dan pressed the enhanced recording and turned down the sound of the caller's voice in order to make the music clearer.

'We should probably talk about last night,' Alex said quietly. 'Not here, though.'

'I don't want this to affect our work.'

Dan pulled his chair closer to the desk, widening the gap between them. 'Neither do I, but I can't do this now, all right. I'm sorry.'

'I'm the one who should be apologising.'

'You've got the 999 call back then?'

Alex turned to see Chloe just behind them, her focus on the paused audio clip on Dan's computer. She felt a flush creep up her throat, hoping Chloe hadn't overheard any of their conversation. Turning from both women, Dan clicked the file and waited for them to listen to the clip again.

'That's not a ringtone, is it?' Alex said. 'Not a standard one that comes with a phone, anyway.'

Chloe pulled a chair over to the desk. 'You can download pretty much anything as a ringtone now.'

Dan paused the file and played it back, repeating the six seconds that held the best quality of enhanced recording. 'Can anyone make out the words?'

The three listened closely again.

'Got Shazam on your phone?' Dan asked Chloe.

'Shazam? Check you out, down with the kids.'

Dan smiled, though Chloe noticed it didn't reach his eyes. 'You learn a lot having daughters.'

Chloe turned to the room, searching out Jake and calling him over. She didn't have the app on her phone, but knew that Jake did. He held the phone to the speaker as they replayed the recording.

'There's not enough,' he said when the app returned no result. 'You'd need a longer clip.'

Alex's eyes followed Jake as he returned to his desk. 'Why is he still here? He's about as much use as an ashtray on a motorbike.' She leaned across Chloe and pressed the recording again. '"Impractical",' she said. 'Does that sound like "impractical" to you?'

Chloe shrugged. 'Could be.'

Alex wrote down the word in the notebook in front of her. 'And "death". Listen.' She played the recording for a final time, pausing at each distinct word in turn. They were the only two that were clear enough to identify. 'That's bound to be a lot of help.' She pushed back her chair and stood, leaving Chloe and Dan at the desk. Neither spoke for a moment. Chloe noticed that Alex had barely made eye contact with her, and she hadn't seemed to acknowledge Dan once during the conversation.

'Whatever's going on with her, I hope she snaps out of it soon,' she mumbled. 'She told me someone cut the brake fluid line on her car.'

'Yeah?'

Chloe narrowed her eyes, assessing Dan's response. 'Did you know?'

He shook his head, but it was an unconvincing denial.

'She hasn't said much. I wonder why she hasn't reported it.' Chloe pressed further.

'You'd have to ask her.'

Chloe got up and crossed the incident room, returning to her own desk. She glanced back at Dan, who had returned his focus to his computer but didn't appear to actually be doing anything. She looked to her own work. Feedback from the three shops in which the skeleton outfit was stocked had so far proved fruitless: no one recognised anyone matching the description of the suspect captured on CCTV. Not that it was much of a description. Male, around five foot nine. It described a quarter of south Wales's population.

And was this all a waste of time anyway? she wondered. The outfit was available quite widely online, which broadened their search to a near-impossible scale. Some of the team were looking into it, but no one expected their inquiries to lead to anything.

Feeling dejected and frustrated, Chloe got back up and headed for the staff toilets. As she entered the ladies', Alex was leaving one of the cubicles. She barely acknowledged Chloe as she went to the sink to wash her hands.

'Has something happened?'

Alex looked up from the sink. 'Other than the fact that this investigation is so slow it might as well be going backwards?'

'I know,' Chloe agreed, frustrated by Alex's evasion of the question. 'But I don't mean that. Is this about the car? You should report it, you know.'

'So you keep saying.'

'And what's going on with you and Dan? You could have filed nails on the atmosphere earlier.'

Alex shook the excess water from her hands and went to the dryer, allowing the blast of warm air to halt the conversation. Chloe waited. If Alex thought she was going to give in that easily, then she obviously didn't know her well enough.

'You've been acting weird all day. I know something's up.'

'Just leave it, please.'

'What did you have to apologise to him for?' Chloe asked. 'I heard you say something about needing to—'

'That was a private conversation,' Alex said defensively. Too defensively, she realised. If anything, it only made Chloe increasingly suspicious.

Chloe narrowed her eyes. 'Have you two argued or something?'

'Chloe, just leave it, for God's sake.'

She couldn't. Alex's behaviour was uncharacteristic and had only served to heighten her curiosity. 'Has something happened between you and Dan?'

When the words left her mouth the question seemed a ridiculous one, but Alex's immediate reaction suggested it was perhaps less ludicrous than she'd assumed, and that she'd been closer to the truth than she'd realised.

'No way,' she said slowly. She sought Alex's face, forcing her to make eye contact. 'Is there something going on?'

Alex opened her mouth to lie, but she couldn't bring herself to do it. Chloe knew her well enough to spot when she was trying to evade the truth, and besides, Chloe hated liars. She was going to be annoyed enough by what Alex had done; lying would only make things worse. She didn't need to say anything anyway; the truth was already out, stamped in the guilt Alex realised she was wearing all over her face.

'He's married,' Chloe said, as though Alex needed reminding of the fact.

'I'm aware of that, thank you.'

Chloe shook her head in disbelief, eyeing Alex as though she didn't recognise her. 'You work with him.'

'If all you're going to do is point out the bloody obvious then I think we're done here,' Alex said, heading towards the door.

Chloe stepped in front of her, blocking her exit. 'Have you slept with him?'

'No.'

'But ...?'

Alex sighed, but her lack of words spoke volumes.

'Why would you go anywhere near him?'

'Because I could,' Alex snapped, frustrated by the stream of questions. 'Because the opportunity was there and because I'm a sad, lonely old cow no one else would look at. Does that answer your question? Remind me when I became answerable to you anyway? It was nothing, all right. So don't go blowing it out of proportion. We all know you can't resist a drama.'

Chloe looked at her as though Alex had just slapped her. If she wasn't already so angered by what Alex had done, she would have been upset by her animosity. 'What has happened to you? You know, I used to respect you, but this morning you made me look stupid in front of everyone, and now this. There's not much to respect really, is there?'

She moved aside as Alex reached for the door handle. 'I'm your superior,' Alex reminded her. 'Whether you like it or not. Perhaps things would work better if we all remembered that fact.'

They were interrupted by the appearance of a female constable, who almost walked into Alex as she opened the door. 'Sorry,' she said. 'I've been looking for you. Richard Peters is in reception.'

CHAPTER THIRTY-EIGHT

The man waiting for Alex in Interview Room 2 was probably in his mid fifties, but his choice of clothing suggested he was still trying to pass as a man decades younger. He was wearing trainers and tapered jogging bottoms, with a parka jacket that he kept zipped up to his stubbly chin. His hair was gelled and styled in a failing attempt to hide the balding patch at the back of his skull. When Alex entered the room, he stood hurriedly, knocking his knee against the desk.

'Mr Peters,' Alex said, gesturing for him to sit back down. 'I'm Detective Inspective King. You may have some information for us?'

She placed the file she was carrying on the desk and took a seat opposite. The man nodded and shifted uncomfortably. He seemed uneasy at the formality of the setting and she wondered whether he'd had much experience of police interview rooms.

She opened the file and withdrew a still taken from the CCTV footage at the café in Tonypandy. Richard Peters looked down at the photo as she put in front of him.

'It's definitely him,' he confirmed with a nod.

'Him being …?'

'Gary. My brother. Changed quite a bit since I saw him last, mind, but that's definitely him.'

'When did you last see your brother, Mr Peters?'

Richard Peters placed a finger under the neckline of his parka and ran it along his throat as though wiping away sweat. Why didn't he just take the coat off? Alex asked herself. Time had made her suspicious of everyone, and she wondered whether he had something to hide or whether recent events were making her increasingly paranoid.

'Good few years back, I reckon.'

'You don't live far from here, though?' Alex asked, tapping a finger on the photograph.

'Only up the road,' Richard admitted. He sat back and sighed. 'Easy to lose touch, though, isn't it, especially under the circumstances. Do you reckon it's him then who they found up at the hospital?'

'These circumstances,' Alex said, avoiding the question for the moment. 'How did you come to lose touch with your brother?'

'Same old story really. Nothing unusual. Gary had a problem with the drink, had for years. Lost him everything – his wife, his job, the house. She gave him plenty of chances, but he was always his own worst enemy.'

'Where's his wife now?'

'Moved away after the divorce. Think she went somewhere Cornwall way, to be nearer to her sister.' Richard reached for the photograph and slid it towards him to take a closer look. There was no sadness in his expression, almost as though he had expected to one day be sitting in a police station having this conversation about his brother.

'Any children?' Alex asked.

Richard shook his head. 'You think it's him then?' he asked again.

'We don't know at this stage, although we know the victim had been sleeping rough up at the hospital. I'll need to take a swab from you if you're willing, although there's a strong possibility the fire may have made a DNA test impossible. Now that we have your brother's name, we can check his dental records. If it is him, we'll be able to identify him that way.'

Richard nodded. 'Poor sod. What a way to go.'

'Was your brother in debt, Mr Peters?'

'Christ, aye … plenty. That's what caused all the trouble.'

Had this been a random attack, or had Gary Peters – if their victim was in fact him – got himself involved with someone who had set out to murder him? Money was often a motivation for crime, and it all too often took little to escalate to murder.

'I realise you haven't seen him in a long time, but is there anyone you know of who may have wanted to cause Gary harm? If it turns out that your brother is in fact our victim, we have to consider all possibilities.'

'Sorry, I didn't have much to do with him even back even. Enough problems of my own without taking his on as well.' He pushed the photo back across the table to Alex. 'If it is him, do you know what happens now, with the funeral?'

'When the body will be released, do you mean?'

'Well, no, not really. I mean, who's responsible for it, like?'

'I'm not following.'

Richard Peters leaned forward and rested his hands on the desk. 'I'm his next of kin now, what with his divorce and everything. Gary didn't have a pot to piss in … He's not going to have left a funeral fund stashed away anywhere, is he?'

Alex folded her arms across her chest, exasperated by the man's insensitivity. There was a possibility his brother was dead – murdered in the most horrific of ways – and yet his main concern was his own finances.

'There must be something in place when this kind of thing happens,' Richard continued. 'A government scheme or something?'

Alex stood as she fought to hold in the angry tirade she could happily have allowed to escape her. She was still smarting from the argument she'd had with Chloe, and Richard Peters was a prime target on which to take her frustrations out. 'I'm afraid I can't help you there. You'll have to work that one out for yourself. If you could follow me, please … I need that swab from you.'

CHAPTER THIRTY-NINE

The following morning, the atmosphere at the station continued to intensify. Forensics had finally got back to Alex to let her know that nothing useful had been found in the samples taken from Corey Davies's fingernails, nor from those taken from the man who had intercepted the attack. Although it proved no surprise, it was disappointing nonetheless. A lack of development in each of the cases was causing frustration, and the friction between Alex and Chloe was beginning to be noticed by others in the team.

Alex sat in her office nursing a cup of coffee that had been left to go cold. She was reading once again the fire investigators' report that had been submitted following the incident at the hospital the previous week. She realised she was searching for the impossible: some missed detail that might somehow make sense of all the things they were currently unable to fathom.

She and Chloe would be paying a visit to the Hassan home later that morning, but she didn't want to leave until she had received the results on Gary Peters' dental records. It had been confirmed that the fire damage to the body had meant a DNA test was impossible. She pulled up Peters' police record on the computer database. He had been arrested twice, each a number of years earlier and both for shoplifting. According to his brother, Gary had developed a drinking habit that had gone on to cost him his marriage and his home. He had cut ties with his family; or, it seemed, his family had cut ties with him. Either way, his tragic ending had been a brutal finale in a life that had apparently been wasted in so many ways.

Studying the image stored on his record, Alex felt sure it was the same man captured on CCTV at the café in Tonypandy. What was as yet impossible to tell was whether Gary Peters was the man whose beaten and burned body had been recovered from the derelict hospital building.

Clicking from the page, she opened up another record: that of Syed Hassan. The Hassan brothers' names kept recurring, yet there was currently no known link to any of the cases they were investigating. Syed Hassan had been in trouble with the police as a teenager, cautioned on a number of occasions for a series of minor offences. His record suggested he might be capable of more, but Gavin Jones was still refusing to make a formal statement regarding his assault. Then there was the link with Faadi and Corey Davies. Syed and Jameel would have known that Corey Davies was at the house on Saturday evening. Had one of them followed him home with the intention of harming him? And if so, why had they done it?

From what she already knew of the Hassan brothers, she didn't think either was foolish enough to jump on a bus after carrying out such an attack.

On the desk, Alex's phone began ringing, its noisy vibrations jolting her from her thoughts.

'DI Alex King.'

'We've got the results on Gary Peters' dental records,' the man at the other end of the line told her. 'He's your man.'

'We could do with a warrant,' Chloe said as she and Alex pulled up outside the Hassans' home. She didn't make eye contact when she spoke, still angry about their exchange at the station the previous day. She hadn't forgiven Alex for what she'd done, or for the words that had been spoken in anger. The comment about drama had been particularly hurtful. She had never thought

Alex would use what had happened to her months earlier against her in that way.

Alex and Dan didn't make sense. The Alex she knew was fair and honest. She didn't go around kissing other people's husbands. Her own ex-husband had messed her around, even after the marriage had long been over. Chloe couldn't comprehend Alex even contemplating bringing the same kind of troubles to another family.

So far, all conversation had been confined to the case. As far as both women were concerned, things were better kept that way.

'Not enough to justify it at the moment,' Alex replied.

Alex cut the engine of the Audi. She had picked it up that morning, reluctant to drive it from the garage and resolving to sell it as soon as possible. The car had been an impulse purchase after her divorce papers had been signed years earlier: a two-finger salute to the years of joint decision-making that had gone before. Like every other impulsive choice she'd ever made, it had turned out to be a regrettable one.

'So where does Gary Peters fit into all this, if we're considering a link between these incidents?' Chloe pondered as she closed the passenger door behind her.

'You're looking for a connection between the victims. I don't think there is one, not in the way we might like. Someone found out where Gary was and they attacked him, knowing he was incapable of fighting back. Same with Corey Davies. We're looking for someone who preys on the weak.' She pressed the Hassans' doorbell. 'I'm not sure that's this pair,' she said, giving a nod to the house. 'Not if Gavin Jones's claims are anything to go by. Our victims have all been vulnerable. Not exactly a fitting description of Gavin, is it?'

The door was answered by Mahira Hassan. This was her third encounter with Chloe and her face fell at the sight of police on her doorstep yet again.

She stepped aside to let the two officers into the house. 'Faadi's already told you everything he knows about Saturday night,' she said, pushing the living room door open. Her youngest son was sitting on the sofa watching television.

'We're not here about Corey,' Alex told her. 'Are your other sons at home, Mrs Hassan?'

'What do you want with them?' Youssef Hassan appeared in the hallway. He was a middle-aged man, older than his wife by several years, and he wore a shirt and tie beneath a heavy coat. Either he had just arrived home or he was about to leave.

'Are either of your older sons home?' Alex asked, ignoring the question.

There was a clatter at the top of the staircase as Jameel Hassan, dressed in a pair of pyjama trousers, came from his room to see what was going on. 'I'm here,' he said, trudging slowly down the staircase.

'Nasty bruising there,' Alex said, noting the fading shadows that marked the young man's left eye.

Jameel shrugged. 'It's nothing.'

'Souvenir of your encounter with Gavin Jones last Thursday, is it?'

Jameel stopped at the foot of the staircase, stalled by Alex's comment. His eyes narrowed as he looked from one woman to the other, wondering how they knew about the fight. 'It was nothing,' he said again.

'Where were you on Sunday evening at around seven thirty?' Chloe asked.

'Here.' Jameel folded his arms across his chest. He was just like his brother, Chloe thought; the same arrogant self-assurance and the same disregard for authority. She looked at Mahira, who nodded.

'We had dinner together at six o'clock,' she said. 'The four of us.'

'The four of you?'

'Syed isn't staying here at the moment,' Youssef explained.

Alex glanced at Chloe. 'Where is he staying?'

'No idea,' his father said. 'You'd have to ask him.'

Faadi appeared in the living room doorway and looked questioningly at the adults gathered in the hallway.

'If we could have a contact number for him then? A man named Gavin Jones was attacked on Sunday night,' Alex continued, turning her attention back to Jameel. 'You don't know anything about that, do you?'

'Why would I know anything? We just told you ... I was here. Have you charged him with torching the shop yet?'

'Jameel ...' Mahira began.

'The fire happened just after the fight,' Jameel said, cutting his mother short. 'It doesn't take a genius to work out it was Gavin who started it.'

He held Alex's gaze, staring her out in the same way his older brother had challenged Chloe.

'Were you here on Saturday evening as well?'

Gavin Jones's alibi for Saturday had proved rock solid: he'd been in the Wetherspoons in Pontypridd as he claimed, with plenty of witnesses and CCTV footage to prove it. As such, it looked as though his claim that the petrol can had been stolen from the garage along with other of his possessions might be an honest one. Either that or he knew the person who'd attacked Corey Davies and had given them the petrol can, though that didn't necessarily mean he had known they were going to use it to carry out the attack.

'Yep,' Jameel said, unable to keep the smug tone from his voice. 'All night. Watched a bit of TV after dinner, then went up to bed.'

Alex glanced at Mahira, who nodded again at her son's response. Was she giving him an alibi in an effort to protect him?

'So you saw Corey Davies here on Saturday before he left to head home?' Chloe asked.

'Briefly,' Jameel said. 'Only when he walked past the living room to go up to Fatty's bedroom.' He cast his younger brother a smile that quickly stretched into a sneer.

'Jameel,' their father said, his tone laced with a warning note. 'Look,' he said, turning to Alex, 'my sons have both told you everything they know. I'm sorry we can't be more help to you.'

Chloe held Jameel's stare, regarding him with contempt. He'd obviously picked up a lot of bad habits from Syed, she thought, including bullying their younger brother. They were unpleasant enough alone; put together, poor Faadi probably didn't get a minute's peace.

'If you do think of anything else,' she said, handing a card to Mahira, 'my number's on there.' She looked to Faadi as she spoke, knowing he would understand her intention. He might be shy, but Chloe reckoned he was far from stupid.

CHAPTER FORTY

Later that day, Chloe was in the staffroom showing Jake for the third time that week how to use the coffee machine when her mobile phone began ringing in her pocket. She gestured to the button Jake needed to press, waving a hand in despair when his impatience had him jabbing at it in a way that would turn an already slow process into an impossible one.

'That's how you keep breaking it,' she said, swiping a finger across the screen of her mobile. 'DC Lane speaking.'

She moved to the other side of the room, keen to escape the noise of Jake's fight for a simple cappuccino. It would have been quicker and easier for him to use the café over the road. Not for the first time, she wondered how he survived day-to-day life.

There was silence at the other end of the line.

'Hello?'

'Hello,' a voice eventually said. It was a male voice, young. 'You said to call.'

'Faadi?' Chloe sat at one of the tables in the corner of the staffroom. 'Is that you?' She thought he might hang up, and wondered for a moment whether he had changed his mind and gone. Then she heard breathing at the end of the line, heavy and laboured.

'Thank you for calling, Faadi,' she said, keen to keep him talking. 'Did you think of anything else you wanted to tell us?'

'You asked about the gaming. Who we played against at the weekend.'

'Okay,' Chloe said, searching the clutter that littered the table for a pen and a scrap of paper. 'Tell me about it. Did you play someone different on Saturday?'

'I don't know,' Faadi said, his voice still quiet; his reluctance to speak obvious. 'Maybe … I think so.'

*

Alex entered the building through the main doors and scanned the room. It was an old-fashioned pub with round wooden tables and a brown patterned carpet that might have once been red. The air smelled of stale beer and disappointment. The place was quiet; a couple of men stood drinking at the end of the bar, and in the far corner the manic tinkling of a fruit machine cut through the silence, its multicoloured lights blinking frantically in the otherwise dimly lit room. The man playing the machine cursed loudly and kicked the base when his luck failed to come in.

Reaching into her pocket for her ID, Alex went to the bar, where a young man was crouched at the fridges bottling up. 'What can I get you?' he asked without looking up.

'Detective Inspector King. Can I have a minute?'

The young man looked up. Alex flashed her ID, and he stood, arching his back as though he was decades older.

'Know this man?' She put a photograph of Christian Coleman on the bar in front of him: the image that had been splashed across the front of the local newspapers following his sentencing.

The young man nodded. 'Seen him in here.'

'Was he here at the weekend?'

The barman pulled a face as he tried to recall. 'Couldn't say for sure. We were pretty busy over the weekend.'

'Know who he drinks with?'

The man cast a glance along the bar as though to check no one was eavesdropping. He was out of luck: the two older men who were drinking there had paused their conversation when Alex had produced her ID, and neither bothered to hide the fact that listening in on what was happening at the other end of the bar was far more interesting that whatever they'd been talking about.

'I don't know. Sorry.'

He didn't sound it, and it was obvious to Alex that the unwanted attentions of the men had brought his side of their brief conversation to a premature end. Christian was a regular here, or had been before his prison sentence. Despite his notoriety throughout the town, it seemed there were certain places and certain people that were still willing to accommodate him. She wondered whether they did so through loyalty or fear.

'Pass me those please,' she said, gesturing to the notepad and pen that were resting on a shelf beside the till.

She wrote her name and number on the pad, ripped off the top sheet of paper and handed it to the barman. 'When he comes in next, I want you to call me.'

The man nodded, though Alex knew the chances of his calling her were as likely as Christian having rehabilitated during his time in prison. Shooting a glance at the men standing at the end of the bar, she wondered just how many people Christian still had on his side. He would more than likely have a rock-solid alibi, but as far as Alex was concerned, that would mean nothing. He might not have been the person to actually cut the brake fluid line on her car, but that didn't mean he hadn't been behind it somehow.

Stepping back outside the pub, she swallowed down a gulp of fresh air. A part of her had wanted to find Christian there, yet at the same time she recognised the relief she'd felt when she found the pub next to empty. She knew what the man was capable of. Despite everything she suspected of him, she knew she wasn't ready yet to face him alone.

CHAPTER FORTY-ONE

Chloe found Dan in the incident room with Jake. They had Syed Hassan's record open on the database and were discussing their failed attempts to find out where he had been staying since his father had kicked him out of the family home.

'Seems he got himself involved with some notorious names down in Cardiff,' Dan said, referring to the array of faces that filled the computer screen. 'This lot have got more than fifty convictions between them.'

'Faadi just called me,' Chloe said, pulling up a chair and sitting beside them.

Dan turned to her. 'How come?'

'I knew he was hiding something,' she said. 'He's so nervous, that boy. Here.' She slid a piece of paper across the desk. On it was scrawled 'bottleman4000'.

'What's this?'

'Xbox username. Faadi and Corey played FIFA on Xbox Live on Saturday. He said they mostly played against usernames he recognises – I've written those on the back of the sheet, there – but there was someone new this time, someone who struck up a conversation with them on one of the message boards.'

'A conversation about what?' asked Jake.

'Just general stuff, Faadi said. But by the sounds of it, this person would have gained enough info to know that the boys were together at Faadi's house, if they knew who Faadi's username belonged to.'

'So they would have known where to find Corey, or near enough,' Dan said.

'If they knew where Faadi lived, yes.'

'Why didn't Faadi mention this before?'

Chloe shrugged. 'Could be a number of reasons. I think he's scared of his brothers, for one – he may have been too frightened to speak to us in front of them. I think his mum might keep him a bit mollycoddled as well. Perhaps she wouldn't be too pleased to know he chats with people online.'

'Bottleman,' Jake said, looking at the name on the sheet. 'Strange username.'

'Think there may be a clue in there somewhere?' Dan suggested.

'Not unless our suspect's a milkman,' Jake said.

Chloe rolled her eyes. Sometimes it was easy to see why Alex had so little patience where Jake was concerned. 'Are we dealing with a paedophile here?' she asked, ignoring Jake's remark. 'Why else target kids online?'

'Corey wasn't sexually assaulted,' Jake said.

'But was that only because the attack was intercepted.'

Dan shook his head. 'The petrol. That would have come after, surely.'

'Unless it was a response to the interruption,' Chloe suggested. 'What if he'd been intent on sexual assault, but threw the petrol once he realised he wasn't going to get what he wanted?' She gestured to the username on the paper and looked to Dan. 'Can you do something with this?'

He pulled a face that immediately quashed any hopes she might have had. 'I can try. It's not that easy to locate a user by IP address when it's an individual. They make it look easy on TV.' He shrugged apologetically. 'I'll do my best.'

Jake returned to his own desk, leaving Chloe at Dan's.

'She's told me,' she said, knowing that if she waited any longer she would only talk herself out of broaching the subject. If they were going to salvage the team they'd been building during the past year, they were going to need to get everything out in the open. In Chloe's experience, secrets and lies only ever resulted in disaster.

'Told you …?' Dan glanced at her. He was wearing guilt like a second skin. Her raised eyebrow told him there was no point in attempting to evade the subject. 'Right.' He looked around the room, checking there was no one near enough to overhear the conversation. 'Look, it was my fault, all right. I don't know why it happened, it was a moment of madness—'

'You don't have to explain yourself to me,' Chloe said, cutting him short. 'I just think you should sort it out – people are going to start noticing there's something going on.' Her tone was clipped; her disapproval obvious.

'It was just a kiss,' Dan added.

'So I heard.' She stood and gestured to the Xbox usernames. 'Let me know if anything shows up from those.'

CHAPTER FORTY-TWO

She sits in the darkness, only the light of the laptop illuminating the room. When she looks down at her hands, she knows they'll never look the same again. She feels more powerful now than she ever has; more in control than she could ever have imagined. Those hands are capable of anything. When she closes her eyes at night, she sees the things she has done play out before her, bright and alive and real once more. She knows she should feel something else – some fear or sense of wrongdoing – but she is incapable of either. There are spaces where she knows there should be feelings; there are voids that can only be filled by violence.

All she feels now is a burning power that craves more with every act. She is strong and fierce. She is destructive. She is just like fire.

And she knows she can do it again. Better this time.

She scrolls down the page of images in front of her. She knows these people, she sees them daily, but they don't know her. No one really knows her, not like they should; not in the way that she deserves to be known and celebrated. Looking at each face in turn, a festering resentment eats away inside her. She is invisible. None of these people notice her. She passes them by, just another face in the crowd of so many faces, but she could be anyone to them.

She deserves to be noticed, she realises that now.

She stops at the girl's image and studies her for a moment. With her sweeping dark hair and sharp bright eyes, she is the kind of pretty that seems to fit in with what is expected. This girl is everything that goes noticed in a world where she herself is mostly ignored.

She wonders if this girl has ever looked at her. Has she ever really noticed her?

She flips the lid of the laptop shut and pushes it away.

Soon enough, she will make her notice. She will make them all notice.

CHAPTER FORTY-THREE

She had just settled down for the evening, the dishes washed and put away and the kitchen table cleared of the newspaper she had been reading as she ate her dinner. *Coronation Street* would be on soon, and though eight o'clock seemed far too early to go to bed, what she fancied more than anything was to head upstairs afterwards and curl up beneath the quilt with the book she'd started at the weekend. She would boil the kettle and do herself a hot-water bottle to take up with her.

The local newspaper that she had folded and put to one side made for depressing reading. That poor man killed up at the hospital, then the young boy attacked near the park on Saturday night. What was the world coming to? She remembered a time when this little corner of the planet had been a safe place, when front doors had been left unlocked and children had gone in and out of neighbours' houses without their parents having to worry about where they were or whether they were safe. Everyone had looked out for each other back then. But not any more. The world was different now. Hostile.

But there were still the traditions, she thought, and they offered at least something to hold onto. The box of sweets she had bought from the shop up on the main road was sitting on the table in the hallway, waiting for the arrival of the children who came every year, their plastic pumpkin-shaped buckets already half filled with chocolates and lollipops. She loved to see their little outfits: the tiny witches and the miniature devils who would gather on the pavement outside the front door.

She glanced at the clock. Nearly half past seven. They were late this year. No one was coming. Perhaps, like so many others, this tradition was also dying out.

Turning up the sound on the television, she settled back on the sofa. The ringing of the doorbell interrupted the voices in her living room, and she got up to answer it, arming herself with the box of sweets on the way.

'Trick or treat!'

The skeleton at the front door held out his bare hands, thanking her as she scooped handfuls of sweets from the box. He was on his own – unusual for a trick-or-treater, she thought – and he seemed tall for a child, although the black costume might have made him look bigger than he was.

'Happy Hallowe'en!' the voice behind the mask said.

She glanced down at the hands, at the long, thin fingers that held the sweets she had given him.

'Happy Hallowe'en,' she returned.

Closing the front door, she put the box of sweets back on the side table before checking that she was double-bolted in for the night. The *Coronation Street* theme music had begun playing out from the living room, inviting her back to the comfort of the sofa.

As she turned back from the doorway, ready to settle down again, a sound startled her; a movement further along the hallway, something out of sight. Then she saw it, there at the end of the passage, blocking the entrance to the kitchen. Framed by the doorway stood the skeleton, come back.

She opened her mouth to speak, but nothing came out. Fear gripped her insides, rendering her silent.

'Trick or treat?' a voice said.

CHAPTER FORTY-FOUR

Alex and Chloe followed the directions given by the satnav, aware that the journey was taking them in a direction that was becoming all too familiar to them that week. The skies above the Rhondda valleys hung heavy and looming, their greyness weighing over the towns below with an inescapable claustrophobia and a sadness that seemed to be spreading.

'Did you see that?' Alex asked as they passed a block of council flats along the main road. 'Christmas decorations. We're not even in November yet.'

It was an attempt to soften the increasingly fractious atmosphere between them, but one that Chloe appeared unwilling to respond to. Other than to discuss details of the case, they hadn't really spoken properly since their bitter exchange in the ladies' toilets at the station the previous day. Chloe's comment about there being little to respect had stung. One thing Alex knew for sure was that the younger woman had until recently admired and looked up to her, something Alex had probably gained more satisfaction from than she cared to admit.

Something else she hadn't wanted to admit was how much it would hurt her to lose that respect.

She was beginning to understand why people put Christmas decorations up so early. Under a weight of grey skies, they offered a false optimism that could be hidden behind until January reared its head.

'Let's not keep this up,' she said.

'Keep what up?'

'This. I know what I did was stupid. I don't need the permanent reminder. And you can't possibly make me feel any more guilty than I already do.'

Chloe was no longer listening. She had leaned forward and was tapping a finger at the touchscreen of the satnav. 'Hold on. Ivor Terrace. That's just behind the hospital. We were there on Friday.'

There was a police cordon stopping people from entering the street when Alex and Chloe arrived. They parked on the next road and were ushered to the scene by a uniformed officer. The narrow street was teeming with fire crew and the air was still thick with smoke. The fire had started in the third house in the row of terraces, but the residents in the adjoining houses had been evacuated safely. Neighbours were huddled together outside, and crying could be heard among the crowd of people being kept back by police.

'Doris,' Alex said quietly. She scanned the scene for someone she could speak with; someone who could tell her whether anyone had been inside. Whether anyone was still inside.

'One woman,' one of the firefighters told her.

'And?'

The man shook his head. 'She was found in the hallway. They got her out before the fire reached her, though. I'm sorry ... that's all I know.'

'We spoke with her last week,' Alex said distractedly. She looked to the front of the burning building, its front window blasted onto the pavement from the force of the heat. She imagined Doris inside, watching television with her own fire turned up, oblivious to what was about to happen.

'Bastards.' She turned to Chloe. 'Cowardly bastards.'

'We don't know how this started yet,' Chloe tried to reason.

They both knew the reassurance that it might not have been arson was futile.

'Fine,' Alex said, anger flooding from her. 'But it was no accident, was it?' She stepped back and crossed the road, knowing there was little they could do until the blaze had been put out. Fire-scene investigators would be able to tell them how it had started, but she knew she didn't need to hear their words.

The old lady had already been taken by the ambulance crew. The firefighter Alex had spoken with hadn't seemed to know much about what had happened to her. Was there a chance she was still alive?

She knew in her heart that there wasn't.

A series of questions flooded her brain. Had someone put something through the letter box knowing that Doris was inside the house? Had she answered the door to someone and the fire been started then? Why had she been targeted?

The wave of questions engulfed her. Alex pressed the heel of her hand to her eye, knowing she couldn't let her emotions impact on the investigation. 'Let's speak to the neighbours,' she said, heading back to Chloe. 'Perhaps someone saw or heard something.'

CHAPTER FORTY-FIVE

First thing the following morning, the team gathered in the incident room to discuss the latest turn of events. Doris Adams had been pronounced dead at the scene and Alex had already heard from fire-scene investigators that the fire had been started from inside the house. The information triggered an immediate surge of murmurs among her colleagues.

'Signs of a break-in?' someone asked.

Alex nodded. 'Back door had been forced. Fire was started with petrol – a brand test is being carried out; the results should be with us by tomorrow.'

'This is showing all the same hallmarks as the fire at the hospital then?' DC Jake Sullivan said.

'So far, yes. The test on the petrol will give us a stronger link.'

'Was she beaten before the fire was started?' Dan asked.

Alex nodded. She had already spoken with the pathologist and had gleaned enough information to know they were looking at yet another brutal attack. 'We'll have more details when the post-mortem report comes back.'

A moment of silence fell over the team. Each attack had been vicious, but this latest seemed particularly callous. Doris Adams had been a blameless victim; an elderly woman murdered in her own home for no apparent reason. Whoever was responsible for her death, and that of Gary Peters, was guilty of the worst kind of crime. This was murder for murder's sake, and there was little doubt in Alex's mind that the same perpetrator was responsible.

She turned to the evidence board. 'SOCOs have lifted a print from the front door frame of Doris's house, although the fire was started at the back. It's not come up as a match with any on the database. We have Gavin Jones's fingerprints on the petrol can located near the attack on Corey Davies, but as we know, his alibi for Saturday evening is solid. The Hassan brothers,' she pointed in turn to photographs of Syed and Jameel, 'keep cropping up.' She pressed her fingertips to her left temple and stepped away from the board. 'Syed Hassan has previous cautions, but his prints aren't a match either. By all accounts he got himself involved with a few gangs when the family lived in Cardiff. Keeping their son on the straight and narrow was a motivation in their move to the valleys.'

'That was a success then,' Jake quipped.

Alex's top lip curled. 'The more this case escalates, the more I think we should be separating the fire at the Hassan shop from the rest of the investigation.'

'How come?' asked Chloe.

'The fire at the hospital holds several similarities to the arson at Doris Adams's house last night. Vulnerable victims, as we've already discussed, and both targeted in their homes.' Alex made inverted commas gestures at the last word. 'It seems Gary Peters may have been using the hospital as a base for some time, which would suggest he felt safe there, or at the very least safer than anywhere else. Gary and Doris were both attacked in places they might have least expected it – places where they would have been caught off guard. There was no victim at the shop fire – not in the physical sense, at least. It was targeted at night, at a time when whoever was responsible would have known there was no one inside.'

She paused, her attention still focused on the images of the Hassan brothers. 'Do we know anything about the Hassans' finances?'

Chloe shook her head. 'You think Syed or Jameel might have started the shop fire?'

'We know they've both got form, particularly Syed. Gavin Jones has admitted to fighting with them on Thursday evening. Perhaps one of them hoped to frame him.'

'But why destroy their own family's shop?' asked Jake.

'That's why I'm questioning their finances. If they have money problems, they might have seen this as a way to kill two birds with one stone. Or with one petrol-soaked rag, anyway.'

'And you still think the attack on Corey Davies might have been a copycat?'

'It doesn't follow the pattern. That incident was more frenzied. The perpetrator was clumsy. It doesn't match the other attacks in any way, other than the use of petrol. Dan, did you manage to get anywhere with the Xbox username Faadi gave to Chloe?'

Dan shook his head. 'The name's no longer registered. Whoever Bottleman was, he knew exactly what he was doing – there's no way of tracking the username to an IP address now the account has been deactivated.'

'So if the account was used to target Corey on Saturday night and find out where he was, this person could do the same thing again to trace another victim?'

Dan nodded. 'Unfortunately, yes. If the account exists, the user can be tracked. Once it's no longer up and running, that's it.'

'I might have found something else.'

All eyes turned to Chloe, who stood and went to the laptop at the desk near the evidence board. Alex stepped aside, allowing her to access the internet search engine. The web page was projected onto the screen behind her so that the rest of the team could see what she was viewing. She typed the word 'bottleman' into the search bar, then pointed to the fifth result that was thrown up. 'Catfish and the Bottlemen. They're a band from north Wales.' She returned to the search bar and extended her request with the words 'Kathleen lyrics'. 'Look,' she said, pointing to the screen behind her. Her fingertip scanned the page of lyrics, stopping at the start of the second verse. 'Impractical. Death.'

'The 999 call that was made on the night of the fire.'

Chloe gave Alex a nod. 'Listen.' She searched for YouTube and found the track titled 'Kathleen'. After skipping the first minute of the music video, the short sound clip that had been enhanced from the 999 call could be heard. 'It's definitely the same song.'

Alex shot her a smile; the first she had given anyone in days. 'Well done, Chloe.'

'You know what this means, though,' Dan said. 'Whoever made that call on Thursday evening may be the same person who played FIFA against Corey and Faadi on Saturday.'

'So the attack on Corey might be linked after all?' asked Jake.

Alex nodded. 'Seems possible. But there's still something not right about it. The incidents were so different. Maybe we're looking for more than one person.'

'So what do we do now?' Chloe asked.

'Let's step up the pressure on the Hassan brothers, for starters. Dan, we need some background checks on their finances – let's find out how the shop's been doing recently. Anyone we speak with now, I want the ringtone on their phone checked out. I don't care how you get it done – just think of any excuse, okay? Chloe ... great job.'

Chloe gave her a nod to acknowledge the praise. Under the circumstances, Alex knew it was the best she could hope for.

CHAPTER FORTY-SIX

Faadi sat back on his heels and sighed. He had emptied nearly all the contents of his bedroom drawers, as well as having searched through his wardrobe, but the Xbox game he was looking for was nowhere to be found. He hadn't played it in a while; he had bought a few new ones recently and had been kept so engrossed with them that he'd forgotten all about it. A couple of months ago, back in the summer, his mother had suggested doing a car boot sale in order to clear the house of some of its clutter. Now he wondered whether the game might have got mixed up in the things he had packed away.

They had never done the car boot sale. It had rained every weekend for a month during August and no one had fancied standing in a muddy field for the sake of a few extra quid. Everything had been put in the garage at the end of the garden to wait for the following summer, which would probably be as wet as the last.

He was distracted from his thoughts by the beep of his mobile phone. He searched for it among the debris that lay strewn across the carpet, wondering who might be texting him. No one ever texted him; only his mother, and she was downstairs.

Hi, Faadi. You having a nice half-term? Rebecca x

He stared at the text message for a long time, not quite believing what he was seeing. He only knew one Rebecca. She had spoken to him a few times at school, each time resulting in the inevitable twist of tongue and loss of words that Faadi suffered every time someone addressed him. And with Rebecca it was even worse. She was a girl. She was a pretty girl; a girl he had liked since he had first met her at school.

Good thanks, he texted. *How are you?*

He knew he wouldn't send it. Even if he wanted to – and he really did want to – he knew it would mean unthinkable embarrassment the next time he was face to face with her, which would likely be in full view of a corridor full of other kids; kids who would love to watch him die a slow and painful death in front of this girl and then tease him relentlessly about it for months afterwards.

Faadi knew what his problem was: he couldn't communicate with people. Not face to face anyway, and not with anyone who wasn't his mum. Recently he wondered whether he was even able to speak to her any more. She was so wrapped up in other things: the problems with Syed, the fire at the shop, his dad always being away with work. That was why he loved being online so much. He could speak to people there. It was like being someone else: someone who wasn't awkward and clumsy and embarrassing.

He supposed there was no difference with a text, really. Texting someone a message was just like talking to them online.

His thumb lingered over the send button. Then he did something he had never done before. He acted on impulse and sent the text.

Shoving his phone into his pocket, he stood and made his way downstairs. He could hear his mother in the kitchen and could smell dinner wafting from the open doorway; the heady scent of spices behind which his mother always hid. No matter what was going on, his mother would cook. They could be told the world was coming to an end within hours, but that wouldn't stop her preparing one last dinner for her family.

He left the house through the kitchen and went down the back garden to the garage. He didn't like it in there: it was cold, and there were too many cobwebs, and everything was coated in a thick layer of dust that caught in the back of his throat and made him cough. With a sigh, he began to open boxes, rummaging among the contents. After every box, he would move it aside before opening the next. He strained under the weight of one, exhaling loudly as he put it on the ground with a thud.

He was just wondering whether his efforts were worth it when something caught his eye. Something red. Something much cleaner than anything else in the garage. He leaned over the boxes and craned his neck for a better look.

It was what he'd thought it was. It was a petrol can.

Faadi stood on the pavement outside his parents' burned-out shop, wondering where everything had started to go wrong. He had thought it had been the move from Cardiff that had sent his family spiralling into chaos, but looking back now, it seemed the problems had started before then; he had just been too young to see them for what they were. Syed was a bully; he always had been. Their mother preferred to blame his behaviour on the older kids he'd got involved with back in Cardiff, but doing so was only a desperate attempt to avoid an inescapable truth: Syed had been bad long before any of those boys had appeared on the scene.

Faadi had heard of a mean streak before, and he guessed that was what his oldest brother had. He was passing it on to Jameel now, gradually getting him to think and act more like him; slowly poisoning all the nice parts that Jameel had once had. Faadi could remember the times when Jameel had played on the Xbox with him. He could remember, not that long ago, when Jameel had listened to him talk about school, about his fears over not fitting in. He'd been sympathetic, once. Now he just used all the things Faadi had told him as weapons, beating him about the head with them and using them to make him look stupid every time Syed was near.

Faadi looked at the boarded-up window and the blackened signage that hung above the door. He glanced at the black bin bag in his hand and knew what he had to do. He took his mobile phone from his pocket and searched for Chloe Lane's number.

CHAPTER FORTY-SEVEN

It felt colder inside Corey Davies's house than it did on the street outside, and Chloe found herself pulling her jacket close around her in a bid to stave off the biting air. It was a wonder Leanne Davies didn't feel the cold; she had barely any fat on her to keep her warm and was wearing only jeans and a T-shirt. Chloe gave a thought to her own expanding waistline. Since meeting Scott, dinners out and evenings in on the sofa meant she had gone up a dress size. She had resolved not to waste too much thought on the fact. If anything, it meant that she was happier than she'd been before, when stress and worry had been responsible for keeping her thin.

Alex was sitting on the sofa; at the other end, Corey was huddled beneath a grey blanket, wrapped so tightly in it that only his neck and head could be seen. He hadn't spoken a word since Alex and Chloe had arrived, despite the ongoing encouragement of his mother.

'See what this has done?' Leanne said, looking to Alex as though she was responsible. 'Things were bad enough before. I can't get a word out of him now.'

Chloe scanned the room. It was sparsely furnished, with bare floorboards that needed sanding. Wallpaper was peeling from the walls and at the windows the curtains moved with the cold that pushed through the single-glazed frames. Working long hours that kept him away from home for great stretches of time didn't seem to be paying off for Corey's father, or for his family.

'Corey, you must remember something,' Leanne said. She sat down beside him and snatched the TV remote control from his hand before muting the screen. 'You want him to do the same to someone else, do you?'

Corey's pale eyes looked past his mother, but for the first time there was a sign of something behind them. The boy blinked back tears and glanced down at the blanket, shaking his head as though willing her away.

'Shall we all have a cup of tea?' Alex suggested. She gave Chloe a nod before turning to Leanne. 'Come on, I'll give you a hand.'

Chloe knew what Alex was doing. Leanne was trying to be helpful, but her presence was overbearing and it was little wonder that Corey was still refusing to talk to anyone. Though she would probably have been upset at the suggestion, she was treating Corey as though he was in some way to blame for the attack, and doing so meant he would never open up to her about the incident.

'I like this show,' Chloe said, gesturing to the muted television. 'They're funny.'

Corey stared at the silent screen, refusing to acknowledge Chloe's presence. He was small for his size, skinny like his mother, and he seemed crippled by an awkwardness he was unable to control. Chloe wondered what sort of person they were looking for; what sort of man would attack someone so obviously vulnerable and unlikely to fight back.

On the television, a group of men stood huddled by a row of bushes in a park, watching in stitches of laughter as their friend tried to get passers-by to sign up to a fake charity called 'Save the Seagull'.

'You know the tall one?' Chloe said. 'He's related to Donald Trump. He's his second cousin or something. He doesn't like people to know. Well, you wouldn't, would you? You can sort of tell, though, when you look at the hairstyle.'

There was a flicker of a reaction at Corey's lips. 'You know the short one?' he said without looking at her. 'He's related to Elvis.'

'Is he?'

'No,' Corey said, his voice flat and unchanging. 'I just made it up, same as you did.'

Chloe smiled. 'Ah, I've been caught out. Too smart for me.' She sat back and faced the television. 'Listen, Corey. It's because you're smart that you know your mum's right. You don't want what happened to you on Saturday night to happen to anyone else, do you?'

The boy shook his head. The motion was slow and methodical, any emotional response he might have had kept carefully forced back by a tensed jaw and a steely determination.

'The thing is, we think it already has.'

Now she had his attention. Corey turned to her, making eye contact for the first time.

'Last night, someone's house was set on fire. Someone who lives not too far from here. She was an elderly lady, she lived on her own.'

Corey had already looked away, unable to hold her gaze for long. She waited for him to say something, but he didn't speak. He was moving his head from side to side as though in slow protest. Chloe didn't know much about his condition, but she could remember being fifteen. She hadn't liked being spoken down to or talked to as though she was a child. If she was going to gain Corey's trust, she was going to have to treat him like an adult.

'We think whoever attacked you was the same person responsible for the fire last night,' she continued. 'We also think they're responsible for the fire up at the hospital last week. You're the only one who's able to tell us anything about this person. I know it was dark and I know everything happened quickly, but anything you might be able to tell us could make a massive difference. This person needs to be stopped before they hurt anyone else.'

The boy's head-shaking had increased in speed; his eyes were closed and his arms had emerged from beneath the blanket. He moved his hands together, twisting his fingers in his lap and clenching his fists until his knuckles whitened.

'Did your attacker speak to you, Corey? Did he say anything at all?'

The more Chloe spoke, the more the boy shook his head. 'No.'

'No, he didn't say anything to you?'

'No. No, no, no, no, no, no!'

The word filled the room, louder with each repetition. The living room door opened and Leanne appeared carrying two mugs of tea, Alex following behind with another two.

'Corey. Stop.'

'No!' The word escaped in one long scream this time, the single syllable stretched into an ear-splitting screech.

Leanne leaned down to put the mugs of tea on the table beside the sofa, but Corey lashed out before she got there, sending one of the drinks flying into the air. The mug smashed on the wooden floor, shattering into pieces and sending hot tea splashing against the women's ankles.

'What the hell have you done?' Leanne asked accusingly, glaring at Chloe as she wrapped her arms around her son in an attempt to stop his shaking. 'It's all right, love,' she said, though her words of comfort were unconvincing.

'I …' Chloe glanced to Alex for help. 'We were just talking. I'm sorry.'

'You need to leave now,' Leanne said, firing the words out as Corey struggled to free himself from her grip. 'Go on. Now!' Her arms tightened around the boy and tried to control the frantic rocking that was taking over his body.

As Alex closed the front door behind them, Corey's cries could still be heard.

'Do you think he remembers anything?' she asked.

Chloe shook her head. 'Probably not. If he does, he's not likely to tell us, is he?'

Alex unlocked the car. 'Whoever this bastard is,' she said, getting into the driver's seat, 'he's running rings around us at the moment.'

CHAPTER FORTY-EIGHT

Alex sat in her office thinking about the visit to Corey Davies's house. She had hoped that Chloe would be able to persuade Corey to speak to her, but the boy's condition was more complex than either of them had realised. Even had his autism not affected him socially, the attack would have been enough to render him speechless. Was he reluctant to talk about it because he didn't want to return to the event, or did his fear run deeper?

She was pulled from her thoughts by the ringing of her mobile phone on the desk in front of her.

'Alex King.'

'Alex, it's Helen.'

She reached for a pen and a notepad. She had been anticipating this call from the pathologist all day, hoping that details of the post-mortem analysis might offer clues about the person responsible for Doris Adams's death.

'I've just sent the PM report over,' Helen told her. 'We're looking at another vicious assault, I'm afraid.'

Alex's thoughts returned to Gary Peters' post-mortem. Lung disease brought about by years of sleeping in damp and cold conditions had rendered him unable to fight back against his attacker. Similarly, Doris had been frail and elderly. It wouldn't have taken much of an assault to disable her, and little more to end her life.

She felt a sickening anger surge through her once again. Whoever they were hunting was a cowardly bastard.

'Blunt-force trauma to the front of the head – the details are all in the report. I have found something of significant interest, though. The victim sustained a prolonged assault, mainly to the torso. She was stamped on. Despite the bruising, a very clear print has been left just beneath the ribcage.'

'A print? From a shoe?'

'Looks like a boot print. The images are in the email I've sent you.'

As Helen continued to speak, Alex logged into her email account. She opened the post-mortem report, quickly moving on to the images that accompanied it. Her stomach turned at the sight of Doris's corpse laid bare on the pathologist's table, her pale skin stained with a smattering of black and purple bruising. Helen was right: a visible boot print had been left upon the victim's body.

'You're lucky she was removed from the building before the fire spread any further,' Helen said.

Alex understood the implication, but the word 'lucky' seemed inappropriate under the circumstances. She studied the image of the pattern imprinted on Doris's frail torso. With a match, would it be enough to convict? They would need to find the old lady's DNA on the boot, and she realised the chances of doing so were slim. With every turn the case took, Alex felt herself grow less and less confident. Whoever the killer was, it seemed that yet again he was getting the better of them.

'Thanks for this,' she said, unable to keep the lack of enthusiasm from her voice.

She ended the call and left the office to get a coffee. Reading the details of the report was going to require a caffeine hit at the very least. She passed the incident room hurriedly, not wanting to see Dan. Their contact had been minimal during those past couple of days, and if the case permitted it that was how she wanted things to stay. She felt bad enough as it was, and seeing him only made the guilt worse. It wasn't just the kiss that was getting to her: it was the knowledge that if Dan had allowed her to, she would have willingly taken things further.

She returned to her office, focusing her thoughts back on the case. When she got there, Chloe was waiting for her. 'Listen,' she said, holding her mobile out in front of her.

'You have one message,' said the voicemail.

There was a long beep, followed by a moment's silence. Someone could be heard clearing their throat.

'Um … it's Faadi. Faadi Hassan. Please don't tell anyone about this, but there's something I need to tell you. It's Syed. Syed started the fire.'

The message ended abruptly, as though Faadi had changed his mind too late.

'Have you called him back?'

'No answer. I'll keep trying.'

Alex opened the door to her office, ushering Chloe inside. 'We need a search warrant for the Hassan house. Ideally, we need to get our hands on their laptops. If that skeleton outfit was bought online, there'll be a history of it somewhere.'

'Why is Faadi saying this now? This can't have just come out of the blue.'

'Keep trying his phone. Let me know when you manage to get hold of him. We don't even know which fire he means – we're only assuming he's referring to the shop.'

Alex sat down and pushed Doris Adams's post-mortem report across the desk to Chloe. 'This'll be keeping me busy for the next couple of hours.' She turned her attention to the computer and pulled up the image of the boot mark left on Doris's body.

'Jesus Christ,' Chloe said, shaking her head.

'Have you seen Dan? How's he getting on with the check on the Hassans' finances?'

'You should ask him. You can't keep avoiding him forever.'

'I'm not.'

Chloe raised an eyebrow. 'Just sort things out. This is a good team. It'd be a shame to lose it all over a stupid mistake.'

Alex was grateful for the interruption of Chloe's phone. She took her mobile from her pocket and glanced at the screen.

'Faadi,' she said. 'Thanks for calling me back.'

In the incident room, Alex sought out Dan. Chloe was right: they were a good team. What had happened on Sunday had been stupid and shameful, but they couldn't let it interfere with the case.

'Any joy with the background check on the Hassans?' she asked him, lingering at the side of his desk.

'So far, it seems the shop has been doing fine. No one's going to retire a millionaire off the back of it, but no signs of debt either. No apparent reason for an attempt at an insurance claim.'

Alex noticed that Dan didn't look up when he spoke to her, avoiding any eye contact. She wanted to talk to him, to clear the air, but there never seemed an appropriate time and there were always other people around; people neither of them would want overhearing what needed to be said. She wondered whether there would ever be an appropriate time for such a conversation.

'Who does the shop belong to?' she asked. 'Legally.'

'Everything's registered in Mahira Hassan's name.'

Alex nodded. Something wasn't adding up, and it hadn't since the arson attack. She knew the family had been the victims of hate crime – their complaints of harassment had been logged, though there had never been sufficient evidence to lead to any convictions – but the arson attack bore no similarity to any of the family's previous complaints.

'Youssef Hassan has another job, doesn't he?'

'Works as a sales rep for a stationery company. They sell to offices and schools.'

'What about the two older sons?'

Dan shook his head. 'Unemployed on paper, but they help out at the shop apparently.' He turned back to his computer.

'Dan,' Alex said, looking over her shoulder to check there was no one close. 'Can we talk now?'

Without looking up, Dan shook his head. 'Probably not the best place here.'

'My office?'

There was a pause. 'Give me five minutes.'

Ten minutes later, Dan came into the office. He closed the door behind him, but didn't move any further into the room, making it clear the conversation was to be a brief one. It was the way Alex wanted to keep things too.

'I'm so sorry,' she said, the words escaping hurriedly.

'So am I.'

'I don't know what I was thinking. I mean, I wasn't thinking. I just—'

'It's my fault,' Dan interrupted.

'It's really not.' Alex sighed and ran her hand through her hair, pushing it away from her face. 'Look ... we're a good team. All of us, I mean. I shouldn't have ... I just don't want this to get in the way of our work. All our focus should be on this case.'

'Chloe knows.'

Alex nodded.

'She won't say anything to anyone, will she?'

Alex shook her head. Chloe might be angry with her, but one thing Alex could depend on was her word. She would just have to hope that the younger woman would eventually forgive her.

She watched Dan leave the office, knowing his guilt was likely to be even worse than hers. Chloe might come to forgive her in time, she thought, but forgiving herself was going to take a lot longer.

CHAPTER FORTY-NINE

Tyler Morris was sitting on his father's sofa watching television. His younger brother Curtis was playing on the carpet behind him, barking instructions to a row of toy robots and dinosaurs he had lined up against the wall at the back of the living room. It was the first time Curtis had been over to their dad's new house, and the first time Gavin had spent any time with his younger son since the Christmas before last. Within an hour of the boys getting there, it was obvious Gavin didn't know what to do with Curtis. He was loud and uncontrollable and, unlike Tyler, he couldn't be bribed with pizza and cash handouts.

Gavin had called for a takeaway, which had recently arrived. He was at the back of the house in the kitchen spooning chicken curry from a plastic carton when his mobile started ringing. He didn't recognise the number, but he had applied for a lot of jobs over the past fortnight and he wasn't prepared to run the risk of losing out on an opportunity for the sake of a Chinese. Balancing the phone between his shoulder and his chin, he lifted a handful of chips from their bag, dumped them on a plate and carried it through to the living room. He nudged Curtis with his right foot, pointed to the sofa and handed his son the plate.

'Gavin Jones?'

'Yep.'

'I'm calling from the Royal Glamorgan Hospital. It's regarding your partner.'

For a moment, Gavin thought the woman had called the wrong number.

'Partner?'

'Sian Foster. I'm afraid there's been an incident. We asked for a next of kin … she asked me to call you.'

Gavin went into the living room and took his jacket from the bottom of the staircase, searching the pockets for his keys. 'What's happened?' he asked. 'Is she okay?'

'It's probably best you come to the hospital and we talk here. The police are currently with Sian.'

'Police?'

'I'm afraid Sian has been attacked.'

Pulling his keys from his pocket, Gavin ended the call, cutting the woman off. 'Tyler, you'll have to plate up your own food.'

Tyler watched his father put on his jacket. 'Where are you going? We only just got here.'

'I'm sorry. I'd take you with me but I've only got the bike. Just keep an eye on Curtis, all right? I won't be long. And if your nan calls, do me a favour and just tell her I'm upstairs. You know what she's like.'

He had known what to expect when he arrived at the hospital, but when he saw Sian, Gavin realised he hadn't been entirely prepared for what would greet him there. Her room was quiet – the police must have already made themselves scarce. Gavin wasn't surprised. In his experience, they were good at showing up too late and disappearing again too soon.

Sian was lying on her back with her face turned to the window, staring at an expanse of dark night sky. There was movement beneath the hospital sheet at the sound of his arrival, but she didn't turn to see who was there. When he went around the bed and saw her face, Gavin realised why. She didn't want anyone to see her, not in the state she was in.

'I'm going to fucking kill him.'

He grabbed a chair from against the wall and dragged it across to the bed before sitting down and reaching for her hand. Her left eye was circled with a vivid purple bruise, the white of the eye bloodshot and bleary. She had a swollen top lip, wet with tears, and the grey T-shirt she was wearing was stained with dried blood.

'Not now, Gav.'

'You've reported him to the police this time, right?'

Sian winced as she moved beneath the sheet. 'There's nothing to report.'

Pulling his hand away from hers, Gavin pushed back the chair and stood. 'Well if you won't do it, I will.'

'Gavin, please.' She pushed herself up on the pillows, but the effort of moving left her moaning in pain and clutching her ribcage. 'You'll make things worse.'

'Look at the state of you. How can things get worse?'

He stood at the end of the bed, not knowing where to look as she cried. Mascara streaked her cheeks, smearing across the purple bruising that stained her pale skin. 'Just listen. Please. It's over, all right? Please, for me. Just leave it. I don't want you to do anything, I just want you to be here.'

Reluctantly Gavin went back to her. He sat down and allowed her to grip his hand in hers, not knowing whether he really wanted to be there or not. He'd had enough of his own problems over the years, and being dragged into hers was probably the last thing he needed.

He watched her as she closed her eyes and tightened her grip on his hand.

Why wouldn't she report Christian? And why was she still protecting him?

CHAPTER FIFTY

Alex and Chloe were once again heading up the valley; a journey that had become all too familiar to them during the past week. A swell of mountains loomed in the background, their green and brown bodies standing tall against a grey sky that promised rain. Rows of houses snaked at their feet like interweaving train tracks, with towns built in clusters in the curves of the hillsides. Alex imagined there was a certain brooding beauty about the place, but with murder lingering in its shadows it was impossible to see anything but darkness.

'So the petrol used to start the fire at Doris Adams's house was the same brand used at the hospital?' Chloe confirmed.

Alex nodded. 'And the same brand used during the attack on Corey Davies. The only thing that doesn't match is the petrol used to start the fire at the Hassans' shop.' She slowed the car for a set of red traffic lights. 'Guess who I got a call from last night?'

'Go on.'

'Gavin Jones.'

Chloe raised an eyebrow. 'About?'

'You know about Christian Coleman, do you?'

Chloe's face was blank. She hadn't been with them when Coleman had been poisoned; she had joined the team later, after a transfer from the Met. Her return to Wales had been motivated by a desire to discover the truth about her brother's death years earlier, something she hadn't told Alex until her investigations were already under way. It had put both women in a difficult situation, though for Chloe, events had gone on to be life-changing.

'I've heard of him.'

Alex gave her a brief rundown of the story.

'So where does Gavin Jones come into all this?' Chloe asked.

'He's seeing Coleman's ex-wife, the one he put in hospital. Gavin reckons he's done it again.'

Chloe pulled a face. 'Surely the police are already involved. Why's he contacting you about it?'

Alex pulled the car up to the kerbside, stopping near the Hassan home. 'You'd think so, but he says she's refusing to report it. I think Gavin might be genuine about this wanting a fresh start business, for him and for Sian. He doesn't need any more trouble at his door.'

The two women got out of the car, neither relishing the prospect of yet another visit to the Hassans. Alex imagined the reception they would receive would be less than welcoming. Sure enough, their presence was met with a succession of sighs and rolled eyes. Even Mahira Hassan, who had until then been patient and accommodating, was visibly exasperated.

'Syed's still not here,' she said, stepping aside to allow the detectives into the house.

Alex produced the search warrant she'd had to fight for earlier that afternoon. The petrol can that Faadi had told Chloe about was evidence of nothing, but Alex had managed to persuasively argue that the fight between the Hassan brothers and Gavin Jones, followed by the arson at the shop, was sufficient motivation for Syed or Jameel to have sought revenge on Gavin. Had one of them taken the petrol can that was found near the attack on Corey Davies from Gavin's shed, knowing his fingerprints would incriminate him in the attack?

And why was there another one in the Hassans' garage? Gavin's motorbike gave him justification for owning a petrol can. As far as Alex was aware, there was no reason for anyone in the Hassan household to have one.

'We won't be needing Syed,' Alex said.

'What now?' Youssef appeared from the kitchen. He looked even more tired than he had when Alex and Chloe had last visited, and the dejection in his voice suggested he felt in some way defeated.

'We have a warrant to search the premises, Mr Hassan.'

'What? No, you can't.'

Alex showed him the warrant. 'We won't be long. Could you show me to Syed's bedroom please, Mrs Hassan.'

Youssef stepped in front of his wife, blocking her path to the stairs. 'You have no right to be here,' he said, firing the words at Alex. 'My sons haven't done anything wrong.'

'Then you won't mind us just checking their rooms,' Chloe said.

'Mr Hassan,' Alex said. 'I appreciate that we're intruding on your time. You look tired. Long week at work?'

Youssef studied her accusingly, his dark eyes narrowed. 'Yes. So if we could just get this over and done with.'

'You work for a stationery company, is that right?'

Youssef looked from Alex to Chloe. 'Yes, that's right.'

Alex smiled. 'Perhaps you could show me to Syed's room?'

Knowing they would search the property with or without his say-so, Youssef sighed and began to head upstairs. Alex followed, leaving Chloe downstairs with Mahira. They passed Jameel's bedroom and Alex glanced past the opened door; he was inside, sprawled face down on the bed watching a television that was turned up too loudly. He must have heard their voices in the hallway and their footsteps on the stairs, but he did nothing to acknowledge them.

Youssef stopped at the next door and hesitated for a moment. 'What is it you think Syed has done?'

'I can't go into that, I'm afraid. Does he have access to a laptop or a computer here? We'll need to take it.'

They still hadn't found out where the skeleton fancy-dress outfit had been purchased. If Syed or Jameel was the person on the CCTV footage, there was a chance one of them had ordered the costume online. Alex believed Syed to be the more organised of the two brothers. Ideally, she needed his phone.

Without responding, Youssef opened the door to Syed's bedroom, allowing Alex to enter. The room had been tidied, the bed made, and a pile of ironed clothes was waiting on top of a chest of drawers. Mahira had obviously been in here, Alex thought. Despite the events of the last week, she was clearly keen to maintain as much of a sense of normality and order as possible.

From Jameel's bedroom, a mobile phone started to ring. Alex turned back and listened for the ringtone, but it was a generic tune that came with an iPhone. The tune stopped when he answered.

'I'll be okay from here,' Alex said. 'Thank you.'

Reluctantly, Youssef turned to leave, doing nothing to disguise the exhalation of breath that gave voice to his frustrations.

'Mr Hassan,' Alex said, stopping him. 'One last thing. When are you planning on telling your wife you've lost your job?'

CHAPTER FIFTY-ONE

Alex hadn't seen Sian Foster since her son's sentencing two years earlier. Communication between the two had been tense: Sian blamed Alex for Nathan's arrest, and her anger had been directed at her in the aftermath of his sentencing. Alex seemed to make a hobby of attracting people's anger. Youssef Hassan had watched her with contempt as she'd searched his oldest son's room, furious with the knowledge that he had little choice but to tell his wife about his lie. Yet in Sian's case, Alex didn't blame the woman for her animosity. Had Alex had any control over the situation, Nathan would have been back at home with his family by now, where he belonged. Once he'd been charged, she had had no involvement in the case. What happened next was in the hands of the judge.

It wasn't the first time a legal professional had made a poor decision. Nathan had been used as an example. People couldn't take the law into their own hands, and his twelve-year sentence was a clear deterrent to others.

On Wednesday evening, Alex headed over to the hospital in Llantrisant. The decision to visit Sian hadn't taken long to come to. The car accident that could easily have been so much worse still preyed on her mind. If Sian Foster still had contact with her ex, there was a slim chance she might know whether he'd had any involvement in cutting Alex's brake line. Sian knew better than anyone just what Christian was capable of.

She asked at the hospital's main reception desk which ward Sian was in before heading upstairs. Finding the right corridor, she pushed open a set of doors and scanned the area for a member of staff. Finding no one, she walked the length of the corridor, slowing at each room to look through the windows.

Turning a corner, she stopped when she saw a teenage girl outside one of the rooms. She was sitting on a plastic chair to the side of a closed door, a pair of earphones shoved into her ears, its wire disappearing into her pocket, attached to the mobile phone hidden there. She looked up as Alex approached. Casting a glance at the window, Alex saw Sian Foster lying in the bed, her eyes open and staring listlessly at the ceiling.

She wouldn't have recognised the girl had she seen her elsewhere, but Alex realised now that this was Keeley, Sian and Christian's daughter. Nathan's sister.

'Keeley.'

The girl pulled the left headphone from her ear and looked at Alex questioningly. She didn't remember her. Alex hadn't expected her to: Keeley had only been young when her brother had been sentenced, and being a minor meant she had been kept sheltered from much of what had gone on. She had changed so much in the two years that had passed, no longer a little girl.

'I know your mum,' Alex said by way of explanation.

Keeley nodded. 'You can go in. I've just come out here to cool down – it's boiling in there.'

Alex went into the room. Keeley was right: the air was sticky and uncomfortable. Despite that, Sian kept herself hidden beneath a hospital blanket, concealing her injuries.

'What are you doing here?' she asked, her hostility tangible.

Keeley might have forgotten her, but Sian never would. She still blamed Alex, even now.

'Did Christian do this to you?'

Sian turned her face away and looked to the window. Her nose was blocked and her breathing laboured; every time she exhaled through her mouth, a chesty wheezing filled the otherwise silent room. She was only in her thirties, yet she looked and sounded much older.

'You don't have to let him get away with this,' Alex said. 'He's not supposed to go anywhere near you, he knows that. One word from you and we can put him back inside.'

'How did you find out?'

'The hospital has a duty to inform the police.'

Sian shook her head. 'I told them last night I don't want it to go any further. So who really told you?'

Ignoring the question, Alex went to the other side of the bed and sat on the chair there. Sian turned away and faced the ceiling, closing her eyes as though able to somehow block Alex from her mind. Alex wondered if this was how she spent most of her life, hiding from problems in the hope that one day they might just disappear.

'Don't let him do this. What happens when he meets someone else? There will be a next time – there always is with men like Christian.'

The feeling she'd had when she had pressed her foot flat to the brake of her car and found it useless returned to her then: that feeling of fear and helplessness that she had felt before, in different circumstances. She never wanted to feel it again, but if she had to, she didn't want it to be at the hands of a person like Christian Coleman. She studied the pattern of bruises that mottled Sian's skin. She had pitied the woman once, but now she felt an overriding frustration that cancelled out any sympathy she might have had for her. For whatever reason, Sian seemed intent on protecting her ex-husband. But why? She owed him no favours, and she had nothing to lose if Christian was to return to prison.

Realising her words were lost on Sian, Alex stood. She glanced to the doorway. Keeley was still outside in the corridor, her head bowed as she listened to the music playing from her phone.

'What about Keeley?' she said in a last attempt to change Sian's mind. 'She'll be a woman before you know it. What if he does something to hurt her? If you say nothing now, what are you teaching her?'

The irony of her own words wasn't lost on Alex. She thought of Dan, and of Dan's two daughters. She knew she should have thought of them sooner, before she had allowed Dan into her home. She should have thought of them before she went ahead and kissed him. It had been pathetic and desperate.

What the hell had she been thinking?

Sian's eyes remained closed. 'Just go.'

Alex stood up and walked round the bed. She stopped for a moment and glanced at the file that was hanging from the end of the metal frame. At the top was written Sian's full name, scrawled in biro by one of the nurses.

Sian Kathleen Foster.

CHAPTER FIFTY-TWO

There was shouting coming from downstairs again. Raised voices seemed to form a soundtrack to the daily routine of the Hassan household, and there was no place to escape it. Faadi sat in his bedroom with a pair of headphones clamped over his ears, lost to the sounds of the game he was playing. He hadn't gone online that day, or any day since Saturday. He didn't want to and he hadn't needed it. He glanced at his phone. He and Rebecca had been messaging each other all day, though it was still taking him at least half an hour to deliberate over each and every reply.

He still couldn't believe that she would want to talk with him. Whenever she had spoken to him in school – just a general question about something a teacher had been saying or something they had been due to hand in that day – Faadi had found himself speechless, not knowing how to talk to her or what to say. And every time, afterwards, he had regretted his shyness and hated himself for being so awkward around other people.

*

Downstairs, beneath Faadi's room, Youssef Hassan was pacing the length of the kitchen. Mahira was sitting at the table, her eyes following her husband as he passed back and forth in front of her. Since the police had left, they had barely said a word to one another. DI Alex King had returned from the shed with a petrol can, the existence of which neither Mahira nor Youssef had been able to explain. She had taken it away with her when she had left;

for testing, she had told them. All fingers seemed to point to Syed, who hadn't been there to defend himself or explain why his name kept recurring during their investigations.

'Did he do it?' Mahira asked, breaking the silence. 'Did he start the fire at the shop?'

The thought made her feel sick. Everything she had worked for had been brought to ruin with a single malicious act. Their new life away from trouble was already a farce. To think that her own son might have been responsible for that was something Mahira hadn't prepared for and wasn't ready to accept, yet she had to admit that the possibility was all too plausible. She didn't know why Syed would do it, but she knew he was more than capable of it.

'All those reports I've made to the police,' she said quietly. 'We wanted to be taken seriously here – we wanted things to be different. All I've ever wanted is to be treated as an equal, to be shown some respect, and he goes and does this and undermines everything we've worked for. The graffiti on the shop ... was that him as well? Did he try to cover himself by making it look like a racially motivated attack?'

She stopped talking, realising her words were pouring from her too quickly. This wasn't like her. She approached things methodically, with a calm head and rational thinking, but this was more than she was able to comprehend. Syed had brought trouble to their home on many occasions, but he had never targeted them directly. Not like this.

'You're not going to say anything?'

Youssef turned to the window and folded his arms across his chest. 'There's something I haven't told you.'

'What?'

'I lost my job.'

Mahira pushed her chair back and stood, crossing the kitchen to stand beside her husband. 'What? When?'

'July.'

She stepped back as though he had just burned her. 'July? But … you've been away with work since then. You've hardly been here.'

He put his hands to his face and rubbed his tired eyes. 'I'm sorry.'

She didn't know what to say. Returning to her seat at the table, she waited for some sort of explanation, but none came. 'Where have you been?' she asked, sinking into the chair. If she didn't sit down, she feared she might fall over. Everything else, and now this. She wasn't sure how much more she could take.

A knotted tangle of thoughts lodged in her brain, the clearest of them being that during the nights he'd been away from home, he had been staying with another woman. There was someone else, and he couldn't bring himself to admit it to her.

'Youssef?'

'I stayed in hotels to begin with,' he said, turning to her. 'At first I thought I could act normal, pretend things were fine, find another job and there would be no need to tell you what had happened. The longer it went on, the harder it became to tell you the truth. I've been sleeping in the car most nights. I thought I'd find something else. You've been so worried about the boys, I didn't want to burden you with anything more.'

'Oh, so this is my fault?'

'No.' He sat at the table opposite her. 'Mahira,' he said, trying to get her to make eye contact with him. 'Look at me. Please. I never meant for any of this to happen.'

'Any of what?' She asked the question knowing there was more to come. He had been lying to her for months and he was continuing to conceal the truth now. She didn't need to hear the words; she knew what he was going to say.

'I had to do it,' he said, tears gathering at the corners of his eyes. 'Please, believe me, if there had been any other option then I would have taken it, but things had got in such a mess and I couldn't see a way out. There are debts … the house. We needed the money.'

Scraping her chair back across the tiled floor of the kitchen, Mahira stood. She could feel her whole body shaking and couldn't be sure whether it was with anger or sadness. Everything was broken. Everything she had worked for was lost, and everyone she loved was lying to her. Nearly everyone.

'The police suspect Syed,' she said, her voice flat and shallow. 'You will go to the station tomorrow and you will tell them what you've done.'

*

Upstairs in his bedroom, oblivious to the conversation taking place below, Faadi had received another message.

Want to come to a party with me tomorrow night? It'll be fun x

He had never been to a party; not like the type the other kids in his year group went to anyway. The last party he had gone to had involved jelly and ice cream and pass the parcel and had been about seven years earlier. His mother had tried to get him to mix with the other kids, but she'd seemed to learn quickly that socialising really wasn't for him and she had thankfully given up not too long after.

Things were different now. He wasn't a little kid any more. And another thing: he knew he couldn't hide away in his room for the rest of his life. He might have spent a few hours with him the previous Saturday, but Faadi didn't want to end up like Corey Davies. He liked him well enough, but he knew that Corey didn't have any friends, not real ones, and he didn't seem to want any. But Faadi wanted to have friends. He wanted to have a girlfriend, and to be able to talk to her.

He was going to have to do something he'd never really done before. He was going to have to be brave.

His fingertip lingered over the phone.

Yeah, that would be good. Thanks x

He hid the phone guiltily when there was a knock at the bedroom door. 'Faadi,' his mum said, entering the room. 'Pack a bag with some overnight things, please.'

'What? Why, where are we going?'

'Just do it.'

She had never snapped at him before, not like that. He watched her leave before taking his phone from beneath the cushion he was resting against, watching its dulled screen as he waited for a reply. He didn't know what had gone on downstairs, but his mother's appearance had made him even surer that he wanted to go to this party. He loved his family, but he needed to escape the drama.

His phone vibrated in his hand.

I'll send you the address.

Faadi smiled, stood and put his phone in his pocket before reaching under his bed for an overnight bag.

CHAPTER FIFTY-THREE

The sky looks full and dark from where she lies, stretching past the window in a midnight-blue sheet that weighs heavy over the lives below. There are no fireworks tonight, only the ones that exist in her brain. They explode in plumes of colour and light, warming the chill that sits within her.

It is easy to start a fire. One strike of a match, one flick of a lighter. It is so much harder to stop one, and that is one of the things she loves about it. Fire is difficult to contain and difficult to control. In so many ways, it is just like her. She won't be stopped either. She will surge and spread and make herself known in every corner she can reach, and when she does come to an end, finally, she will leave a mark on the landscape; a deep, blackened scar that can never be fully erased.

She will remain even after she has gone, forever spoken of. She will be the stuff of legends.

They can try to stop her if they like – she'll enjoy watching them – but she will leave her mark.

She stands and returns to packing the rest of her things. She doesn't need much really, not where she's going. It will be so easy to start again.

She stops in front of the mirror and smiles. Her reflection smiles back at her, unassuming. Like a method actor, she has perfected this role. She knows she is good at what she does.

There is one final job to be done before she leaves. Tomorrow, she will complete it.

CHAPTER FIFTY-FOUR

On Thursday morning, the team sat in the incident room, the mood one of general dejection. It had been a week since the fire at the hospital. Too much time had passed and too little evidence had been uncovered. The killer they were hunting had been allowed to get away with too much in the time that the team had spent chasing their own tails, leaving them unable to join the dots between the various points and people of interest that had arisen.

Alex's tiredness was ingrained in the furrows of her brow, and despite the two coffees she had already consumed since arriving at the station, she feared it was set to remain with her for the duration of the day. She had barely slept. She hadn't been able to tear herself away from thoughts of Gary Peters and Doris Adams. The gruesome details of their post-mortem reports had lingered through the night, haunting her with their horrific truths. Corey Davies, terrified of his own shadow. And then there was Christian Coleman. Alex had no evidence to suggest that he had been responsible for the abusive graffiti that had been scrawled across the front of her home, or the cut brake line that had caused her car accident; just an aching, relentless suspicion that couldn't be shaken off.

She knew she should have been to see him by now, but a deep unease was keeping her from going to the house. It wasn't just Christian, she realised that. What had happened to Chloe earlier that year still haunted Alex as much as it did Chloe. They exposed themselves to new dangers with every case. It was only a matter of time before something caught up with her, and perhaps that time was now.

Alex had arrived early at the station that morning, but Youssef Hassan had got there before her. His admission was unexpected; it came as little surprise that he was responsible, but she hadn't anticipated the guilty party coming forward to confess his crime. The family's financial problems – ones that he had managed to keep hidden from his wife for months – had driven him to the arson attack, but with his eldest son under suspicion he had been forced to admit what he had done.

Despite her increasing doubt, she told the rest of the team what she had seen on Sian Foster's file at the hospital the previous evening. The more she'd thought over it, the more unlikely it had become. Kathleen. It was just a name, surely.

'It could just be a coincidence,' she said.

'It's not that common a name, though.' Chloe stared at the board behind Alex, perusing the gaps that showed a lack of connections between the faces staring back at her. Sian Foster had now been added, alongside Gavin Jones. Other than being in a relationship with Gavin, it was unclear where Sian might come into any of this.

'Was someone trying to leave us a clue through that song?' Jake asked. 'Literally naming a suspect?'

Alex shook her head. 'I don't think so. The sound was very unclear before the recording was enhanced, and the call was cut short not long after it started. Unless we're way off the mark here, Sian Foster is a victim. She has no links to these cases other than being Gavin Jones's girlfriend, and at the moment his alibis are solid. I think Chloe's theory that it's a ringtone is probably our best one.'

'Bit of a weird coincidence, though,' Dan said.

Alex nodded in agreement. 'Are there any updates on Syed Hassan's laptop?'

'Two Hallowe'en outfits purchased online,' Dan told her. 'Neither of them a skeleton.'

Alex pursed her lips. She had been hoping for a result there, despite the fact that Youssef Hassan had now admitted to the arson at the shop. The other three attacks were linked, she was convinced of it. What she still wasn't sure of was that they were carried out by the same person.

'We don't know that Syed and Jameel didn't carry out the attack against Gavin Jones,' Chloe said. 'Could the outfits have been bought for that?'

'Good possibility. Bit old for trick-or-treating, aren't they? Gavin doesn't want to make a statement, though, and we've got no evidence. We can't take it any further.'

A silence fell over the room. The lack of progress was making everyone frustrated, and the more time that passed, the more the faces on the evidence board seemed to loom over the team, watching each and every one of them accusingly. It was 2 November, just three days until Bonfire Night. They were anticipating another incident that weekend. How many more names might be added to the board? Alex wondered. How many more innocent victims would fall prey to this murderer?

'This has all the markings of a killing spree,' she said, thinking aloud. 'Gary Peters on Thursday, an attempt on Corey Davies on Saturday, Doris Adams Tuesday. There's a regular gap between each crime and each attack has occurred in quick succession. We've been concentrating our focus on these faces,' she said, passing a hand across the images of Jameel and Syed Hassan, before resting it on Gavin Jones. 'But what if we've got it wrong?'

'What do you mean?'

'We've spoken before about the fact that our attacker preys on the vulnerable. Victims who are unable or unlikely to defend themselves.' She returned the team's attention to the board. 'These are all grown men, young and strong. It didn't need strength to kill Gary Peters, nor Doris Adams.'

She moved away from the board and ran a hand through her dark hair, pushing it back from her face. She wished she could give them more – that she was able to say 'this is who we're looking for' – but they just didn't have the details needed.

She turned back to the montage of photographs pinned on the board, stopping at the image captured on the CCTV of the bus that had picked up their skeleton figure.

'*This*,' she said, tracing a finger over the image before moving it to the close-up of the boot print that had been left on Doris Adams's body, 'doesn't seem to add up with *this*. The driver guessed the man in the skeleton outfit to be around five foot nine. This boot print is a size six.'

She stepped back from the board and folded her arms across her chest.

'We've already considered the possibility that we may be looking at two suspects here – one responsible for the deaths of Gary Peters and Doris Adams and the other for the attack on Corey Davies.'

'So they're not working together?' Dan asked.

'Not necessarily. They could be. It may be that the two of them were together for the first and last attack, but not for the incident involving Corey. Jake, what size are your feet?'

'Eight. Why?'

'Dan?'

'Size nine. What are you thinking?'

'I'm thinking one of our killers is a woman.'

They were interrupted by a man in uniform entering the room.

'DI King,' the officer said. 'Gavin Jones has been found dead.'

CHAPTER FIFTY-FIVE

The scene that awaited King and Lane at Gavin Jones's house was macabre. The man was lying face down on the living room carpet, encircled by a dark pool of his own blood. Arterial spray stained the walls and the furniture, suggesting he had been stabbed multiple times in what had been a frenzied attack. Boxes that had been stacked waiting to be unpacked in his new home had been knocked over, their contents spilled across the floor. Signs of a struggle were obvious, and bloody handprints marked much of the furniture.

'He put up a good fight,' Chloe said, studying the array of smeared fingerprints that patterned the arm of the sofa.

A pathologist was crouched by Gavin's body, his bagged feet steeped in the victim's blood.

'How many wounds, do you think?' Alex asked.

'At the moment, I'd say at least eight.'

Alex went back to the front door. It had been forced open by uniformed officers earlier that morning when the 999 call from Sian Foster had been received. Before their arrival, there had been no sign of any forced entry.

'Whoever did this,' she said, 'Gavin knew them. He let them in.'

She turned to face the scene. The first evidence of blood spatter was a few feet inside the living room. Someone had followed Gavin into the house and attacked him there, presumably not long after entering. There had been a struggle, during which he had tried to make it to the kitchen, but he had been quickly disabled by a succession of fatal stab wounds.

Studying the scene, Alex knew there was no chance that evidence wouldn't be lifted from the body and the room. The attack was too messy. Looking at the results of the fight that had taken place, it was likely that they would find the killer's blood here as well as the victim's.

'We need to find Syed Hassan,' she said, turning to Chloe.

'You think he came back to finish what he and his brother started?'

'They'll know about their father being responsible for the fire at the shop. We know Syed is capable of violence. He'll be angry. By all accounts he spends most of his life angry. Perhaps this is the result of it.'

'Inspector?'

Both women turned to the pathologist, who was holding Gavin's right hand in his own. Deep cuts were slashed into Gavin's palm.

'He grabbed the blade,' Chloe said.

'Not just that. Look.'

The pathologist turned Gavin's body so that his face could be seen. His eyes were still open, which made the sight all the more chilling. Had his killer stayed with him as he'd died, watching what he'd done?

There were two stab wounds to the side of Gavin's neck, both of which would have finished him off if nothing else already had. He hadn't stood a chance of fleeing his attacker, no matter how much of a fight he put up.

'Two different knives,' the pathologist continued. 'I'll be able to tell you more for certain once I get him back to the lab, but these wounds weren't made with the same blade.'

'Two attackers?' Alex asked, her thoughts jumping straight to the Hassan brothers. If Gavin's claims had been correct, he had already survived one assault at the hands of either Syed or Jameel. Superiority in numbers would have meant he had no opportunity to escape an attack this time.

'Either that, or a killer armed with a knife in each hand.'

Chloe followed Alex from the room. Outside, Sian Foster was waiting in a marked van at the roadside. Both women got into the back of the van, where Sian was sitting with a blanket wrapped around her shoulders, her pale face contrasting with her puffy red eyes.

'Tell us what happened,' Alex said gently.

'I've told the others,' she said, barely able to get the words out. She was still in shock, and beneath the blanket officers had draped around her body her shoulders were shaking.

'We need to hear it again, Sian.'

She closed her eyes, squeezing them tightly shut as though trying to blank out the horrors of what she had found waiting for her.

She took a deep breath. 'I left the hospital this morning and came straight here. I was trying to call him all morning, but it kept going straight through to answerphone. I thought I'd just show up, surprise him. There was no answer when I knocked on the door. I tried his phone again, and when I pushed open the letter box I could hear it ringing inside. That's when I looked through the window.'

Alex studied her. There seemed something rehearsed about Sian's retelling of events, though Alex realised she was now suspicious of everyone. 'There was no one else here when you arrived?'

Sian shook her head.

'Why didn't you go home first after leaving the hospital?' Alex asked.

'I don't know,' she said defensively. 'I just didn't fancy being on my own. You know those Hassan brothers attacked him, don't you? Shouldn't you be asking them some questions?'

Alex held the woman's stare for a moment. 'Thank you, Sian.'

She and Chloe got out of the van. 'She's right,' Chloe said. 'We need to chase them up before they have time to do a runner.'

Alex nodded. 'Get Jake and go to the house.'

'You're not coming?'

'I'll meet you back at the station. There's someone else I need to see first.'

CHAPTER FIFTY-SIX

Alex left Gavin Jones's house and headed back down the valley. She hadn't told Chloe where she was going, knowing there was little point until her suspicions were proved correct. She had found out the previous day where Christian Coleman was staying, intent on paying him a visit. Gavin's murder made the need to see Christian more urgent. Maybe everyone else was right: perhaps the Hassan brothers were responsible for the murder. But Alex wasn't so sure.

Had Christian found out about the relationship between Sian and Gavin? From what Alex knew of the man, he wouldn't be happy about Sian moving on with anyone. He might not have wanted to be with her, but that didn't mean he wanted her to find happiness without him. Christian was a man who liked to maintain control, and everyone knew what he was capable of. To Alex's mind, the bloody scene they had just encountered was more likely to be the handiwork of Christian Coleman than Syed Hassan.

She might not have been prepared to face him for her own sake, but for the case she was ready to swallow her fears.

Perhaps it was stupid going to see him alone, she thought as she pulled up outside his address, but stupid seemed to be her speciality that week. She had already resolved not to go inside the house. She would stay on the doorstop, on the street where people could see them.

With clammy hands and an unease she didn't want to make visible, she knocked on the front door. A moment later, a woman in her mid sixties answered. She had lanky hair that was dyed black, with a strip of grey roots racing down the middle of her scalp like a runway. She was holding a cigarette in one hand and a half-eaten sandwich in the other. This was Christian Coleman's aunt, Mandy Lewis.

'Yeah?'

'Christian in?'

'Who's asking?'

'I am.'

The woman raised an eyebrow and stood her ground, moving the hand that held the burning cigarette to her hip. Alex reached into the pocket of her jacket and produced her ID. 'We spoke on the phone.'

The woman sighed and turned back to the house. 'Christian!' she called. 'Some copper wants you.'

She disappeared back down the hallway, leaving Alex waiting at the front door. A moment later there was a thundering of footsteps on the stairs and the bulk of Christian Coleman loomed towards her. He hadn't changed in the time since Alex had last seen him, other than for the widening expanse of gut that strained beneath his T-shirt.

'What the fuck do you want?'

'Nice to see you too. How's freedom treating you?'

Christian narrowed his eyes and glared at her. The scar on the side of his face glinted beneath the orange glow of his aunt's hallway lighting: a single bulb that dangled naked from the ceiling, dressed only with a thick cobweb that stretched to the picture rail.

'What do you want?' he asked again.

'Sian's been in hospital,' Alex told him. 'You've probably heard.'

Christian shook his head. 'Nope. Not heard a thing. What's wrong with her?'

'You put her there, Christian. You don't need to ask.'

His eyes darkened. 'If I'm being accused of something, you'd better come out and say it. I haven't seen Sian.'

'Now we both know that's a lie. You've been to the house.'

'I didn't touch her,' he said, his story altering under duress. 'So whatever the lying cow has said to you, you'd better check your facts.'

'We've heard that one before. "I didn't touch her."'

'Look,' he said, stepping out of the house and standing on the pavement in his socks. 'When I left her house she was fine. Your lot would know that … they saw me out. We talked about Nathan a bit, that was all. Whatever happened to her, it weren't nothing to do with me.'

Alex stood her ground, her confidence growing. She would never get an admission from him, but she wanted him to know she was on to him.

'Gavin Jones,' she said. 'Know him?'

Christian's mouth curled into a sneer. 'Not exactly an unusual name, is it? How many Gavin Joneses are there knocking about?'

'Do you know him?' Alex asked again, her lack of patience obvious.

Christian said nothing, enjoying his little moment of power over her. 'Can't say I do,' he eventually offered. 'Sorry.'

'Let's talk about my house then. The car. Must be disappointing to see me standing here unscathed.'

Christian folded his beefy arms across his chest and sighed. 'What the fuck are you talking about?'

'"I'll fucking kill you, you ugly whore",' Alex said, her fingers raised to make inverted commas in the air.

A second sneer spread across his face. 'Stand here talking shit much longer and I might just carry out the threat.'

Alex felt another ripple of unease pass through her. She pictured him in Gavin's living room, raining a flurry of brutal stab wounds upon his victim. Had he attacked Gavin armed with a knife in each hand? Gavin hadn't stood a chance.

She held his gaze. There was no way she was going to allow him to witness her fear.

'Are we done here?' Christian asked, dropping his hands to his sides.

'No. Sian's middle name – Kathleen.'

'What about it? Christ, these questions are getting weirder by the minute.'

'Family name, is it?'

He exhaled loudly, making it clear that Alex was wasting his time. She wondered what television programme she was keeping him away from.

'Yes,' he snapped. 'After her grandmother. A tradition, apparently. Stupid, if you ask me.'

'What do you mean, tradition?

'Tradition,' he said, slowing his voice as though Alex was either thick or hard of hearing, 'as in something that's been passed down to the next generation. Nathan was spared, mind, what with being a boy. Now are we done?'

Alex stepped off the pavement to return to her car, leaving Christian to go back inside the house. Her mind had left Sian; it had left the graffiti on her house and the cut brake line on her car. Her thoughts were instead stuck in one place: one awful idea that was already starting to unravel as a terrifying possibility.

Keeley Kathleen.

CHAPTER FIFTY-SEVEN

Alex got two streets away before pulling the car to the kerb and stopping just past a pedestrian crossing. She cut the engine dead and called Chloe.

'Where are you now?' she asked.

'At the station. Syed and Jameel have conveniently gone AWOL. Both parents are saying they don't know where they are. What's the matter?'

'Nothing. I mean, I don't know yet.'

Alex's thoughts were racing away from her, moving faster than she was able to keep up with. Two people: a man and a woman. Was that woman really a child? Could Keeley Coleman have been responsible for the boot mark that had been stamped on Doris Adams's body, and the prolonged and vicious assault that Gary Peters had endured before his death? Children had been known to kill before, though such cases were rare. When they did occur, they left an aftermath that would be felt by families and communities for years.

She had met Keeley on a few occasions during her father's trial. She had been eleven years old then – quiet and unassuming – and she had struck Alex as a girl who had fallen silent in the aftermath of Christian's reign of terror over the family. To think that she was involved in any of this seemed madness, but the more Alex's mind directed her to the idea, the more of an awful possibility it became.

'Teenage boy has been reported missing,' Chloe told her. 'His nan said he didn't come home last night.'

'Where's the grandmother now?'

'At home. There are a couple of officers with her. The thing is, it's Gavin Jones's son.'

'Send me the address,' Alex said. 'I'm on my way.'

Julie Morris was sitting on the sofa in her living room, a mug of untouched tea going cold on the carpet at her feet. Her younger grandson was curled up in a chair near the television, watching a cartoon and eating a chocolate biscuit. The liaison officer that had been assigned to the family following the news of Gavin's death was also there. Officers had taken a statement from Julie, as well as a couple of recent photographs of her older grandson, Tyler.

'He didn't come home last night?' Alex confirmed.

Julie shook her head. 'And before anyone bloody asks me again, no, he's never done anything like this before.'

'Has Tyler had contact with Gavin recently?'

'Yes, unfortunately. I know you're not supposed to speak ill of the dead and all that, but he's been nothing but bad news from the start. I tried calling him this morning to see if Tyler was with him. There was no answer.'

Alex's thoughts strayed again towards the Hassan brothers. Surely they weren't involved in the disappearance of Gavin's son too?

She glanced at Curtis, who seemed oblivious to everything going on around him. His mouth was smeared with chocolate. 'Does Tyler know about his father?'

Julie shook her head. 'He can't do. Not unless he's heard about it from someone else.' She put her head in her hands.

'When did you last see him?' Alex asked, taking a photograph from one of the uniformed officers.

'Yesterday lunchtime, before I went to work.'

'Where do you work?'

'The Royal Glam. I'm a nurse.'

Alex wondered whether Julie had come into contact with Sian Foster at the hospital, and if she knew Sian was involved with Gavin. 'Must be tough going with the two boys to look after on your own.'

Julie shrugged. 'We're managing. Haven't got much choice, have we? Look, I know there's something wrong, okay. Tyler doesn't just go off like this.' She picked up a mobile phone from the end of the sofa and brandished it towards Alex like a weapon. 'I can't even bloody call him either.'

'That's his phone?'

Julie nodded and passed it to Alex. 'He's bloody useless with the thing. I'm always nagging him about it.'

'You only contacted the police this morning?' Alex asked, putting the mobile phone in her pocket. 'Why was that? Why not call last night when he didn't come home?'

Julie looked to the floor. 'I stayed on late at work – they were short-staffed. I didn't get back until gone midnight.'

'But you checked on the boys then?'

Beneath the previous day's make-up that she had been too tired to remove the night before, Julie's face flushed. She spoke quickly, her words falling out and tripping over her obvious guilt. 'I should have, all right – I know that now. But I was knackered and it was late … I didn't want to disturb either of them.'

'Who was looking after them while you were at work?'

Julie sagged. 'I'm a shit grandmother, all right? There – is that better? I'm trying my best. If I don't work, we lose this house, and if I do work, there's no one to watch the boys. I can't win either way, can I? I thought Tyler was grown up enough now to look after Curtis for a bit. I thought you were police, not the bloody social.'

'I'm not here to judge, Julie. I'm just trying to build a picture.'

'No? Well it sounds like that's what you're doing.' Julie stood and went to the window, her back turned to Alex. 'Why are we all just standing around talking, anyway?'

'Are there any friends Tyler might have stayed with?'

Julie shook her head. 'Only his girlfriend, and I can't get hold of her either.'

'What's his girlfriend's name?'

'Keeley.'

Alex glanced at Curtis, who had got up from his chair and was now playing with a plastic toy car, ramming it repeatedly into the side of the TV unit. Each time it made contact with the glass panel, the boy made a sound like an explosion.

She looked down at the photograph that was still in her hand. A child's face looked back at her.

'Keeley Coleman?'

Julie turned sharply. 'Yeah. You know her?'

Alex's mind was running two steps ahead of her once again. A picture was beginning to fall into place: one far worse than any of them might have imagined. 'How tall is Tyler?'

Julie looked exasperated. 'What sort of question is that, for God's sake? I don't know, about five eight, five nine. He's always towered over me.'

'I need to see his bedroom.'

Julie glanced at the other officers before looking back angrily at Alex. 'Why?'

Alex headed for the living room door. 'You can show me or I can find it myself.' She left the room and headed out into the hallway.

'I don't understand what's going on,' Julie said, following her towards the stairs. 'How's this supposed to help find him?'

Tyler's bedroom was easy to find: there was a sticker with a toxic warning label stuck to the door and a sign that read 'Danger – Keep Out'. Inside, dirty clothes lay strewn on the carpet and the single bed was unmade, the duvet in a pile at the end of the mattress. A TV and an Xbox games console sat on a chest of drawers at the end of the single bed.

Alex scanned the room, her eyes stopping at the wall above the head of the bed. A collection of posters formed a montage that covered the wallpaper that lay beneath. At its centre, there was a poster of four young men, all clad in leather jackets and posing against a brick wall. A series of dates was printed across the bottom.

Catfish and the Bottlemen, the poster read. *UK Tour 2018.*

Alex turned and left the room, not answering Julie when she asked where she was going. The other officers were still waiting in the hallway, one keeping an eye on Curtis, who was still playing in the living room.

Out on the pavement, she called Chloe. She reached into her pocket and took out Tyler's mobile phone.

'We need to find Tyler Morris as soon as possible.'

'You think he's in danger?'

Alex glanced at the phone gripped in her hand. 'I think he *is* the danger.'

CHAPTER FIFTY-EIGHT

The mood in the incident room was sombre. The idea that two children might be responsible for the horrific series of crimes they were investigating was something none of the team had prepared for. None of them had ever encountered a case in which children had been the suspects. A search for Keeley and Tyler had begun, though Alex knew they had to tread carefully. With both suspects being minors, no details could be released to the press or on social media. Any leak of information might later jeopardise a trial, and after everything else that had happened, watching this killer duo get away with their crimes was something Alex wasn't prepared to risk. It meant they would be unable to ask for help from the public, which in turn meant the job of finding the pair would be made all the more difficult.

Did Tyler know about his father's death? Alex wondered. And an even more chilling thought … was he responsible? It seemed anything was possible now.

Jake had been sent with other officers to search the home of Keeley Coleman. A warrant had been granted quickly, and under Alex's instructions Sian was to be kept unaware of the suspicions surrounding her daughter. The importance of it staying that way had been emphasised to everyone on the team. If Sian knew where Keeley and Tyler were, there was a chance she might protect them. And there was no doubt in Alex's mind that the two teenagers were together somewhere.

She and Chloe sat at Chloe's desk in the incident room.

'Do you think Sian knows about all this?' Chloe asked.

Alex shook her head. 'I doubt it. But if she finds out, there's no knowing how she'll react. She's already got one kid in prison, remember.'

'So Tyler broke into his own father's shed to take the petrol can? Surely he would have known it might incriminate his dad?'

'Perhaps Keeley did it. It wouldn't matter to her, would it?' Alex stood and looked at the board. 'Tyler's clumsy,' she continued. 'He attacked Corey Davies alone and he messed things up. My guess is that it's probably his fingerprints that were lifted from the front door of Doris Adams's house. The fact that he left his phone behind at his grandmother's house suggests he's disorganised. My bet is that Keeley is the brains behind all this.'

The irony of her phrasing wasn't lost on her. The kind of brain that could plot and orchestrate such brutal and senseless attacks was the type she knew she would never comprehend, regardless of how many years' service she might give. Grown men had scared her. Child killers would haunt her.

'Shit,' she said. Her own words echoed, taking on a greater meaning than she had intended.

'What?' Chloe asked.

'It wouldn't have mattered to her,' Alex repeated. She turned back to Chloe. 'What if Keeley killed Gavin?'

'A teenage girl against a grown man?' Chloe asked sceptically.

'If Keeley's responsible for the other deaths, we're not dealing with a normal teenage girl. Two knives, the pathologist said. He didn't stand a chance.'

'Why would she kill her own boyfriend's father? The other victims weren't known to her. She would have known Gavin, or known of him at the very least.'

Dan approached them. 'Listen.' He held up Tyler's phone. A clip of the song 'Kathleen' played; the same clip they had heard on the 999 call recording. The words 'impractical' and 'death' were unmistakable now. 'It's stored as the ringtone for Keeley's number.'

'So what are we thinking?' Chloe asked. 'They beat up Gary Peters, the fire was started, and then what? Tyler had a change of heart and called 999?'

'Looks that way perhaps,' Alex said. 'He disappears and Keeley calls him, wondering where he is. He's smart enough to make the call from a phone box rather than from his mobile, but not smart enough to turn his own phone off while he's doing it. She inadvertently led us to them.'

'Either that or Tyler made the call because they wanted to watch emergency services turn up?'

'Could be.' Alex sighed. 'Anything's possible now.'

'Be interesting to see what shows up on Sian Foster's laptop. If she's got a bit more about her than Tyler, Keeley won't have done anything from her own phone, will she? She's been a lot cleverer at covering her tracks than he has. If she's the one who ordered that skeleton outfit, it had to have been done somewhere else.'

'What if he told his dad?'

'Tyler?'

'You just said he may have made that 999 call after having a change of heart. He was feeling guilty enough then to alert the authorities.' Alex pressed her fingertips to her lips. 'Did he need to confide in someone … someone who wasn't Keeley?'

'You think he told Gavin, and Keeley found out about it?'

'Makes sense, doesn't it? Gavin wouldn't have come to us. He wouldn't have been able to report Keeley without incriminating his own son. You okay?' Alex looked at Dan, who had fallen silent beside them. He didn't appear to have taken in any of the conversation. He was still holding Tyler's phone and had been scrolling through its contents, but had stopped at something. His face had paled.

'What's the matter?' Alex asked.

Dan held the mobile up. 'My daughter's number. It's stored on his phone.'

CHAPTER FIFTY-NINE

Faadi would have liked to have had something different to wear, but he had only packed an overnight bag and he didn't have much to choose from. There was a Coke stain on the front of the T-shirt he had been wearing the day before; he had tried to scrub it off but now there was a thick waterline that was much bigger than the original mark and he had only managed to make it look worse. He zipped his jacket up to the neck, deciding not to worry about it. If the party wasn't too hot he could leave his jacket on, and if it was dark then hopefully no one would notice anyway.

Anticipation clenched in his stomach like a fist. He stood at the station in Cardiff and waited for his train to arrive. The night before, he and his mother had stayed with one of Mahira's old friends; a neighbour they'd had years ago when they had lived in the old house. He had thought they would only be there for one night, but his mother had shown no signs of heading home that day. He knew what was going on. His father had started the fire at the shop, although no one would just come out with it and tell him so. He was fed up of being treated like a little kid.

He had snuck out through the front door while his mother and her friend had been talking and drinking tea in the kitchen. He didn't want to cause his mother any worry, so he sent her a text saying he was sorry and that he was going home. He had his front door key with him and planned to go back to the house after the party. Jameel and his father would be there, so he wouldn't be on his own.

He had never been on a train on his own before. He sat near the window and watched the world as it sped past in a blur, all the time thinking about Rebecca and what he would say to her when they met up. He would probably get all tongue-tied and either not be able to speak or end up saying something stupid. Either way, there was no backing out now. He was on the train and he was heading back towards the valleys.

The train got busier as the hour passed. Commuters in sweaty suits and shoppers with arms laden with carrier bags filled the seats and stood crammed in the aisle, blocking Faadi's path to the toilet at the end of the next carriage. By the time the train reached his stop, he desperately needed to pee. Stepping onto the platform, he looked for a toilet, but there was nothing but the bridge and a fence that cyclists used for chaining their bikes to. He knew most boys his age would have relieved themselves up in the bushes on the other side of the bridge, but Faadi had never peed like that out in the open and he wasn't about to start tonight.

With his hands shoved into his pockets and his right hand clutching his phone, he forced his thoughts away from his bladder and headed towards the main road. Rebecca had asked him to meet her outside the church; he had googled it that morning and had recognised some of the nearby street names. He could feel his heart rate increasing as he neared the road. He was a bag of nerves. What was he doing? Whatever it was, it was too late to back out now.

When he turned the corner, he saw a figure in the distance. As he got nearer, he could see it was Rebecca. She was dressed for the night air, in a pair of jeans and a red padded jacket. She was wearing a beanie hat and her hair was falling to one side of her face in a mass of dark curls.

'Hi, Faadi.'

Her voice was like an angel's, he thought. In fact, she was just like an angel, standing there at the side of the church, waiting for him.

'Hi, Rebecca.' He didn't even recognise his own voice. It sounded stupid and embarrassing; even more embarrassing than usual. Heat raced to his face despite the cold nip of the evening air.

'Thanks for inviting me,' she said.

Faadi smiled. He didn't know what to say. She had been the one who had invited him, but now didn't really feel like the time to point that out. Instead, he continued to smile at her, knowing the smile was probably now bordering on the insane. He looked away, down to the ground, and lifted his left foot from a patch of muddy earth.

When he looked back up, he saw something move behind Rebecca: a fleeting shadow that was barely visible in the darkness of the side of the church. For a moment he thought he might have imagined it. There was a sound, the snapping of a twig beneath a shoe, and then the shadow was there again, real this time and moving swiftly towards them; so quickly that Faadi barely had time to think.

The shadow raised an arm. Faadi tried to scream, but nothing left his mouth, the noise kept trapped by his own fear. Rebecca stared at him for a moment, her expression questioning, a smile still stretched across her lips, oblivious to what was about to come.

Then the blow to the head arrived and she crumpled to the ground at Faadi's feet.

CHAPTER SIXTY

'She's not answering.'

Dan exhaled loudly and put his mobile on the desk. Alex wondered whether he was overthinking things. Tyler and Keeley went to the same school as Rebecca; they were in the same year group. Tyler probably had the names of countless other students stored in his contacts list. It didn't have to mean anything. It didn't mean Rebecca was in any danger.

Yet she could only imagine how she would be feeling if she had found her own child's number stored in the mobile phone of a boy they suspected was a murderer; or, at the very least, an accomplice to one.

Dan snatched his phone back from the table when it began to ring, its vibrations shaking Alex back from her veering train of thought.

'Steph.'

Dan's wife. He had been ringing her for the past half an hour, his anxiety increasing with every call that had gone unanswered.

'Is Rebecca with you? What ... when? Okay ... where is it?' His voice was becoming increasingly frantic. If Steph hadn't been worried about their daughter, it wouldn't be long before that changed. Alex wanted to intervene, to tell Dan to calm down, but it wasn't appropriate; particularly not with his wife at the other end of the call.

At his side, Dan's left hand had balled into a fist. His right was clutching the phone to his ear, his knuckles white.

'What do you mean, you don't know? You dropped her off, didn't you? No, just …' He reached for a pen from Alex's desk and waved his hand at her, motioning for some paper. Alex grabbed a sheet from the printer and passed it to him. 'I don't know,' he said, scrawling down an address. 'No. Just stay where you are, okay?'

He cut the call. 'Steph says she took her to a party.'

'A house party? She dropped her off there?'

Dan laughed, but there was no humour in the sound. 'No, she dropped her off "nearby". Apparently Rebecca didn't want her mother showing her up in front of her friends.'

He pressed a hand to his forehead. 'Put this in there for me,' he said, pushing the paper towards Alex and gesturing to her computer. 'She told her mother the party was here, but said she was getting a lift home with a friend's mum.'

Alex pulled up an internet search engine and typed out the address Dan had noted. 'There's nothing coming up,' she told him.

'Of course there's not. Did you always tell your mother the truth when you were thirteen?' Dan's voice was fraught, laced with a mixture of frustration and panic. 'You think I'm overreacting, don't you?'

Alex shook her head. 'Under the circumstances, no. Look, get yourself home and get on the phone to anyone you can think of – friends, family … anyone who might have seen Rebecca. I'm sure she's fine. You've tried her number again?'

'Still no answer.'

'Go on,' Alex prompted, nodding to the office door. 'I'll get a trace on her phone and let you know as soon as anything comes in. I'm sure she's fine, Dan,' she said again, trying to reassure him. 'This is probably just an unfortunate coincidence.'

She didn't believe her own words. Tyler had already attacked a fellow teenager – a boy who was known to him – and there was nothing to say the next victim wouldn't be another child. There was no doubt that Keeley and Tyler had chosen their victims well in advance. With this pair, nothing happened by chance.

'You'll let me know straight away if you hear anything?'

'Of course. You'll do the same?'

Dan nodded and hurried from the office. Alex knew him well enough to know the first thing he would do was drive to the place where Steph had dropped Rebecca off. He wasn't thinking straight. If Rebecca was with Tyler or Keeley, there was no knowing what Dan would do or what he might be capable of, knowing everything the young couple were guilty of.

Alex knew they had to find them before Dan did.

CHAPTER SIXTY-ONE

When consciousness returned to her, Rebecca found herself thrown into darkness and tied to a chair. Her head was pounding and she could feel something sticky on her neck and cheek. Blood. For the briefest of moments, she couldn't work out where she was. Then everything came flooding back, the recollections of a nightmare. She remembered meeting Faadi outside the church, and how nervous she had been at seeing him there waiting for her. She remembered how nervous he had been too.

That was where her memories stopped.

She recognised their voices, though she didn't know why they were doing this to her. All she knew was that she was cold and scared and she wished she hadn't lied to her mother about where she was going. Her mum would never have allowed her to go out to meet a boy, even though Faadi was the nicest boy anyone could imagine. Now she wished she had just been honest. She would rather have been in her bedroom sulking than here, cast into darkness and not knowing what was happening on the other side of whatever it was they had tied around her eyes.

'My dad's a policeman,' she said, her voice trembling with uncertainty. 'He'll know where we are. He won't let you do this.'

She heard Keeley laugh. She had never liked the girl – there had always been something different about her, as though she thought herself too good to bother with anyone else in their year group – and now Rebecca knew that her instincts had been right. Was she the one who had hit her over the head, or had it been Tyler? Either way, Rebecca felt sick with the pain. But it was nothing compared to the fear that was holding her rigid.

But how had they known where to find her? she wondered. Faadi, she thought, her mind racing now. Was he still here? She couldn't remember hearing him, not since she'd been hit. Had he run away and left her? Was he a part of all this?

'You think?' Tyler said, his voice somewhere near. Then he moved so close she could feel the heat of his breath against her cheek. It made her feel sick. 'Let's play a game.'

His voice sounded muffled, as though she was hearing it under water; Rebecca's ears were still ringing from the blow to the head she had suffered. If her eyes hadn't been covered and her vision cast into darkness, she would have recognised too that her short-lived unconsciousness had also rendered her sense of sight temporarily impaired. She realised she had never felt scared before, not properly; not like this.

'I'll count to three, and after three, one of us is going to touch you. All you have to do is guess which one of us it was. Easy.'

Rebecca felt her tears escape from under the fabric pulled across her eyes. She didn't like this game. She wanted to go home. She tried to cry out, but whatever was stuffed into her mouth made the sound escape as little more than a muted sob.

'You like Rebecca, don't you, Faadi?'

'Come on,' Keeley said, her voice cold and hard. 'Do it. Touch her.'

Knowing she couldn't free herself, Rebecca's body tensed, every limb shuddering with fear. Faadi was still there. This couldn't be happening to her. She had heard about things like this – had seen the stories on TV, things she hadn't wanted to see – but they didn't happen round here. They didn't happen to her.

'Come on,' Tyler said, repeating his girlfriend's words. 'You like games, don't you? And all those computer games you play must mean you're good with your hands.'

Keeley snorted, a horrible sound that pierced the cold air of the room. 'Show us how good you are,' she taunted.

The sound of a slap, sudden and sharp, cut through the horrible silence that had fallen over the room. It echoed around them, and Rebecca realised then that they were no longer outside. They were inside the church. She felt nothing when the sound came, but heard a small whimpering noise somewhere else in the room, the sound of a caged animal, trapped and tortured, before a scuffling crossed the floor, the noise falling towards her.

She felt a hand on her arm, shaking, and then a quiet voice that whispered in her ear. 'I'm sorry.'

Faadi. They were making him do this, she thought. He didn't want to be there any more than she did. Had they set this all up? Was that why Faadi had looked confused when she had thanked him for inviting her to the party?

He didn't want to do what they were telling him to. But he was going to do it anyway.

There was a scream of pain, so close it made Rebecca start with fright.

'Just so you know what's happening in here,' Keeley said, the girl's face so close that Rebecca could feel her hair brushing against her face. 'Your little boyfriend needs to follow our instructions first time. He hesitated. That's not in the rules, I'm afraid. There's been a forfeit.'

Rebecca heard Faadi's sobs, choked and pained. She tugged at the ties that bound her arms, not knowing what was happening to him but desperate to help him, but she was held fast and had little choice other than to listen to the sound of Faadi's fear.

'Now then,' Keeley said, moving away from Rebecca. 'Do it.'

Rebecca waited an awful moment, wondering just what they were instructing him to do. Her young mind pictured things she would never have thought it possible to imagine, but suddenly these things were real and they were closer to her than her dad could ever have warned her. He had talked to her about men like this. Women like this, even. She had known not to trust any adult who wasn't known to her.

But no one had ever told her anything about not trusting other children.

Her body tensed again as she heard a snipping sound. Something cold touched her chest – something hard and metallic – and for a heart-stopping moment she thought it was a knife. Then she realised it was a pair of scissors. Someone was cutting through her coat, exposing her. A sob caught somewhere in her throat, unable to escape.

'You do it.'

Keeley was talking to Faadi. There was quiet for a moment before the snipping of fabric continued, but it was quickly broken by the sound of Faadi's tears. It wasn't his fault, Rebecca told herself, repeating the words in her head over and over like some kind of mantra that might get her through whatever would happen next. He didn't want to do this; they were making him.

It wasn't his fault.

She heard a laugh – Keeley again – before everything changed.

The snipping of the scissors stopped.

'I'm not doing this,' she heard Faadi say. 'I'm not like you.'

And then everything happened so quickly.

CHAPTER SIXTY-TWO

Rebecca's phone had been traced to a road in Ystrad, just a few streets away from the train station. It was a five-minute walk from the road her mother had dropped her off on. Wherever she had been going – or whoever she'd been meeting – it was obvious that she hadn't wanted her mother to know about it. And why was that? Alex wondered. There were numerous possibilities.

Taking the iPad from the glove box of Alex's Audi, Chloe googled the location and scanned its details.

'They're at the church,' the voice on the radio told them.

A boy and girl matching Tyler and Keeley's descriptions had been seen in a shop in the town just an hour earlier. It might have been a coincidence, but Alex wasn't prepared to take a chance on it.

She glanced at the satnav. They were still ten minutes away, despite the speed she was driving. Chloe found the church on the iPad. 'Derelict,' she told Alex. 'Set back from the road again, by the looks of it, just like the hospital.'

Everything had been planned. Keeley Coleman and Tyler Morris had spent a week executing crimes that must have been plotted well in advance: the wheres, the hows, the whos. Everything about them was premeditated. They had targeted the most vulnerable people they could find: people that society should have kept protected. The acts these children had committed reached levels of evil Alex had rarely been witness to in almost two decades of service with the police. It was hard to believe that any adult could be capable of such evil. For children, it was inconceivable.

'Why are they doing this?' Chloe asked.

Alex shook her head. 'Keeley Coleman is obviously her father's daughter.' She fell silent for a moment, considering the brutalities this child was capable of. Monsters came in all shapes and forms, and age was no barrier to evil. Why hadn't they seen it earlier? Alex cursed herself. The answer had been there in front of them, yet nobody had seen it. Perhaps no one had wanted to see it, not when the truth was so difficult to accept.

'Blame the parents,' Chloe said. 'That's what people say, isn't it? If only it was that simple.'

'Her father is a notorious thug,' Alex said, thinking aloud. 'Brother in prison for attempted murder. Perhaps in this case we can blame the family, in part at least. Both of them have had extensive media coverage over the years. Is this to do with fame?'

'Christ,' Chloe said. 'What a way to make a name for yourself.'

'Maybe she thought she would get away it. There's a history of violence in the family. Perhaps she's become a product of her childhood.'

Alex's mobile started ringing, distracting her from her thoughts. She swiped the screen hurriedly. 'Dan.'

'They've just told me where she is, Alex. What the hell is she doing there? She told us she was going to a party.'

His voice was fraught, thick with worry for his daughter. Neither Alex nor Chloe had ever heard him like this, and doing so brought the case far too close to home. If Rebecca was with Keeley and Tyler, she was yet another innocent victim. When Alex had considered the previous day how many more lives their killer might claim, she could never in her most horrific imaginings have contemplated this scenario. She pushed her foot further to the accelerator. 'Where are you, Dan?'

The line was bad, the conversation thwarted by poor signal at his end. He was in the car, she thought. He was heading to the church now.

'I'm on my way there.'

'Please, Dan, listen to me,' she said, knowing her words would be ignored. 'Do not go in there until we arrive, okay? Please.'

'For fuck's sake, what do you want me to do – sit outside and wait for everyone else to show up? She's in fucking danger, Alex.'

Alex glanced at Chloe, a knowing look passing between them. Neither of them wanted him to get there before they did. If he barged in there without considering the consequences, he might unwittingly put Rebecca in further danger.

'Dan, wait for backup. Please.'

They heard something neither woman had been witness to before. At the other end of the call, Dan had started to cry. 'I swear to God, if they hurt her, I will kill the little bastards. I will rip their evil little heads off their fucking shoulders with my bare hands.'

Alex shot Chloe another glance as she drove through a set of red lights. The driver of a car coming from their left sounded his horn as he was forced to slam on his brakes. Dan's emotions were exactly why he couldn't arrive there before them. He could end up getting himself and Rebecca killed.

Still following the directions provided by the satnav, Alex could see their destination now just streets away. She hoped they wouldn't be too late.

CHAPTER SIXTY-THREE

Faadi had set out to meet Rebecca with the intention of being something he'd never been before – someone he had never been before – and he knew now that if he didn't do just that, then neither he nor Rebecca would see beyond the four walls of this church again.

He had a pair of scissors in his hand. Keeley had passed them to him, instructing him to remove Rebecca's clothing. But he wasn't like them. He would never be like them.

He lunged forward and thrust the opened pair of scissors at Tyler. One of the blades caught the side of his neck, piercing the skin below his ear. Faadi saw blood bubble to the surface of the wound. Tyler cried out in shock and staggered back. For a moment, Faadi was too stunned to move. He had never hurt anyone before. He had never wanted to hurt anyone, and even now, even under these circumstances, knowing he had done so made him feel sick to his stomach.

But Tyler was coming at him and there was nothing else he could do. He drew his hand back and lunged towards the other boy again, this time plunging the scissors into his chest.

'You fat little prick.'

As Tyler fell back, Keeley came racing towards him. She had something in her hand that Faadi hadn't noticed in the room with them until now: a petrol can. With the scissors now embedded in Tyler's chest as the boy sprawled on the church floor crying in pain, Faadi had nothing with which to fight her off. He threw his hands up to protect his face, screaming as Keeley threw the contents of the petrol can towards him. Then she turned her attention to Rebecca and doused the girl in the liquid. Its odour seemed to fill the room, lodging in the back of Faadi's throat. He could taste it, foul and toxic.

There was banging at the far end of the room and voices calling Rebecca's name. There was the distant sound of sirens – a sound that should have filled Faadi with a sense of relief – but he feared they were too late. He shouted back, begging them to hurry, to help them. He couldn't see. The petrol was burning his eyes. He had no idea what was going on elsewhere in the church and no idea what was happening to Rebecca. But he could imagine.

There was a crash at the far end of the room and then a female voice shouted Keeley's name. Faadi blinked frantically, his sight coming back to him as patches of the darkened room reappeared like the visions of a nightmare. And then everything seemed to happen in slow motion. There were two women, women he had seen before. The pretty police detective was there, but this time it was the other woman he couldn't take his eyes off. She raced through the church towards Keeley. The petrol can was raised again, the last of the liquid thrown at the detective, who shoved Keeley with a blow so hard it sent the girl thudding to the cold stone of the church floor, but not before a spark of light lit the darkened room, circling like a tiny Catherine wheel as it was flung towards the chair on which Rebecca still sat tied.

He didn't notice Keeley flee the church, leaving Tyler bleeding on the cold stone floor. All he saw was the woman as she moved in front of Rebecca and blocked the flight of the match, pushing the chair on which Rebecca was tied towards Chloe, who smothered the girl with her own body, shielding her from a further assault.

And then the flame caught the woman, racing up her arm as though devouring her, quickly enveloping her clothing and catching at her shoulder-length hair. And all Faadi could hear was her screams, echoing through the wide emptiness of the church.

CHAPTER SIXTY-FOUR

Jake and Chloe stood in the corridor between the two cells in which Keeley Coleman and Tyler Morris were being held. Tyler had spent the previous night in hospital; the wounds Faadi had inflicted had required staples and monitoring for infection, but Tyler had been lucky to avoid any serious or long-term harm. Keeley had been detained after being charged, but Tyler was yet to be formally interviewed.

'Let's put them both in there,' Chloe said, referring to the interview room.

'Together?'

Chloe nodded. They had guessed at the dynamic of the relationship between the two, but seeing the teenagers together might confirm their suspicions.

Ten minutes later, Chloe and Jake sat in the adjoining room and watched Tyler and Keeley via the two-way glass. Both detectives were still stunned by the brutality that two children had been capable of, and the events of the previous evening had left the entire station contaminated with an anger Chloe couldn't imagine would disperse any time soon. Threats of violence had been made by a couple of officers who'd had to be removed from having any contact with either child. In any other circumstance their reactions would have been criticised, but Chloe understood all too well how they were feeling. It was impossible to regard these two as children.

They knew the stories of children who had maimed and killed – heard news reports and read case studies regarding crimes committed by the most unlikely of young offenders – but those horror stories always took place elsewhere, far enough from home that they were never sufficiently close to feel truly real. Here and now, they were real enough to have reduced Chloe to tears. She had kept them hidden, shedding them alone at home with no one to witness them, but there had been plenty of them: for the victims and their families, for the killers' families; for Alex.

Chloe's thoughts hadn't strayed too far from Alex all day. The sound of her screams as the flames had swept the upper half of her body had been bloodcurdling, and Chloe knew she would hear them and relive those moments in her nightmares for months to come.

She studied Keeley Coleman as the girl paced the small interview room. She wanted to do pretty much what Dan had threatened. The apple never falls far from the tree, she thought. Alex had been right: Keeley Coleman really was her father's daughter. She had shown no remorse for the things she had done, nor any hint of a reaction to the suggestion that they had evidence against her that connected her to the murders.

'What do we do?' Tyler asked her. He had sat on one of the chairs at the desk, his elbows on his knees and his head in his hands. Every so often he would lift his head to seek his girlfriend's eyes, desperately searching her face for answers. He looked vulnerable, despite everything he was guilty of. It was a misleading disguise; one Chloe wasn't going to fall for.

'No comment.'

'What?'

'That's what you say,' she told him. 'To everything. No comment.'

'Keeley, they know we were there. They've got my prints, they've looked on your mam's laptop and they know you bought the outfit. You said they wouldn't be able to trace us.'

Keeley turned sharply, leaned over Tyler and pressed her face against his. 'They're watching us now, you know that, don't you? Why do you always have to be such a fucking idiot?'

Tyler stood. 'You left your boot print on that old lady and I'm the fucking idiot?' he spat.

Keeley didn't answer him. Instead, she crossed the small room and stood to face the mirrored wall. She stepped towards it and pressed her face against the glass, a slow, chilling smile spreading across her pale face. She might have been able to wear innocence like a second skin, but she was equally able to shed it when it suited her. 'No comment,' she mouthed slowly.

In the next room, Jake turned to Chloe. 'She's pure evil.'

Chloe forced her anger down, swallowing it like a bite of rotten apple. 'Forget her for a minute. Let's get Tyler on his own.'

'Interview with Tyler Morris commencing at 15.17,' Chloe said. 'Present in the room are DC Chloe Lane and DC Jake Sullivan. The accompanying adult is duty solicitor Amy Barton.'

Julie Morris had refused to so much as be in the same room as Tyler since his arrest. She had crumpled into Chloe's arms at the news that her grandson had been involved in the series of attacks that had plagued the town, and she was still stating she wanted nothing more to do with him.

Tyler hadn't been told of his father's murder until that morning. Unless he was an exceptionally talented actor, his reaction suggested he had known nothing about it. The fact that he hadn't mentioned it to Keeley when given the chance also suggested he had no idea that she might be involved. Like everyone else, he had most likely assumed that the Hassan brothers had finished what they'd started.

'Tell us about Keeley,' Chloe said. 'How long have you two been going out with each other?' When Tyler said nothing, Chloe leaned forward. 'Whatever she said to you, Tyler, this "no comment" business isn't going to work. You know we've got enough evidence against you both. If you want to help yourself, you'd better start talking.'

Tyler glanced at the duty solicitor as though looking for a lead. Alex had been right: Keeley was the driving force behind everything. The boy was a follower, but that didn't make him any less evil. Only evil could have stood by and watched as he did, and nothing less than evil could have actively participated.

'Are you in love with her, Tyler?'

Chloe spread a couple of sheets of paper out on the desk in front of her: transcripts of WhatsApp conversations between the two teenagers. Beneath them sat transcripts of the messages that had been sent to Faadi Hassan and Rebecca Mason; a conversation the two had innocently believed to have taken place only between the two of them. Tyler had been clever enough to send them from a pay-as-you-go mobile phone rather than from his own, and Keeley had been devious enough to let him keep it in his possession rather than hide it in her own home.

'It's a funny thing, isn't it?' Chloe said. 'Love. It makes you do things you never thought you would.'

'That's a very leading question, DC Lane,' the duty solicitor intercepted.

'She's not that nice to you, is she?' Chloe said, running a finger along the transcript and ignoring the woman. '"Fucking useless … not man enough … good for nothing …" Do you think you might like her a little bit more than she likes you?'

'She loves me,' he said, his voice a cold monotone. 'She's the only one who does.'

Chloe put out a hand to Jake, who passed her a series of photographs. In turn, she laid them out on the desk in front of Tyler, allowing sufficient time for him to absorb the details. The first was a photograph of Gary Peters' burned and battered corpse; the second a photograph of Corey Davies. The third was a close-up photograph of the boot mark printed on Doris Adams's body.

'For the purposes of the recording, I am showing Mr Morris images of Gary Peters, Corey Davies and Doris Adams. We know you made the 999 call on the night of the fire at the hospital, Tyler. We've got the skeleton outfit you wore when you attacked Corey, and we've got your prints from Doris Adams' house. The game's up. So start talking.'

Tyler sat back and folded his arms across his chest. 'No comment.'

'I thought you might say that,' Chloe said. She reached into the file on her lap and took out another couple of photographs. 'For the purposes of the recording, I am now showing Mr Morris stills of the CCTV footage taken from the Royal Glamorgan Hospital in Llantrisant, captured on 2 November 2017. Do you recognise the two people in the images, Tyler?'

Tyler glanced at the photographs, perusing them with his unusually bright green eyes. There was a flicker of a reaction, but still he said nothing.

'The stills I'm showing Mr Morris show Keeley Coleman and Gavin Jones. Now,' Chloe continued, pressing a fingertip to one of the images. 'If you were to watch the recording in full, Tyler, you would view quite a heated exchange between your girlfriend and your dad. Any idea what they were arguing about?'

'No.'

'When did you tell him, Tyler? When did you tell your dad what you and Keeley had done? I'm guessing it was after Doris Adams was beaten to death, am I right?'

The boy said nothing, but the expressionless glaze that had covered his face was fading now, replaced by a dawning realisation.

'He couldn't report her without involving you, could he?' She tapped the image again. 'They were both at the hospital to see Sian, and it looks as though your dad couldn't hold back. Once Keeley was aware that Gavin knew what the two of you had done, she had to find a way to keep him quiet, didn't she?'

Tyler sat frozen in his seat, his eyes fixed to the image on the desk in front of him. The truth was beginning to take shape in front of him, and it was clearly a truth he hadn't anticipated or prepared for.

'She left plenty of evidence at your dad's house to see her put away for a very long time.' Chloe reached into the file and produced something else: email confirmation of a one-way flight to Spain, booked in Keeley's name. She described the item for the recording before placing the printout in front of Tyler. 'You thought you were going with her, didn't you, Tyler? But it looks as though Keeley had other ideas.'

She sat back and watched as the boy's resolve began to crumble.

'Now,' she said, sliding the email back into the file. 'Talk.'

CHAPTER SIXTY-FIVE

The boy sitting on the chair at her bedside looked so much older than the one she'd seen just days earlier. He had a mark across his cheek; a cut that Keeley had made when he'd refused to do as she instructed. Alex gave him a smile. In spite of all the evil they'd encountered, he was a reminder that there was still plenty of good in the world.

Faadi shifted uncomfortably, still unable to meet her eye. It was obvious he blamed himself for Alex's appearance, and she knew that no matter how many times she tried to reassure him that he was not at fault, he would take home the burden of responsibility with him. And where was home now? she wondered. Mahira Hassan was refusing to return to the family home, and she and Faadi were currently relying on the kindness of old friends.

She glanced through the window, where Mahira was waiting in the corridor. Like Faadi, it had been obvious she hadn't wanted to look directly at Alex's burns for longer than she had to.

'Have you seen Rebecca?'

At the mention of the girl's name, Faadi's face flushed. The events of the previous few days might have forced him to grow up, but he was still the awkward, innocent boy beneath it all. 'Yes.'

'How's she doing? She okay?'

Faadi nodded. 'She'll be okay.' He looked to the door. 'I'd better go.' When he turned back to her, he still couldn't bring himself to make eye contact. Instead, he scanned the floor nervously, not knowing what to do with his hands. 'Thank you. I'm sorry.'

'Thank you for the chocolates, Faadi. And stop saying sorry. Nothing is your fault.'

He gave her a sad smile and left the room, Alex watching as he pulled the door shut gently behind him. She slid from the side of the bed and went to the window, making sure not to glance at the mirror as she passed. She still hadn't been able to look at herself. It was bad, she knew it was; much worse than anyone was letting on. Everyone from the doctors to the nurses had told her it could have been so much worse, and Alex knew they were right. The majority of petrol Keeley had thrown at her had missed, splashing instead across the stone floor of the church. And had Chloe not been there – had she not pushed her to the ground and smothered the rapidly spreading flames so quickly – things could have been very different.

But she wasn't ready to look at herself, not just yet.

She still had dressings on her right arm, the side of her face and her neck. She had been told not to move them, but she had pushed a finger beneath one that morning and traced her tip along the scarred flesh that ran in winding rivers across her jawline and down her neck. She didn't need to see it to know she would never look the same again. Alex had never thought of herself as particularly vain – no more so than the next person – but the thought that she might be disfigured for life filled her with sadness. She forced herself to think of Gary Peters and Doris Adams, desperate to find some kind of perspective. It worked for a while, but the sadness always returned.

She had been at the hospital for two days now; two long days that had felt like weeks, with nothing but pain to interrupt the boredom. She wanted to be at the station. She had missed the interviews with Keeley and Tyler, but had been updated by Chloe on everything that had happened. As they'd suspected, every attack had been planned well in advance. Keeley and Tyler had followed Gary Peters over a number of evenings, finding out that he was using the hospital for shelter. It turned out that Doris Adams had recently been discharged from hospital and was still receiving home visits from nurses, one of whom had been Julie Morris. Tyler had taken her details from one of his grandmother's files, finding out that Doris lived alone.

With her father and brother already infamous, Keeley had wanted notoriety for herself. She had bought a ticket for a flight to Spain with birthday and Christmas money she had saved, intending to disappear and start a new life, leaving her crimes and her family history behind her. She had naively believed that she would be able to run away from everything she'd done, and Tyler had naively believed her when she had told him he was booked on the flight to go with her.

Alex shuddered at the thought of what might have happened to Rebecca Mason had she and Chloe not arrived when they did. She was lucky to have had Faadi there, but he alone wouldn't have been enough to stop what Tyler and Keeley had been planning.

Alex returned to the bed and stared at the television, trying to distract herself from thoughts of what might have been. She hadn't been watching the TV when Faadi and his mother had arrived, and it was still muted – but with it switched on, she was unable to catch a glimpse of her reflection in the screen.

There was a knock at the door and a nurse entered. 'Stephanie Mason is here to see you. Am I okay to send her in?'

Alex wanted more than anything to say no, but she knew there would be only so long she could avoid meeting with her. 'Yeah, of course.'

A moment later, Dan's wife was standing in the doorway. It had been raining and her windswept dark hair was clinging to the sides of her face. Alex had met her once before, just briefly months earlier, when Stephanie had picked Dan up from the station one day. She could never have imagined that the next time they would see each other would be under these circumstances.

Stephanie tried to hide her shock at Alex's appearance, but Alex didn't miss the widened eyes and the involuntary intake of air. She didn't know whether to be hurt or grateful for the honest reaction. For the past two days she'd had people tiptoeing around her, whispering outside the door of her room as though she couldn't hear what was being said just feet away from her. A part of her wanted someone to just be honest, yet now it had happened, she already wished the reaction could be taken back.

Stephanie came into the room and closed the door behind her. 'I am so sorry. I don't know how to thank you.'

Her gratitude stung. Alex couldn't shake the thought of Dan in her kitchen, her body pressed against his. Blaming him would have been the easy option, but it would have been a lie. If Dan hadn't stopped things, Alex might have allowed them to go much further.

'Please don't be nice to me. How's Rebecca doing?'

Stephanie lingered by the doorway, not knowing where to look. She fumbled with her bag for a moment before finding somewhere to put it down, using it as an excuse to avoid making eye contact with Alex. 'She'll be okay. She can't sleep, but that's hardly surprising. When I think about what could have happened to her ...'

She bit her lip. Her face had flushed.

'I didn't mean ...' She stopped mid-sentence, unsure how to backtrack. What had been intended for her daughter had been redirected at Alex, but Alex wouldn't have had it any other way. Rebecca hadn't deserved any of this. She was just a child.

So was Keeley, she thought. So was Tyler. The thought was still sickening, and would remain so.

She opened her mouth to speak, but didn't know what to say. 'Dan's told me.'

She looked up and met Stephanie's eye for the first time. There were tears, but she was holding them back with a stoic determination.

Alex looked away and closed her eyes. 'I'm so sorry.'

Stephanie shook her head, not wanting to hear the apology. Alex realised it was meaningless; the damage was already done. It could have been worse, but that seemed little consolation.

'I was going to come and see you yesterday, but then he told me and—'

'It was my fault,' Alex said hurriedly. 'And it was just a kiss, I swear to you. I wasn't thinking straight. It was completely selfish.'

'He's got a mind of his own. He makes his own decisions.' Stephanie crossed the room and went to the window, placing her hands on the sill and turning her back to Alex. 'You know, if all this hadn't happened, I'd have probably been down that station playing holy hell with you. Strange how a few hours can change everything, isn't it?'

'You still have every right to.'

'You saved my daughter's life. A kiss hardly seems important now, if you're sure that's all it was.'

Alex nodded but said nothing. She knew the good deed couldn't cancel out the mistake that had been made.

A moment later, she heard the door of her room close as Stephanie went out into the corridor, leaving her alone with the heavy burden of her own thoughts. She wondered where she went from here, and whether things would ever return to normal. Normal, she thought. It sounded so boring and yet so appealing, so alien to her.

CHAPTER SIXTY-SIX

Chloe and a uniformed officer got out of the police car outside Sian Foster's home and studied the abuse that had been spray-painted across the front of the terraced house. It hadn't taken long for news to spread, and Julie Morris and her younger grandson, Curtis, had been moved from their home for the sake of their safety and to keep them away from the press vultures that had descended on them following news of Tyler's crimes. Sian had also been offered alternative accommodation but had decided to stay put. Media interest was something she was used to by now, or perhaps she had simply resigned herself to her family's doom.

The words FUCKING SCUM were scrawled across the front door in black paint, and a tin of red had been thrown against the window, running down the glass and drying in thick, guilty trails.

It seemed fitting in more ways than one.

At the sound of the doorbell, there was movement at the front curtains. Chloe waited before pressing the doorbell for a second time. She lifted the letter box. 'We've got all day, Sian,' she called inside.

Moments later, a reluctant Sian opened the front door. She was wearing a dressing gown, and her greasy hair was scraped back from her face and tucked behind her ears with a collection of hairgrips. The bruises staining her face were beginning to fade.

Chloe glanced behind her. There were already neighbours at their front doors, standing with arms folded and waiting for further drama to unfold. 'Shall we do this inside?' she suggested.

The house had been turned upside down by the police during their search and it looked as though Sian had done nothing to address the mess that had been made. In the living room, the cupboards and drawers of a sideboard still stood open, their contents strewn across the laminate floor. Sian seemed to have set up camp on one end of the sofa, where a duvet was piled. A table beside it had gathered a collection of mugs that housed unfinished drinks left to turn cold and grow mouldy films across their surface.

'Have you been to visit Keeley?' Chloe asked.

Sian shook her head.

'I'm guessing you know what we're here about?'

Sian nodded. Her eyes scanned the room and searched out a pair of trainers that had been kicked off and abandoned by the doorway. 'Can I get dressed?'

'Were you hoping Keeley would take the blame for it?' Chloe asked, ignoring Sian's question. 'You must have thought you were in the clear once your daughter's crimes were exposed.'

Sian looked away. It was obvious what the answer was. With everything else Keeley was guilty of, who wouldn't have believed it?

'What did Alex ever do to you, really? All she did was try to protect your family.' Chloe pushed her hands into the pockets of her jacket, fighting to keep her emotions in check. First the daughter, now the mother. The whole family was saturated with cruel intent.

'I wasn't thinking straight,' Sian said, her eyes still fixed to the floor. 'The rejection of Nathan's appeal came through and I just …'

'You just what? You just thought someone needed to pay for it?'

When Sian's laptop had been accessed, her internet search history had been checked. On it had been searches for how to cut a brake fluid line. It was the obvious assumption to think Keeley had been responsible for the searches, but Sian had obviously had no reason to believe that her home would ever be searched or her laptop seized by police.

Chloe stepped forward. She lowered her face to Sian's, forcing the woman to look up from the floor and make eye contact. 'There was nothing wrong with your thinking, was there, Sian? If you weren't thinking straight, the graffiti on her front door would have been enough. That might have been excusable as a moment of madness. But it wasn't enough for you, was it? You went back, and you went back with intent. There's nothing spur-of-the-moment about that.'

'I didn't do anything,' Sian said, the words desperate and pathetic.

'Save it for the jury. Sian Foster, I'm arresting you for the attempted murder of Alex King.'

CHAPTER SIXTY-SEVEN

It was difficult to ignore the looks that were exchanged between the prison officers who ushered her through the security checks, but Alex knew this was something she was going to have to get used to. She had worn a thick scarf; the cold weather meant she was easily able to cover her neck, though she knew that come the summer months, concealing her scars would be harder to achieve. Hiding her face was impossible. She figured that the sooner she faced the world, the quicker she would learn to accept her new self. She would learn, somehow, to deal with other people's reactions.

And this was something that couldn't wait any longer.

She recognised the back of Nathan Coleman's head when she entered the visiting room. He was slouched forward with his shoulders hunched over, defeat oozing from him like an odour; an exaggerated version of the boy she had last seen over two years earlier at his sentencing.

'Nathan.'

She sat in the chair opposite him. She gave him a smile, but it wasn't reciprocated.

He studied the burns that snaked up from the scarf, patterning her skin. 'Tell me what happened,' he said. 'I need to hear it from you.'

The events of the previous two weeks rolled out between them, the reality of what had taken place uncompromisingly brutal in Alex's honest retelling. She watched Nathan's expression morph from confusion to anticipation to horror, each reaction dragging him closer to tears and disbelief. With every detail and with each response received, she grew increasingly confident that the suspicions she had brought to the prison that day were to be proved correct.

'I can't believe it,' Nathan said, pressing a hand to the fading bruises on his face.

'Yes you can.'

There was a moment of silence. Nathan knew her words meant so much more than they said. Alex had worked it out. If she had worked it out years earlier, three lives could have been saved.

'She's been beating your mother. Sian's probably managed to keep the bruises hidden during her visits. Keeley's a clever girl. She wouldn't have left them anywhere too obviously visible.'

Nathan turned to look at the prison officer standing guard at the door before shifting in his seat. He glanced down at his sleeves and pulled them over his hands; anything to distract himself from what he couldn't avoid hearing.

'But why?'

'Control. Keeley's life has been a bit of a mess really, hasn't it? She grew up watching your father beat your mother, never able to do a thing about it. Sian made a decision to stay – Keeley had no say in that. She couldn't control what happened to you either, could she?'

Nathan looked down at his hands, unable to meet Alex's eye.

'I know you didn't do it, Nathan.'

The boy's head hung forward in an attempt to hide his tears. He had protected a girl he had thought innocent; a girl he had believed had been pushed to extreme actions by a set of extreme circumstances for which she was blameless. A girl who had gone on to murder three people and cause fear among the community that had previously shown her family such sympathy and support.

He shook his head. 'She didn't mean what she did back then. She didn't know what she was doing. She was just a kid.'

'She's still just a kid. She's your father's daughter, that's for sure.'

He looked up, finally meeting Alex's eye. 'I don't believe you,' he said, though the statement lacked conviction. 'Mam would have said something.'

'About Keeley beating her? Would she, though? An ex-husband who put her in hospital, a son in prison for attempted murder … do you really think she would have wanted her daughter taken away from her as well? It didn't matter what Keeley did. Whatever your sister is, she's still your mother's child. She had nothing left without Keeley, and Keeley knew it. It meant she could do whatever the hell she liked. Your mother doesn't know, does she? You've never told her that Keeley was the one who poisoned your father.'

Nathan held her gaze, his face seeming to plead with her. With everything his sister had done laid bare before him, he was realising the mistake he had made in protecting her. 'I thought I was doing the right thing.'

Alex sat back. She knew her burns were more exposed now than they had been, but perhaps this was exactly what Nathan needed to see. He needed to be shown what Keeley really was. She hadn't attempted to kill her father because of what he had done to the family. She had tried to kill him because evil was inherently ingrained within her.

'Some people can't be protected,' she told Nathan. 'No one could protect Keeley from herself.' She moved a hand to her scarf and pulled it closer to her throat.

'This is my fault. If I'd told the police what she'd done to our dad …' He broke off for a moment, his thoughts too much for him. 'She should have been here, not me. That homeless man would still be alive. That old lady …' He put his face in his hands, hiding himself from Alex. 'You,' he spluttered through his fingers. 'You wouldn't be …'

'Listen to me,' Alex said, reaching for his arm. 'None of this is your fault, okay. None of it.'

She took her hand away, pushed back her chair and stood.

'What happens now?' Nathan asked, looking up at her with a face that now appeared so much younger than his eighteen years. He was still just a boy, Alex thought. Prison hadn't changed him so much that the damage couldn't be reversed.

She leaned across the table and rested a hand on his. 'Now we get you out of here.'

A LETTER FROM VICTORIA

Dear Reader,

I want to say a huge thank you for choosing to read *Nobody's Child*. If you enjoyed it, and want to keep up to date with all my latest releases, just sign up at the following link. Your email address will never be shared and you can unsubscribe at any time.

www.bookouture.com/victoria-jenkins

It is amazing to think that just this time last year, the first book in the King and Lane series had not yet been published. Writing this third has been powered by the responses I've had from you, the readers, and I am so grateful for every review, tweet and Facebook message that has been written in support of the stories and the characters – they all mean so much and make the experience of writing even more fulfilling.

Nobody's Child sees Alex and Chloe work on a case that takes them further up the Rhondda valleys – a place that over the past ten years has become a second home to me. I have been lucky enough to gain a brilliant, bonkers extended family there and have made some lifelong friends. I hope I've done the place proud.

I hope you loved *Nobody's Child*; if you did, I would be very grateful if you could write a review. I'd love to hear what you think, and it makes such a difference in helping new readers to discover my books for the first time.

I love hearing from my readers – you can get in touch on my Facebook page, through Twitter, Goodreads or my website.

Thanks,
Victoria

victoriajenkinswriter

@vicwritescrime

ACKNOWLEDGEMENTS

A huge thank you to Jenny Geras: a brilliant editor and all-round lovely woman. It is always a pleasure working with you, and thank you for believing in me and the series. Once again, thank you to Anne Williams: without your support, this incredible past year might never have become a reality. A huge thank you to my fellow Bookouture authors: a brilliantly funny group who are always at hand with words of wisdom (and when wisdom's not available, motivational memes). In particular, thank you to Angie Marsons, Kierney Scott and Stephen Edger, who all helped me out in moments of panic. Thank you, as always, to Kim Nash and Noelle Holten, whose energy seems to know no limits. The internet wouldn't be the same without you!

There are not enough thank yous for my family, who have been especially supportive during the writing of this third book. Writing with a baby has been a new and different kind of challenge, and I wouldn't have got this book completed without such amazing support. Thank you to my sister, Nanny McFree, for all the walks around town and for listening to my more-than-occasional meltdowns, and to my in-laws, who have never once complained about the amount of food I take from their cupboards (at least not to my face). To Mum and Dad – I love you both.

To my husband, Steve … you know. Thank you for everything.

And finally, to Norman – thank you for your encouragement, your kindness and your friendship. We will miss you forever. This book is for you.

Made in the USA
Monee, IL
03 October 2020